HOW TO SCORE OFF FIELD

SARA NEY

A NOTE FROM THE AUTHOR...

Please be aware there is subject matter in this book that may be triggering. If you are easily triggered, please contact the author for more info.

COPYRIGHT

Copyright © 2023 by Sara Ney

All rights reserved.

No part of this book may be reproduced in any form or by any electronic or mechanical means, including information storage and retrieval systems, without written permission from the author, except for the use of brief quotations in a book review.

Editing by Jenny Sims, Editing 4 Indies

Proofreading Virginia Tesi Carey

Proofreading by Rachel Rumble & Shauna Casey

Cover Design by Okay Creations

Formatting by Casey Formatting

This book contains material protected under International and Federal Copyright Laws and Treaties. Any unauthorized reprint or use of this material is prohibited. No part of this book may be reproduced in any form or by any means, electronic or mechanical, including photocopying, recording, or by any information storage and retrieval systems without "express " written permission from the author, except for the use of brief quotations in a book review.

This is a work of fiction. Names, characters, places, and incidents either are the product of the authors imagination or are used fictitiously. Any resemblance to any actual persons, living or dead is entirely coincidental.

License Notes

This ebook is licensed for your personal enjoyment only. This book may not be resold or shared with other people. If you would like to share with another person, please purchase an additional copy for each recipient.

Thank you for respecting the hard work of this author.

No part of this book may be reproduced in any form or by any electronic or mechanical means, including information storage and retrieval systems, without written permission from the "author, except for the use of brief quotations in a book review.

PROLOGUE
TESS

I WAS eleven years old the first time I met the Colter twins.

My brother Grady had been signed up to play league football because our mom didn't think he socialized enough, and she was sick of him sitting in his room, gaming all the time.

She wanted him to get exercise.

And meet people.

So that third week of football, she invited all the players over for a pizza party, and I remember the team arriving, one by one, getting dropped off by their parents for the two hours my mother had arranged—and I remember the Colters walking through the door.

Tall, even at the age of thirteen.

Tan from always being outside.

One was quiet and had braces; the other was talking and being loud as soon as he stepped foot in the kitchen where the pizza was being served.

I'd been on the other side of the room, hovering in the doorway where the laundry room was, too intimidated by all the teenage boys to grab a slice of my favorite—cheese, sausage, and pineapple. Mom had ordered it specifically for me, knowing most of the boys wouldn't want pineapple on their pizza, but I was too chickenshit to steal a piece.

"Who's that?" one of them asked. I can't remember who.

Grady had looked in the direction of the kid's finger, glancing at me over his shoulder.

"Oh. That's my sister."

Oh.

That's my sister…

But I mean, I was his little sister, and I was kind of small at that age. And shy.

I remember that once they'd all lost interest in staring at me, and they'd gone back to devouring the pizzas, but I couldn't take my eyes off the twins.

They were so cute.

Literally the cutest boys I'd ever seen in my entire life.

My face turned bright red as soon as the one in the gray tee shirt scanned the small group of boys and caught my eye in the corner, smiling after a few seconds of awkward staring.

I was too freaked out to smile back.

That had been Drew.

I found out his name later—the one with the braces—and lay in bed that whole night, staring up at my bedroom ceiling while saying it to myself. Drew.

Drew Colter.

I wondered what his middle name was.

He was the quiet Colter, who didn't have much to say about anything unless asked. He usually let his louder, more obnoxious brother speak for them, as twins sometimes do.

And I watched number twenty-nine at every game of my brother's that I went to, silently clapping when he blocked a play or took a hit and got back up on his feet without a scratch.

Drew Colter.

Sigh.

When I was fourteen, and we were all in high school, I prayed every day that I would bump into him in the hallway between classes. But we rarely did because freshmen and juniors didn't have class on the same floors, and everything was separated by wings. Freshmen ate with freshmen, sophomores ate with sophomores, and on and on and on.

Then one day when I was eating lunch, there was a commotion at the front of the cafeteria near the vending machines, and a small group of football players walked in, wearing their home jerseys and carrying flyers.

Drew Colter was among them.

I knew it was him instantly. He didn't have the same arrogance his brother Drake had, and he hung back from the group the way he usually did.

I watched as the boys walked around from table to table, handing out those flyers, smiling down at the pretty girls and flirting.

"*Oh my god, they are so. Hot.*"

My friends Charity, Bev, and Tosha stopped cackling about whatever story Charity had been sharing to stare, all of us holding our breath as the football players weaved in and out, like gods among us, for football was the only thing anyone in this town gave a shit about.

Three tables away.

Two.

"Hey, Tess." Drew handed me a flyer with a smile, my name on his full, pouty lips, his white teeth peeking through.

I opened my mouth to reply, but they were already gone.

"Oh. My. God," Charity said dramatically. "Drew. Colter. Said. Your. Name."

I rolled my eyes, pretending to be unfazed. "I'm Grady's sister. He has to be nice to me."

My brother and Drew had become fast friends that night after the pizza party three years ago, spending most of their downtime running plays, hanging out in our basement, or at Drew's house, swimming in his pool.

The Colters lived on a ranch, and their dad was never around, but it was a sprawling house with a massive pool that even had one of those slides you see at the water park—it even had a pool house with a kitchen full of snacks.

I'd only been there once when the Colters hosted a party. Mrs. Colter had wanted help, so Mom dragged me over as an extra set of hands.

I'd refused to take my tee shirt and shorts off to get in the pool.

I was twelve that year and flat-chested, and I didn't want anyone looking at my skinny, pale legs. Besides, my mom would only allow me to wear a one-piece, and I considered it dorky and childish, and it was embarrassing.

So I'd stood there baking in the Texas sun, watching Drew and his glistening skin while he bobbed in the blue pool water.

"He doesn't have to be nice to you," Bev had pointed out. "His brother isn't."

"Drake Colter isn't nice to anyone he isn't dating," Tosha pointed out.

"Drake Colter doesn't date." Bev laughed.

"Exactly." Tosha made her point with a loud laugh, and I glanced over at the boys to ensure they hadn't heard us.

But they were already gone, and I picked up the flyer, my eyes trailing over the words THE GRIDIRON CLUB NEEDS YOU!

The Gridiron Club was the name of the football boosters who raised money to pay for the lights on the football field, keeping the concession stand stocked, and put the team in fancy new uniforms every season.

"They're fundraising for a team that's not even part of the school." Bev snorted. "Lame."

I folded the flyer and tucked it in my lunch box.

I knew I wouldn't get to go to the fundraiser unless my parents planned on attending, but I kept it anyway—because Drew had handed it to me *personally*.

"Hey, Tess."

He'd said my name.

We never spoke, and he remembered my name!

I would take that flyer and doodle his name on it alongside mine.

Drew + Tess.

Tess Donahue + Drew Colter.

Tess Colter.

Tess *Mirabelle* Colter.

Tess Mirabelle Donahue-Colter.

Heart.

Star.

More hearts.

Opened my diary that night and wrote:

> Dear Diary, it's me again.
>
> Drew and his buddies came into the lunchroom today and gave me this flyer. Okay, so it wasn't to me specifically, but he handed it to me and said, "Hey, Tess," and I thought I was going to die.
>
> He is so cute!!!!
>
> I still haven't said anything to the girls about having a crush on him. I don't want them to think I'm out of my dang mind. He's a Colter, and Colters only love one thing—football.
>
> Homecoming is coming up, and Mom said I can go this year with Bev, Charity, and Tosha, but I don't want to go if Drew isn't going, which I doubt he is 'cause he isn't dating anyone I don't think.
>
> Grady is going—obviously—with Beth Newman. I can't stand that B. She's so rude and treats me like I'm a kid and she's only a year older. My brother is an idiot with horrible taste in girls and do you think he takes my advice? No. Because Beth Newman has big

boobs and laughs at every stupid thing he says. I think she caught me rolling my eyes at her but whatever.

Well, Diary, I should get to bed.

I have tennis lessons in the morning, and Mom said I can't skip even though it's going to be hot as Hades. I don't know why, it's not like I'm going to play professionally.

Xx Tess, age 14

I folded up the football flyer covered in hearts and doodles and our names, tucking it neatly into my diary and locking it away.

CHAPTER 1
DREW

"I'M BEGINNING TO THINK I'M SINGLE BECAUSE I NEVER FORWARDED THOSE CHAIN LETTERS I GOT IN HIGH SCHOOL…"

I'm the last man standing.

My three brothers have girlfriends, including my twin—the guy no one ever thought would get himself relationshipped has gone and got himself a better half.

Talk about ironic…

I was always supposed to be the one in a relationship, not Drake. Everyone knows he had zero interest in dating! He's the one who never wanted to date the same person twice or sleep with the same person night after night. Drake wouldn't go on dating apps to find love. He only went on the dating apps to pretend to be me.

Now look at him, gallivanting around campus like a pig in shit when he intended to find a girlfriend for *me.*

The universe is a fickle mistress.

No. The universe is a *bitch.*

Still, I can't be bitter, can I?

I am happy for the miserable bastard.

What?! I am!

I don't have it in me to be anything but—he is my brother, after all, and not just my brother; he is my twin. Honestly, I'm happy for the asshole even though he went behind my back and lied to me and his girlfriend—before she was his girlfriend (obviously).

He was trying to help you out.

But he did it without tellin' you...

He told you. You just didn't take him seriously. You thought he was lyin' when he was telling the truth, then you accused him of lyin' once you found out he was sneaking around.

Because I didn't actually think he was out there dating people and pretending to be me.

Ha!

Whoops.

Anyway. I digress. No sense in getting all bummed out about it. Plenty of people are single, so it's not like I'm the only one. It's just, you know—I feel ready? Yeah, yeah, I know. Love finds you when you're not looking for it, or so my brother—who has now become the expert on love—keeps telling me. He considers himself living proof.

I sigh, shoving my sneakers into my black duffel bag before slinging it over my shoulder. My phone pings with a notification as I push through the gym's front door.

It's Grady Donahue, my best friend.

Grady and I have known each other since middle school when we played Little League football. He's not playing anymore. In fact, he isn't even attending a big university like I am. Instead, he's working a full-time job, renting his own apartment, and paying his own bills.

My heart squeezes.

I'm looking forward to the same independence.

> Grady: Dude, what are you doing this weekend?

He gets straight to the point. No *'good morning'* or *'hey man'* or *'how's it goin'?'* as foreplay for this conversation, no mincing words the way I do when I'm trying to get information from someone.

> Drew: The usual? Hanging out.

> Grady: You should come home. I'm having a bachelor party for Lucas. You should be here.

Lucas Jones is another of our buddies from home. He's working for his dad's construction company and got engaged to his high school sweetheart last year. Must be getting ready to tie the knot if they're having a bachelor party.

I heard buzz about it but wasn't invited to the actual wedding.

> Drew: Bro, wouldn't it be weird to show up when I'm not going to the wedding?

> Grady: Dude, they barely invited his grandma to the vows. They're keeping it small. Told you this a 100 times.

Yeah, he actually has told me this one hundred times, but I'm still not the kind of dude who shows up when I haven't been invited, bachelor party or not.

> Grady: You can afford the flight. Just come home for the weekend. I know you're burned out, so give yourself a break. There are no classes on Monday.

Correct again, I am burned out—from the new relationship my brother is in, from football, from practice, from the gym, from games, from the weight of my family legacy bearing down on my shoulders.

I do need a fucking break.

I'm not sure going home will be the break I need, not if I'm still surrounded by noise and people.

> Drew: How do you know we don't have classes on Monday?

It's a holiday, and most universities aren't holding classes.

> Grady: 'Cause Tess is home from school.

Tess is his little sister, and I can almost hear Grady picking at his teeth with a toothpick. Southern boy to the core.

> Drew: I have to think about it, I guess.

> Grady: What's there to think about? You already said you weren't doing nothin' this weekend.

> Drew: That doesn't mean I want to hop on a plane and fly to Texas, bro.

> Grady: So you'd rather be lying on the couch with your hand down your pants instead???

> Drew: It's cheaper.

> Grady: Don't make me laugh. We both know your mama would pay to fly you home. When's the last time you saw her?

I don't know.

Christmas?

But that's not unusual for out-of-state students who live hundreds of miles from their parents while attending school. And it's not like my schedule is wide open.

Just so happens that right now, it is.

> Drew: Yeah, but for one weekend?

> Grady: Yes, for one weekend. Don't act surprised. I told you about this, so you knew it was coming up. Drake RSVP'd already.

Drew: He did?

That surprises me. Normally, my twin is shit at getting back to people unless they're asking him a question to his face.

Drew: What did he say?

Grady: What do you think he said? He said 'piss off I have better shit to do.'

Drew: LOL

Grady: Just kiddin' Drake wasn't invited - we know he's loved up with Daisy. I know for a fact YOU do not have better shit to do. LOL

Drew: Screw you, dude...

Grady: You wish.

Drew: LOL

Grady: But for real. Get your ass on a plane. You can stay with me. Most of the guys will be here. It'll be a blast, and who knows, you might meet someone.

Drew: Uh. I'm not dating someone in Texas.

Grady: Who said anything about DATING?

CHAPTER 2
TESS

SINGLE SEPTEMBER. ONLY ME OCTOBER. NO MAN NOVEMBER. DON'T DATE DECEMBER...YAY ME, I'M NAILING IT.

"YOU SAID Drew was coming this weekend?" I regard my brother from across the table at the Mexican restaurant where we're having lunch—his treat—and the burrito gets stuck in my throat at the news Drew is coming to town.

Drew Colter.

My childhood crush.

Not that my brother knew that. In his opinion, Drew was like a brother to him. It would never occur to him that I might have harbored fantasies about him since we were in middle school.

Fantasies I kept secret from him, but not my best girlfriends. They all knew I had a mad crush on him and never let me forget it.

But that was then, and this was now.

I'm older, wiser.

Taller.

Not the naive little girl who practiced conversations with him in my bedroom mirror. "Hey Drew, how's it going?" and "Oh me?! I'm so good. Like, totally doing great."

I'm over him.

How can you have a crush on a guy you haven't seen in four years, if not more?

The last time I was in the same room as Drew was at my brother's high school graduation party, and even then, we were mostly on opposite sides of the room. He nodded at me a few times—said hello when he got there, obviously—but other than that…

He had as little interest in me back then as I have in Brian Flanders *now,* the nerdy tech geek who works in the computer lab on campus and stares at me uncomfortably every time I go in for assistance.

And unfortunately, I need a lot of assistance.

Sigh.

"Are you listenin' to a thing I say?" my brother asks, giving me a jostle under the table with the toe of his cowboy boot.

We live in Texas, and cowboy boots and sneakers are interchangeable, though I stopped wearing mine around town the day I left for college.

"I heard you." I bite into the burrito I've taken off my plate and chew thoughtfully. "Drew is actually flying home? For just the weekend?"

He nods.

"How'd you convince him to do that?"

Grady just shrugs.

Grady always shrugs. It's his lazy way of giving a noncommittal answer or not answering at all.

"I think he needs a break."

"A break? From what?"

Another shrug. "School. Drake. Drake and his girlfriend. Football." He rattles off the many reasons Drew Colter "needs a break."

"That's pretty much everything."

"If you ask me, I don't think he wanted to play football in the first place, but you know how his old man was. And he can't escape it, not with every single Colter playin' it."

"So he's flyin' home," I state matter-of-factly. "When does he get here?"

"Thursday. He's skipping his Friday class." My brother picks at his taco, removing half the lettuce. "Can you do me a favor?"

And here it is.

Grady needs something.

"I should have known you asked me here so you could ask me to do something for you." Buying me lunch? Come on now, how transparent could the guy possibly be?

"That isn't true. I wanted to see you anyway, and this gave me the perfect excuse." His smile is charming, so I smile back.

"What?"

"Can you grab him from the airport?"

I throw down my napkin. "Grady, no!" Leaning back, I cross my arms, pouting. "No."

"Come on, sis. I have to work. And he's your friend, too, you know."

Barely.

I would not call a childhood crush and following him around like a puppy dog a friendship. The guy could barely tolerate me, his twin brother even less so. The pair went everywhere together, along with my brother and Lucas and all the other football meatheads who traveled in packs.

They ate together. They hung out together. They practiced together. All their free time was spent together. They lived and breathed for that game, and the Colters still do.

Football is in their blood.

Their daddy played, and the twins' older brothers both play.

They're like one of those famous football families you see on television—the kind where two brothers play on opposing teams, and the cameras always pan to the momma and daddy sitting there cheering. Or cringing.

That's the Colters.

I never got the feeling that Drew cared as much, but nonetheless, it sounds like he'll play professionally anyhow. Whether he likes it or not.

I sigh, nibbling at my burrito. "What time?"

"One o'clock."

Ugh! "Honestly, could you have chosen a more inconvenient time? That's right smack in the middle of the damn day, Grady Donahue."

"I didn't choose it. He did. Calm down. If you don't wanna do it, that's fine. I can see if Sissy Lancaster has the time."

Sissy Lancaster?

Oh hell no.

Sissy is the best friend of Lucas's fiancée and always has her claws in fresh meat—and even though Drew grew up around here—and even though I have no feelings for him anymore, that doesn't mean I want Sissy Lancaster picking him up from the airport.

"You and I both know if Sissy picks him up from the airport, he'll never be rid of her."

That's the truth.

"So?" My brother snorts. "He probably won't want to be rid of her."

Grady says it so nonchalantly—as if he wants to get stabbed with the end of my spork.

I'm not jealous. I'm not.

Like I said, I haven't seen Drew in ages, and in that time, I've dated plenty of other people.

"Do you not *like* her?" he asks smugly.

Um, does my brother not know I had a crush on his best friend at one point in our lives... because he's acting like he does, but it's hard to tell by the expression on his face.

Does he?

Did he?

"Of course I like her. Everyone likes her." Which is slightly annoying, but I'm too polite to say so out loud.

"So I'll just have her pick him up, then. She did offer."

I stop chewing the burrito and gulp it down. "She offered? Oh. Well then, I mean. Why are you asking me, then?"

Seriously.

Inconvenience me even though someone else can grab him from the airport?

Rude.

"Because. Once she gets her claws in him, he won't be able to escape, and I'd at least like to give him the option." Grady laughs.

As if it were so funny that Sissy was way more charismatic than I, and sexier, and better with guys and probably people in general. If there was a party, Sissy was there.

Sorority girl, president of her house.

Rich parents. Pretty hair, nails, and skin.

She's probably never had a zit in her entire life, I'm convinced of it, and she's always wearing the perfect outfit.

I live my life in cute joggers and gray crewnecks and, well, have a zit festering on the tip of my nose that is going to be the bane of my existence once I get my period.

But sure.

Let me go to the airport and fetch the guy I used to have freaking dreams about. The guy who kept me up at night, who I wrote in my journals about.

My journals.

Shit, where are those things?

What the hell did I do with them once I moved to college…?

"Tess. You're doing it again."

"Doing what?"

"Not paying attention."

"Sorry. I was thinkin'."

"Thinking about…grabbin' Drew from the airport on Thursday?"

He's tapping on the table now with the blade of a dull butter knife wrapped with the other cutlery.

"Sure."

His brows go up, and he stops tapping the wood surface. "Really?"

"Yeah. Why not?"

DEAR DIARY...

I got my period at school today and I was NOT prepared for it.

That is the freaking worst and I didn't have a tampon in my backpack. Luckily Kierra, this girl in my bio lab, had one in her bag because it was almost an emergency: I HAD ON WHITE PANTS. Can you imagine? My science teacher Mr D wasn't going to let me out of class because they don't want stragglers in the hallway and three girls had asked to use the bathroom before me, but Kierra blurted out that Aunt Flo was visiting and he got all embarrassed and handed me the hall pass. WORKS EVERY TIME...

x Tess

CHAPTER 3
DREW

"I'M ONLY TWO GIRLS SHORT OF A THREESOME."

THIS WILL BE GOOD.

It'll be good, and I'll have fun.

I need this.

Yup. I made the right choice coming home. Seeing the boys will be exactly what I need.

Not that I don't love my friends at school, but being in my hometown with guys I grew up with just isn't the same now, is it?

Anyway.

My eyes scan the bumper-to-bumper traffic congesting the arrivals at Terminal 4, searching for the silver SUV my best friend told me his sister would be driving and cursing the massive amounts of silver vehicles passing by.

"A license plate number would have been nice, asshole," I grumble, shifting the weight of the duffel bag on my shoulder.

Shit. Am I going to remember what Tess Donahue even looks like? I barely paid attention to her when we were growing up. What if she drives past and I don't see her?

Crap, what color hair did she have? Brown?

Nope—dark, almost black hair, like her brother.

Braces, but those are probably gone, yeah?

I can't remember if she's tall, but that doesn't matter. The only thing I remember about Tess Donahue is that she was always soft-spoken, she was kind of a dork, and she occasionally stammered when she spoke to me.

The duffel bag digs into my shoulder now. It's packed full of everything I need for four days, considering I don't plan on staying at my mama's house. Grady said he's got enough room for me at his place, and couch surfing suits me just fine.

Damn, it will feel good drinking too much, staying up too late, and blasting the music loud.

I scan the street again.

Silver car, silver car…where the fuck is it?

> Grade, tell Tess I'm wearing a bright blue hoodie.

I hit Send, wondering why the hell he never gave me her cell to begin with.

Then.

A gray crossover pulls up—or tries to—getting as close as it can to the curb and myself, the passenger side window rolling down.

"Drew!" The driver yells my name and gives a little wave. "Hey!"

I blink.

I look down at my phone as it buzzes with a reply from my buddy.

> Grady: She'll find you, don't worry. It's not like you blend into a crowd.

I grin, tucking the phone into my back pocket and drop my duffel bag from my shoulder to my hand, carrying it toward the vehicle with Tess Donahue at the wheel.

I grin at her as I pull open the passenger side door. "Why, if it isn't little Tessa Lynn Donahue."

Not so little anymore—if she ever was to begin with.

"No one calls me Tessa Lynn anymore, Drew." She rolls her eyes so hard I'm worried they're gonna get stuck in the back of her skull.

"See, there's the Tess I remember."

"*Please.*" She scoffs. "I never would have corrected you when I was a kid."

Tossing my duffel over the seat and into the back, I fold my massive frame into her car and buckle my seat belt, locking my eyes on the road so I'm not tempted to stare at her.

Dang.

She looks nothing like I remember—not that I could remember shit about her, and not that I would say that out loud. I don't want to insult her by implying she wasn't…memorable.

Clearing my throat, I sneak a glance.

Tess has a pleasant expression pasted on her face. I'm not sure if it's because she's concentrating on the road or what she's about to say next.

"How was your flight?"

"Good."

Uneventful. Boring.

"I slept."

She nods, her long dark ponytail swinging a little.

Tess is tan, and I remember that she used to play baseball. I wonder if she still does, but don't ask her. The last thing I want to do is ask her weird, random questions about herself.

I yawn, doing my best to stretch my long legs in what little legroom her car has, but I was cramped the entire flight here, so another twenty minutes won't kill me.

"Any turbulence?"

"Nothing terrible."

Not like this painful conversation.

I rack my brain. "How is the bachelor party planning coming along?"

Beside me, she lifts her chin and adjusts the rearview mirror as she gives it a hard look at the cars behind her, merging onto the highway from the airport's main drag.

"Good, I guess. Grady is super into it. It's like he's the best man or something."

"How does the best man feel about it?"

Tess smiles. "He doesn't seem to care. Lucas has been celebrating his wedding for the past month."

"My brother is like that for our birthday." Drake celebrates all damn month long as if he were the next coming of the Lord, not just the day or weekend of. "Loves to go out and make it known that it's his birthday for the entire month of May."

By the way, it's May, and I haven't celebrated once.

Our birthday is in two weeks.

Not that I care or am counting.

Tess drives along. "The guys are at the house waitin' for you. I think Grady plans on orderin' pizza this afternoon, plus beer. He usually works until around four, but he's getting done a little early today. You won't be alone long, plus there's the dog." She squints as she goes over the information Grady plied her with. "Tomorrow, the fun begins. Lucas wants to go golfing, but Grady hasn't gone in years, so he took a pass. You're supposed to let them know if you want to join."

All things Grady could have told me himself in a text but was too lazy to. Or too busy.

No matter.

I tip my seat back, reclining. "I'll take a nap when I get there."

This weekend isn't about relaxing. It's about cutting loose and having a fuck ton of fun. But to do that, I have to rest up! Since Grady is still working, I don't have to hit the ground running.

"Thanks for pickin' me up," I lament. "I could have taken an Uber."

Tess laughs. "As if Grady would allow that." She sniffs. "It's no problem. It's not like I had anythin' goin' on today."

"What are you doing while you're home?"

She's quiet while she turns on her blinker and waits for the left-hand arrow to turn green.

"Going to the bachelorette party, obviously. We're all wearin' white, and we're all wearin' veils. It'll be extremely confusin' at the honky-tonk." She laughs.

"Is that where the bachelor party is?"

"I'm not sure if that's where you'll start, but I reckon that's where you'll end up."

I reckon that's where you'll end up…

I lean into my seat and close my eyes for a few seconds. I haven't heard a Texas twang since the last time I was home for the holidays, my brother's not included.

It feels good.

Real good.

"I reckon we will."

CHAPTER 4
TESS

SHOUT OUT TO ALL THE SINGLE LADIES COMPLAINING ABOUT BEING SINGLE BUT NEVER WANTING TO GO OUT, JUST SITTING AT HOME, WAITING FOR MR. RIGHT TO BREAK INTO THEIR HOUSE.

OH MY GOD.

Having Drew Colter in my car was worse than I thought it would be. When I dropped him off at my brother's and headed to my friend Miranda's, I caught a whiff of his cologne. Shooting him a little wave when he leaned through the open window to thank me once again, I couldn't help watching him walk to the house.

Those jeans.

That ass.

Shit.

I thought I was over this stupid crush!

I was.

I am!

Ugh.

I pull up to Miranda's. I'm staying with her over the weekend because I have no desire to stay with my parents. The last thing I want the night of the bachelorette party is to sneak into the house in the middle of the night and get scolded for being out so late. As if I were a child and still had a curfew, my parents keep track of my every move when I'm home.

How quickly they forget I'm twenty-one years old.

"Well, if *that* was one of the most awkward and painful thirty minutes of my life, I don't know what was." I slap my purse onto Miranda's kitchen counter, immediately go to the fridge, and fish out a bottle of white wine.

My best friend walks out of her bedroom, already pulling her hair into a messy topknot.

"It couldn't have been that bad."

Now I'm at the cabinet pulling out a stemless wineglass—two wineglasses—and setting them on the counter with a clink.

"Yes. It actually was."

She laughs, padding across the tile floor in bare feet. "Do tell."

Miranda moved to Belvedere when we were seniors, so she wasn't actually here to witness the most painful years of my crush on Drew. She's only heard a few horror stories.

She plops down at the counter, leaning forward on her elbows, watching me fill our glasses.

"We barely spoke. It was so bad."

"Barely spoke? How is that possible?"

"Erm. Well. He got in, and I asked how the flight was, and he said good. Then I asked if there was any turbulence, and he said no and thanked me for picking him up." I leave out the little details, like how I didn't look at him, not even when I dropped him off. Not even when I gave him that tiny wave goodbye. I was too quick to get the ordeal over with.

Miranda smacks her lips after her first sip of cheap wine as if it were a fine vintage.

"Who cares? You're over him. Plus, you'll barely be seeing him this weekend." She pauses, thinking. "Unless you're the one who has to take him back to the airport, in which case you can redeem yourself."

"Oh, I'll be seeing him this weekend. WE will be seeing him." I tip my wineglass toward her. "He'll be at the bachelor party, which we know is gonna end at Boot Scoot Boogie."

They always do.

BSB has been the most popular dance hall since the late sixties and that hasn't changed over the years. Same floor, same stage, same horseshoes nailed to the Stallion and Little Fillies bathroom doors.

"So." She's still leaning forward, swirling the drink in her glass. "What does he look like now? Did he get uglier?"

I groan. "No." I don't think. "I didn't actually look directly at him, but I'm assuming he's better looking."

That makes Miranda laugh, wine bubbling on her tongue. "You are so awkward."

"See! This is what I'm saying! It was painful. He had no interest in me either, so I guess that makes us even."

"Bro. You picked him up from the airport. Of course he wasn't interested; he was tired."

I pick at an imaginary piece of lint on my tee shirt. "I could have picked him up while I was naked and he still wouldn't have noticed me."

"I'm sorry, I'm confused. Did you want him to notice you?"

Duh. "Doesn't a girl always want a guy to notice her?"

"Not every guy. Just certain guys." She sighs and takes a sip. "You have to make up your mind. Are you going to pretend you don't like him anymore, or will you go for it?"

Go for it.

Say what now?

No.

Going for it has never been my style because NEWS FLASH: I have no style.

I have no game.

"At no point was I ever going to go for it." Not with Drew or anyone.

"See, Tess, this is why you're still single." She sips more wine. Gulps it actually because she already needs a refill.

I pour her more to busy myself, topping my glass as well.

"That is literally not the reason I'm single."

The truth is, I have no idea why I'm single. I mean—fine, I do know. I'm not aggressive enough. Passive, if you will. Never know when a guy is flirting, cannot take a hint unless someone has flat out said the words "Tess will you go out with me?"

Which they haven't.

Not in ages.

The closest I've gotten are a few drunken and the infrequent slobbery, *"You are so hot, wanna come back to my place?"*

Some girls might find any come-on flattering, but I am not most girls.

Um, sir, if your place is a tiny dorm room or a dirty apartment that you share with three of your fraternity brothers, the answer is no.

Hard pass.

"Then why are you single? And don't act like we haven't had this conversation a dozen times before."

I roll my eyes and ignore her question. "Why do you act like it's your job to matchmake for me? I'm perfectly content the way I am."

Miranda snorts. "Then why was it so awkward for you to pick up Drew Colter from the airport and make small talk like a normal person?"

Because.

"I don't even know him. I was basically a glorified Uber driver."

"You don't think he appreciated his best friend's little sister picking him up? Please. I'm sure he would have been glad to flirt."

"The reason we didn't have Sissy Lancaster pick him up was so he wouldn't be trapped in a car with a drooling female fan."

"Oh." She sits back on the barstool, understanding marring her brow. "So that's the reason you didn't flirt? You didn't want to be a simpering female fan? That makes more sense."

"No, that's not…" Ugh. "I give up."

"Yes, it seems like it."

I give her a blank stare. "Easy for you to say since datin' and flirtin' come naturally." Miranda is a hot toddy. Guys love her.

"You don't think I have to work at it?"

"Um, no, you don't work at it."

She preens, taking that as a compliment. "Oh my god, thank you." Flipping her hair over her shoulder, she says, "It takes a lot of work to make it look like I put in zero effort, but trust me, this is exhausting."

I drink my wine, thinking. "Are you tellin' Zero to drop by tomorrow?"

Zero is her boyfriend, and he's exactly how you'd imagine a guy named Zero to be: neck tattoo. Piercings. Black, inky hair. He plays hockey for the university and will probably play pro if he can stay out of trouble on social media.

Basically, Dave Navarro, if you even know who that is, but cooler. He's also the last person you would expect to walk into a dive like Boot Scoot Boogie, but that's the thing about Miranda and Zero: they give zero fucks.

Absolutely none.

I sulk, wishing I were cool.

"Yeah, he's dropping by. He gets a kick out of me wearing cowboy boots." She reaches forward and grabs a grape from the bowl she keeps on the counter. "They're silver."

Of course they are.

Mine are pink—super cute, right?—but I don't think I'll be wearing a pair tomorrow. I left them at my parents' house with no plans to pop in and fetch them.

"Tess, what's the worst thing that could happen if you…you know, tell Drew you're harboring a mad crush on him?"

I laugh. "The same thing that happened the last time I tried."

She tilts her head. "When was that?"

Oh god. "It's not something I want to remember."

"Humor me…"

I pause.

I hesitate, searching for not only the memory but also the words to tell it...

"I was a freshman, and he was a junior, two years older but so nice. Kind. Tall. Good-looking in a non-traditional way. Always had a fresh haircut, always shaved, unlike his twin brother with his unkempt hair and the scruff on his chin.

"He was the boy of my dreams, literally, 'cause I dreamed of him almost every single night."

Miranda listens, spellbound.

"My brother's friends were always at our house. We had a huge pool, and Mom always preferred to have a houseful rather than not know where we were off to. So every weekend, after all the games, Grady would invite his teammates over. Sometimes girls would show up too."

"Anyway, on this particular night, our parents went to dinner. They weren't far from the house, so they thought it would be okay. They trusted us, you know? We weren't allowed to be in the pool, but they let him have people over to watch movies. So that's what Grady ultimately did."

"At some point, I came out of my room, and they had stopped watchin' movies and wanted to play games—seven minutes in heaven or whatever."

God, this is so embarrassing to talk about.

I've never told another soul.

I haven't even written about it in my journal. That's how humiliated I felt.

"Grady hadn't wanted me to play, but his buddies and the girls gave him shit about it. Plenty of other girls there were my age, so it's not like he was tellin' them to sit on the couch by themselves. So I got on my knees on the carpet like everyone else and played the game like everyone else. Lucas had put a book down on the floor and on top of that, an empty Coke bottle. You know, for spinnin'. Drew was there."

Or I thought it was Drew.

When he spun the bottle, and it landed on me, my heart

stopped beatin' completely. Every nerve in my body was hummin', I swear."

Miranda reaches over and grips my hand, squeezing it, mouth pulling at the corner as if to say, *Aw, you sweet thing*.

"My god, I was so nervous." I clear my throat. "This is it, I had thought. This is the moment my lips are going to touch Drew Colter's."

My first kiss.

Or it would have been had he actually kissed me.

"We both stood and headed for the coat closet. Like, why a group of high school kids were playin' that dumb game is beyond me, but I felt like I was going to throw up walkin' through that closet door."

"What happened?" Miranda whispers.

"Ugh. I was so nervous I started babblin'. He was so tall and cute, and in the back of my mind, I was wonderin' how his hair had gotten so long when I'd sworn it was short, but everything was malfunctioning. So instead of playing it cool and just kissing the guy and keepin' my mouth shut, I blurt out, "*I love you, Drew Colter*," right there in that coatroom."

Miranda's hand flies to her mouth, covering it with a gasp. "No."

I nod solemnly. "Yes. Oh yes, I did."

"Stop."

"My lips to God's ears."

Miranda's lips part. "Then what?"

"Then he put his hands on my shoulders, looked into my eyes, and said, real quiet like, '*Then you're about to be real disappointed darlin' 'cause I'm not Drew. I'm Drake.*'" I mimic his deep baritone timbre. "He tapped on his front tooth where the gap was, then said, "*Don't worry, kid, I won't say nothin'.*" I gulp down the horrible memory, then gulp down more wine. "To this day, I'm thinkin' he kept his promise because my brother's never said a peep about it or teased me, and Drew acts the same way around me he always has." I shrug. "So yeah. That's the story."

"Holy shit, Tess. That's a doozy."

"You're tellin' me." I sigh loudly.

Glumly.

"Alright," Miranda allows, avoiding my gaze. "I take back everything I said about going for it. Maybe don't go for him. Go for someone else."

My thoughts exactly.

DEAR DIARY...

    I haven't written in a few days because I've been so busy. Finally had my friends over last night and we stayed up until 2 talking about school and boys, ha ha. Bev is dating Justin Wilder and he tried kissing her under the bleachers at the football game and we were all basically FREAKING OUT. She said he tried sticking his tongue in her mouth and it was disgusting, so we sat up watching videos on YouTube about how to kiss and make out.
    We were dying laughing, it was hilarious.
    Then Bev FaceTimed him and broke up with him because she doesn't have time to teach a teenage boy how to kiss and because he went and told all his friends she stuck her tongue down his throat. But boy he got mad when she called him while she had a room full of her friends instead of in private, but like—we tell each other everything so what difference does it make? Guys are so dumb.
    Grady was home and kept coming into the living

room where we were sleeping. I think he has a crush on Tosha which is SO WEIRD. He better stay away from my friends, they are OFF. LIMITS. PERIOD! The thought of him dating one of my friends is disgusting and plus she's like 3 years younger, GO AWAY GRADY. **GAG**

Anyway.

Going to bed, I have a student council meeting in the morning before school and Mom said she'd take me for a Pumpkin Spice Latte beforehand. I'm SO BASIC ha!

xx
T

CHAPTER 5
DREW

DO YOU BELIEVE IN LOVE AT FIRST SIGHT, OR SHOULD I WALK BY AGAIN?

WHEN GRADY TOLD me he was having a few people over, I assumed he meant like five or six. I definitely wasn't thinking it would be ten or twenty or the full house surrounding me now.

Holy shit.

They party like they're in College Town, USA, and this is a fraternity house.

"Did you invite all the neighbors so they don't call the cops on you later?" I ask him as I heft the newly delivered keg onto the back porch. I lift it as if it weighs nothing.

"No. Should I have?"

Is he for real? "Dude, yes, you should have invited the neighbors. At least some of them might show up, and the other half won't be surprised when it gets loud. You said you were only having a few people over…"

He shrugs like it's no big deal. "I can't help it if word spreads."

Shit.

Do I seriously want to be here when this party gets busted?

Because it's going to, and I'll be standing here with my hand on my dick as the cops bust us for having too many people at Grady's house while families in the neighborhood try to sleep and relax at home.

He eyeballs me. "You sound like someone's mama. You really did need a break, bro."

He's not wrong. On either count.

Honest to God there are people everywhere, none of whom I know besides Lucas, Debts—one of our high school buddies who play football in Kentucky—his girlfriend, Deb, and like four other people.

Plus Tess.

I haven't seen her yet, but her best friend, Miranda, came up and introduced herself the minute they walked through the door. She welcomed me to town, said she'd heard a lot about me, and couldn't wait for the bachelorette party tomorrow night.

The guy with her? Looks as if he were auditioning for a punk metal band after party; like he hangs out in dark basements and does dungeon tours on the weekends.

But I digress.

Plunking the keg down, I wipe my hands on the palm of my jeans, adjusting it so it's in a secure spot and not going to roll back down the steps should someone bump or stumble into it.

Grady adds the hose spigot gadget, and we're off to the races.

When I straighten, my hands get stuffed in my pockets.

Somewhere inside the house, the music gets kicked on. It's country, of course, since we are in the South. I don't know a single soul who listens to anything else, if you don't count that heavy-metal-looking dude, but I don't think he's from here.

I reach for a plastic cup and pour myself a beer.

I'm standing around in the same position, wondering why the hell I'm still standing in the same place when I should be mingling and talking to people I used to know. I should be laughing and whooping it up. I am by no means shy, nor am I a wallflower. But for whatever reason, I'm not drawn to socializing at the moment and just content to observe.

I'm on my second beer when Tess approaches the keg empty-handed. It takes me a few seconds for my brain to register that it's her. The hair she had up in a ponytail is down, falling into long, dark waves around her shoulders.

She lifts a hand and tucks a strand behind her ear, and I notice she's wearing large gold hoop earrings that catch the light. Not a lot of makeup, but her lashes are long and inky black and her cheeks are rosy. Glossy, plump lips.

Tess is much taller than I remember her being when we were younger, and I look down to see that she's not wearing high heels. She's wearing flip-flops, and her toes are painted bright pink.

She catches me looking and wiggles them.

"Hey, stranger," she says with a smile. "Come here often?"

It's a classic pickup line everyone is familiar with. Although I know Tess is just being friendly and not flirting.

At least I don't think she's flirting with me. It's hard to tell by the pleasant expression on her pretty face.

There, I said it. Tess is pretty.

My friend's little sister is *real* pretty.

"I do *not* come here often." I laugh because we both know I haven't been home since our Christmas break, which was less than thirty-six hours since we played in the Tortilla Bowl, a game in sunny Arizona. "Would you like a beer?"

She nods with a wry smile. "It's not my favorite, but if it's all my brother has to offer, sure. I'll take a beer."

"It is all he has to offer." I laugh again, reaching for the hose or spigot or whatever you wanna call it.

"I think the budget for this gathering was nonexistent," Tess provides as she takes the red plastic cup from my hand.

"He must be saving his money for the bachelor party tomorrow night. You know how that goes," she says. "All you bros buying their bro the next round and trying to look cool."

"Bros buying bros beer." I lament. "Actually, I don't. I've never been to a bachelor party before."

Her eyes get wide at my confession.

"What? Are you serious? You've actually never been to a bachelor party before?"

"No, ma'am. None of the guys I hang around with at the moment are even engaged. Only a few of them are dating." I lean back against the porch rail, crossing my legs at the ankles. "Guess most of them are saving themselves until we graduate, although I reckon that sometime soon at least one of my older brothers will get engaged?"

I phrase it like a question, saying the words out loud for the first time. I don't like to think about my two older brothers getting engaged, then married, then possibly having kids—do they even want kids.? We don't talk about it often, but it popped into my mind for whatever reason. Shit, even Drake could get himself hitched in the near future.

"Let me paint you a picture, then, since you haven't been to a bachelor party before." Tess clears her throat and tosses her hair, and when she does, my eyes follow the long hair spilling over her shoulders and down to her breasts. "Picture a raunchy version of a fraternity party," she tells me as I raise my eyes back to her face. "Men acting just as dumb but with more spending money, daring each other to do dumb shit, like go up to a woman for cash—for the groom of course—or drinking themselves into oblivion. Or they just go golfing."

"So either they go out and act stupid or they go golfing?"

"Mostly acting stupid. Driving the golf carts too fast or tipping them. Grady was at a stag party last year and someone drove the cart into the pond. They were blacklisted after that and can't return."

Huh. "I didn't know Grady golfed."

To be fair, a shit ton of my buddies actually do golf in their downtime. But I didn't know my friends from back home did. Maybe tomorrow morning we can take in nine holes…

"He doesn't."

Nevermind, then.

"So what about you?" I ask. "What are you doing in town?"

"Here for the bachelorette party."

I rack my brain for a follow-up question.

Um.

This shouldn't be so difficult. I've gone on plenty of dates with strangers and was able to make idle small talk, so why is coming up with something to talk about with Tess so damn difficult?

Because she's better looking than you remember.

She's older.

Not the kid you remember.

Beautiful.

I shift uncomfortably. Stop thinking about your best friend's sister. Bro code, dude.

Has she changed all that much, or did I just never notice?

Her tank top is bright green—like fresh-cut grass—and her shoulders tan. The fabric dips in front, giving me a glimpse of her cleavage.

She's wearing jeans and looks the kind of casual that comes with being comfortable in your own skin and comfortable in your clothes because they fit well.

"And then I'll stay with Miranda because I have no desire to be at home with my parents this weekend."

Her mouth is moving, but I barely hear a word coming out of it.

"I'm sorry, what?" I have the audacity to ask and feel like a fucking tool for doing so.

She looks as confused as I feel, tilting her head to the side as she regards me. "You asked what I was doing in town this weekend?"

"Shit—sorry, I was listening I swear. I just…"

Can't stop staring at you.

And the Awkward Human Award goes to me.

For being a fucking moron.

CHAPTER 6
TESS

I'M READY FOR MY NEXT TOXIC RELATIONSHIP. WHERE ARE YOU AT, PSYCHO?

WHY IS Drew looking at me like that?

He's not looking at you any kind of way, Tess. He's deciding what to say next.

I can literally see him thinking. That's how expressive his face is.

Suddenly, I wish I'd worn the outfit Miranda had picked out for me; something black and sexy—but not too sexy—rather than this crochet tank top and simple jeans. And flip-flops, ugh, why did I wear these dumb sandals?

My best friend tried to convince me otherwise, but I didn't listen, convinced that when I bumped into Drew, he wouldn't have any interest in what I was wearing. Probably wouldn't give me the time of day, given what little interaction we had earlier in my car.

He barely spoke to me then, and he's barely speaking to me now, but something about the way he's watching me…

Makes me wish I looked sexy.

Instead, I look like someone's kid sister.

If there was a rock beneath my feet, I'd kick at it.

As if conjuring my best friend up, she comes through the back patio door, her gaze flickering between myself and Drew.

Her brows are set in place, though I bet twenty bucks she'd raise them if she didn't think I'd kill her.

"Hey, you two crazy kids." She plucks a red cup from the nearby table and holds it out. "Are you the bartender?"

"I am now." Drew fills her cup; beer foam spills from the plastic rim onto the top of the keg.

He hands it to her when the cup is full.

"So." Miranda takes a long, loud sip of foam. It leaves her with a foamy mustache. "Drew."

Oh no.

I recognize that look.

Drew and I wait to see what she's going to say.

"Are you single?"

If I had been drinking from my beer cup, I would have choked on it.

The fact she can just blurt random shit like that without thinking.

I clamp my lips shut so I don't say something like, "MIRAN-DA," or scold her, giving myself away.

I play it cool, crossing my arms over my chest and fixing my face into a neutral expression.

Drew nods. "I am."

Miranda cocks her head. "Like—*actually single* or single?" She uses air quotes around that second single, implying that he should admit to having a girlfriend stashed away somewhere he's not telling us about.

It's a ballsy question to ask for no apparent reason.

"Like actually single. Anything else you want to know? Like what time I go to sleep and what I had for breakfast?" he teases.

"Yeah, actually, what did you have for breakfast?"

"Well, since I was at Grady's and he is a shitty host, I had six eggs 'cause that's all he had. I woke up at six—force of habit—went for a run, had eggs, took a shit." His brows go up. "Let's see, what else…"

Drew raises a hand to rub his chin.

"Went for a run, had eggs, took a shit. Sounds like a productive morning." Miranda laughs.

"Had to fend for myself. My host wasn't around when I woke up."

"He wasn't? That's so rude."

I stand there like a blob, watching the interaction but contributing nothing.

Get in the game, Tess.

Get in the game.

"You're welcome to stay at my place," she says casually. "We have a stocked fridge. I even have protein shakes and protein bars."

Drew looks impressed. "Protein shakes? You don't say."

"I do say. And I work during the day, too—same as Grady. So like, all Tess has been doing is waiting for me to get home." She pauses. "The two of you should do something in the morning. It's lame to wait around for Grady to get home when you've come all this way to see him."

I swear, if my jaw weren't connected, it would be on the floor. She did not just sidle up here, suggest he come stay with us, then suggest he and I spend the day together tomorrow.

No, she did not.

Did I literally not tell her my Drake Drew Twin Mix-Up Horror Story? Did I not?

She's the one who told me I had her permission to let it go!

The fuu…

"That's not a bad idea." He looks at me. "You can show me around."

Show him around? "Dude, we're both from here."

"I know, but I haven't been home in ages."

"But I go to school in another city, too. I have no idea what's what anymore."

An elbow gets jammed into my rib cage, and I shoot a glare at Miranda.

"*What?*"

Her nostrils flare. "Be nice."

My mouth falls open. When am I not nice?!

This is an outrage.

Pursing my lips, I take Miranda by the arm and give it a tug. "I have to go to the bathroom. Want to come with me?"

She's about to protest, but I pull her.

"Don't go anywhere," she says over her shoulder to Drew. "We won't be long."

"Oh yes, we will," I grumble under my breath as I slide the patio door open and step into my brother's kitchen, my best friend hot on my heels.

I drag her through the house, up the back stairs, and to the second-floor bathroom off my brother's bedroom.

"Dude." I close the door behind me. "What are you doing?"

My arms flap up and down in outrage.

"Stop arguing," Miranda demands. "How did I not notice how dramatic you are?"

I pout, folding my arms across my chest. "What were you doing down there, trying to embarrass me? And wasn't it you who said—and I quote, 'Maybe don't go for him. Go for someone else.'"

Miranda is silent for all of three seconds. "That was before I saw the two of you together."

"Together…by the keg. We weren't flirting. He wasn't about to ask me out. Drew Colter has no interest in me."

The smile on her face is smug. "I wouldn't be so sure about that."

I'm still pouting. "This party is stupid. I want to leave."

"You're leaving over my dead body. You're going to go back down there, find him, and flirt like a normal person."

That makes me snort. "Like a normal person," I repeat for lack of anything more clever to say. "If I knew how to flirt, that would be great. But I don't, and neither does he, if you hadn't noticed."

"Actually, I did notice him watching you. Why do you think I walked over? 'Cause you needed my assistance."

I mean.

Maybe I did; maybe I didn't.

"Maybe what you should do is get warmed up with someone else?" Miranda is by the toilet now, unbuttoning her pants and sitting to pee while I turn to look in the mirror, fussing with my long hair.

"Flirt with one of my brother's friends? Uh, I'd rather stick my finger in a light socket. Have you seen who he hangs out with?"

"Yeah—hotties." She wipes, pulls up her pants, and flushes. "You could do worse than a guy a few years older. That could be why you're still single. Guys our age are just…" She pulls a face, sticking her tongue out. "You're an old soul, Tess, and you probably always have been."

This is true.

I am an old soul.

When I was younger, I'd rather sit in the kitchen when my parents had friends over and socialize with them than kids my own age. Or I'd sit home reading on Friday and Saturday nights while my friends were out toilet papering someone's yard or at the beach sunbathing or going to the movies.

I'm rarely on social media.

"Look. Don't worry about Drew. Yes, he's good-looking. And yes, he's probably going to be rich someday. But so what? Go downstairs and flirt with someone lame—who's never going to move out of this town and will probably end up working for your brother."

I narrow my eyes. "Screw you."

Miranda laughs. "If you want to leave, we can leave. We'll go grab pie and do some adult coloring at Maisie's Pie House. Doesn't that sound more fun than going back down to this stupid party full of people you've known all your life or new friends you haven't met yet?"

I glare at her. I hate when she makes perfect sense. It's annoying.

Friends I haven't met yet.

"Are you gaslighting me into returning to the party and staying and trying to have fun?"

She doesn't even have the decency to look guilty. "That's one hundred percent what I'm doing."

"At least you're not sugarcoating it."

"When have I ever?"

"Never. That's why I love you."

She pulls a face. "Stop. Don't make me gag."

"Too mushy?"

"Way too mushy. I'm not drunk enough for that nonsense."

CHAPTER 7
DREW

DATING PRO TIP FROM MY
BROTHER: JUST DON'T.

I CAN'T KEEP my eyes off Tess Donahue.

I'm trying, trust me—but it's not working.

And I'm trying not to be a creeper. It's not like I'm openly staring, but dude, I haven't seen her in years, and now that I have seen her, the juxtaposed thoughts I have about her in my mind are freaking me out.

Also, I've had a few beers, so that doesn't help dial the thoughts down in my brain.

Grady slaps me on the back, laughing at something stupid. His laughter is loud and obnoxious, mostly because he's approaching drunk. But what else is new? I love Grady, but he can't tip them back as hard as he thinks he can without the blood alcohol level rising quicker than it does for someone my height and weight.

He's not a big dude, not by any stretch, so he cannot drink like one.

He laughs again, snorting.

"You should go over there and talk to her, dude. She keeps looking over here," he's telling me none-too-quietly and in front of other people.

I'm lost. "Who are we talkin' 'bout?"

"Lizzy."

Lizzy who? "I have no fuckin' idea who you're talking about."

No offense to Lizzy. I'm sure she's a nice girl.

Grady rolls his eyes. "I thought the point of you comin' home was to let loose a little. You've been hidin' in a corner all damn night. Don't try denyin' it."

So what if I am? I don't feel comfortable being the center of attention in crowds, and lucky for me, most people have left me alone. No one is hanging on me the way they do at school. Girls aren't trying to grab my junk or grabbing my ass or vying for my attention, hoping I'll take them home.

That always gets on my nerves.

My twin, on the other hand? He used to eat that shit up.

The funny thing is, now that he has a serious girlfriend, it doesn't seem to stop the chicks from hitting on him even though you'd have to live under a rock if you didn't know he was seeing someone.

SportsCenter plastered the story and Daisy's pretty face all over the evening news.

And I'm not getting that desperation here.

No one here cares that I play football because literally everyone here plays football.

A few dudes here tonight play for other schools—a few of them are Wisconsin's conference rivals. The fact is, I'll be back in Texas in a few months to play one of them…

So yeah.

I ain't shit, and they're letting me know it.

"Lizzy is the one over there in the hot pink dress."

I follow his gaze to the other side of the room to the clique of girls near the small entryway, clustered at the base of the stairs, and give the girl in the hot pink dress a quick perusal.

Small.

Compact.

Blonde.

"She's not my type," I finally say to get him to climb down

off my nuts.

"Bullshit. She's everyone's type."

"Not mine." Seriously, just 'cause she's cute doesn't mean my dick will automatically get hard for her.

What an idiot.

I give Grady the side-eye. "What about you, bro? You're single. Why aren't you over there taking your own advice?"

He ducks his head to hide his grin. "I've kind of been talkin' to someone."

"Hold up." My brows lift in surprise. "You've been talkin' to someone and haven't told me about it?"

"Dude, not so loud."

I smack him on the bicep. "Dude, no one's listenin'. Tell me who you're talkin' to. Where'd you meet her?"

"An app." He sounds embarrassed.

"Why are you embarrassed? Drake met Daisy on an app." It's almost impossible to meet someone in person these days. Even when you meet them organically in the wild, there's still no guarantee there will be chemistry on the first date.

I should know.

I spent the first half of this year putting myself out there and asking girls out and look where it got me. My brother is dating the girl he catfished on my behalf.

He has the balls to roll his eyes at me. "Casey's real."

"Kay. I'm just sayin'… I don't want you wasting your time if this Casey person isn't real when the actual thing is right in front of you and you're missing your chances."

He scoffs. "Take your own advice." He gives me a nudge. "You act like an old man whose dick has shriveled off."

I nudge him back. "You should talk. You're standing right beside me, asshole."

Grady laughs. "Hey, we're here for Lucas. Not to get laid."

I clamp him on the shoulder. "I mostly came to see you. I could give a shit about Lucas. You were right when you said I needed to let loose and chill, but…" My shoulders move up and down in a shrug. "Not sure how to. I just need to unwind and not overthink everything."

"Not sure how? Brother, the answer is right here!" He lifts his red cup high in the air. "Listen up, everyone," he shouts. "Our friend Drew here needs your help letting loose. Who wants to be the first one to welcome him home?"

The crowd goes wild, cheers filling the entire house. But considering the place is packed, I'm not surprised.

A stupid grin widens my smile, but I swear to God I would be completely shocked if my face weren't bright red right now. The thought of being the center of attention is almost crippling. I'm not normally so introverted, but my brother is usually with me.

As my brother *and* my twin, we go everywhere together socially. If he goes to a party, I go to the party. If he goes to the library to study, I'll go to the library to study. He went so far as to show up on one of my dates to vet her, the asshole, hijacking the date as if my personal life and who I dated was his damn business.

So the fact that I'm here at this party by myself, let alone the fact that I flew back to our hometown without him for the weekend…

Bonkers, man.

The crowd chants, and people swarm me, and I'm transported to Wisconsin, right back to school, where in public places everyone recognizes me as part of the Colter legacy, the brothers who can do no wrong. Campus royalty.

People crowd me, suddenly want to talk and get me to have a good time. Drinks are being thrust in my hands even though I'm already holding a cup of beer.

Eventually, I forget my inhibitions.

Eventually, I forget that Tess Donahue is on the other side of the room looking wicked cute. Eventually, I forget how pretty she is and how sexy she is in that green top, and I forget that she's my best friend's little sister.

CHAPTER 8
TESS

ON THE FIRST DATE I'VE ALWAYS GOT MY FINGERS CROSSED LIKE, PLEASE, LET HIM BE WEIRD LIKE ME.

I'M up early the following morning.

Not by choice, of course. My original plan had been to sleep in late, considering we were up until all hours of the night and probably didn't get home until after one o'clock. I was even too tired to take off my makeup, if that's saying anything...and I almost always take off my makeup.

Wiped out.

Exhausted from all the laughing and drinking, my ears are still buzzing from the loud music.

The first thing on my agenda for the day was supposed to be: do nothing. Be lazy. Get a cute coffee or latte. Play on my phone. Read. Mindlessly watch *Queer Eye*, my favorite new obsession.

But that's not what happened, is it?

No.

No, it did not because my roommate (for the weekend) was up bright and early at the ass crack of who-knows-when, chipper and chatty, and woke my ass up by bouncing on the edge of my borrowed twin bed.

"Rise and shine, buttercup!"

She is seriously so damn lucky she was sliding a fresh latte in my hand with a smile before I could protest.

I grumbled, but who can be angry with someone who brings you a sweet coffee treat in the morning?

Not I.

"Why are you waking me up? I'm on vacation."

Miranda's laughter makes the mattress move up and down. "You should see yourself. You have the worst mascara and eyeliner bags under your eyes."

Gee, thanks.

I shoot her a look, sipping from the cold latte cup I'm cradling in my palms. "Was too tired to wash my face."

"Well, you can't lie in bed all morning. Drew will be here soon to pick you up."

I swear I shoot off the bed. "Pick me up? For what!"

Miranda only laughs. "Kidding. He doesn't have a car, remember." Rolling her eyes at me. "I just wanted to see the look on your face."

I pick up a throw pillow and chuck it at her. "You're a dick. But also, why is he picking me up?"

"Remember last night when I told him the two of you should hang out since neither of you have anything to do while Zero and I take his grandma to her doctor's appointment and Grady works? Hello, you're going to be sitting around doing nothing, so you're welcome for setting up this date."

"It's not a date, and I'm not hanging out with him today. It's awkward and not fun." I press a hand against my forehead. Does she not see that I'm hungover? If not from alcohol, then from loud noises and fun?

There's something to be said about partying with friends from home versus the ones at college. We're not there to impress anyone, so no one had any inhibitions last night.

"That's not what you told him."

"What's that supposed to mean?" I rack my brain for any memory of a conversation with Drew that could have involved us making plans, and the only one I can recall is the initial mention of it before we'd had all the beer.

Personally, I think Miranda is full of shit but have zero ways to prove it.

"We definitely had a convo with him once I got done lecturing you in the bathroom about being a party pooper."

Yup, she's lying.

"Anyway," she continues, "I have to get going. Zero will be here in like three minutes. But you have to zip by your brother's and grab Drew since he doesn't have a car."

"Yes, I'm aware."

I blink. "So what are we doing on this day…date of ours?"

"Don't know. Killing time, probably."

"Oh great. Killing time. Awesome, that won't be like watching paint dry."

"Dude, stop complaining. You're spending the day with your crush. Consider yourself lucky!"

"He was my crush in middle school, okay? I'm over it."

Mostly.

Sort of.

Miranda doesn't believe me. "Are you trying to tell me your girl parts didn't tingle when he looked at you last night?"

I nod. "Yup, that's what I'm saying."

"Yeah, okay liar." She stands, smoothing down the short denim skirt she's wearing with a cropped concert tee shirt. "Be at his place by eleven."

When she walks out of the little guest bedroom I'm occupying, I can only stare with an open mouth.

She's bamboozled me. Pulled a fast one.

Did a bait and switch.

Dammit!

Throwing back the covers, I rise from the bed and pad to the bathroom, getting a first look at my reflection.

"Holy shit." Yikes.

Eyeliner everywhere.

I grab a washcloth and spot clean before starting the shower, waiting for the water to get warm before stripping off my tee shirt and sleep shorts and climbing inside.

If I'm going to spend the day with Drew Colter, I should at least look cute, right?

Even if I don't care what he thinks of me.

DEAR DIARY...

    Today was so totally embarrassing and I'll tell you why.
    Mom went out of town for a girls weekend with her college roommates and Dad didn't want to leave me home alone even though I'm old enough, so he took me to football practice with him—LIKE I WANT TO HANG OUT WITH GRADY AND HIS MORONIC TEAMMATES ALL MORNING. Dad's helping the coach count equipment and stuff and brought me along to help and I wanted to crawl into a hole. It was really hot and the guys practiced in just their pads and I swear to God I had actual drool coming out of my mouth. Obvi I texted the girls and Bev was all "pics or it didn't happen" but it's not like I can just freaking start taking pictures without bring obvious. Dad embarrassed the crap out of me when he caught me staring and had to yell my name to get my attention and like, I wanted the ground to swallow me hole.

Why couldn't he have just LEFT ME AT HOME? UGH he's sooooo annoying. I swear, if he takes me to the damn football field any more this week, I'll leave. Not sure where I'd go but that's not the point...
Xx Tess

CHAPTER 9
DREW

YOU KNOW YOU'RE SINGLE WHEN YOUR REMOTES HAVE THEIR OWN SIDE OF THE BED.

"HELLO?"

I hear a voice in the kitchen at the same time I hear the back patio door sliding closed and soft footsteps on the tile floor.

The remote in my hand freezes, pointed at the television.

I set it on the coffee table and rise. "Tess?"

Her head pops into the living room where I've been sitting on my ass all morning, bored out of my fucking mind, counting down the hours until Grady gets home from work and we can get on with this bachelor party everyone has been looking forward to since Lucas got himself engaged.

"Hey!"

She sounds cheery, but the joyful greeting doesn't quite reach her eyes as they glance around the room.

"Grady isn't here," I inform her because clearly that's why she's here.

"I know." She steps all the way into the room. "Um. I thought we were supposed to do something today?"

"We were?"

I'm standing here in boxer shorts and a bro tank that actually belongs to my bro. Barefoot.

Unshaven.

Tired and probably a bit hungover—not that I can recall what being hungover feels like, it's been so goddamn long. But I'm pretty sure that's what this is.

"Miranda told me…" She pauses. "Freakin' A." Her head gives a little shake. "Um. Never mind."

Tess looks torn.

"Let's do it. Let's go do something," I decide, clicking the television power off, then tossing the remote onto the couch. "Give me a few minutes to wash up and change."

Her mouth gapes open as if she wasn't expecting me to acquiesce or volunteer to hang out with her. Even though her friend Miranda was unabashedly pushing us together last night. For whatever reason.

Maybe she actually does feel bad that Tess and I have no one to hang out with during the day while our friends are busy. Yeah, it's Saturday, but Grady had to run to his office for a few hours to file a permit they need on Monday, and it can't wait.

So here we are.

Flying solo.

Together.

I wash my face, run a washcloth under my pits, then slap on some aftershave lotion and cologne even though I haven't shaved. Then I wet my hair and style it so I don't have bedhead.

Standing over my carry-on suitcase, I debate which clothes to put on.

Shit, I have nothing since I only brought clothes for the main event. I didn't even bring clean, fresh airport clothes for tomorrow afternoon's flight back to Wisconsin.

My shorts from yesterday will have to do. Plus this bro tank, which isn't the best but also not the worst.

DAMN, BRO it proclaims. My idiot brother thought it would be funny to get us Colters each one, and I'm certain this one is actually his because this one is white, and mine is gray and buried at the bottom of my closet.

Because it's lame.

When I leave the bathroom, Tess stands in the same spot I left her, fiddling with the keys in her hands and looking as if she were ready to bolt.

"Ready?" She springs into action, stepping back into the kitchen and going to the fridge. Grabbing a water bottle, she hands it to me, then picks up another for herself. "I do kind of want to stop for coffee if you don't mind?"

My stomach growls. "And some food, hopefully?"

"Sure, they have food at the coffee shop." She laughs, leading the way outside.

My eyes trail down her back, over her ass, and continue down her tan legs. She's wearing a short denim skirt, flip-flops, and a white tee shirt with a scoop neck that slouches down off one shoulder.

Stop staring at Tess Donahue's ass, I tell myself. *This is your best friend's little sister.*

Little sister who's all grown up.

Grady would so kick your ass if he caught you eyeballing her.

Would he? How do you know?

'Cause I'd kick his ass if he were gawking at my sister—if I had a sister for him to gawk at.

Not the same thing, plus I've only ever seen him get pissed once.

First time for everything…

I hop in the front seat of Tess's car, buckle in, and stare straight out the window.

"Where're we going?"

She gazes out the window too. Clutching the steering wheel, she taps her fingers on the leather. "I don't really have a plan. I…" She fans out her hands and flexes her fingers, staring at her fingernails. "Fancy a pedicure?"

"I'm sorry?"

"We should get our nails done."

Uh.

"Should we?"

Tess starts the engine of her car with a definitive nod. "Yes.

It's a great idea. Starbucks and the nail salon." She looks over at me, eyes on my lap. Then legs. "Pedi for both of us."

Never heard of it. "What's a pedi?"

"Stop." She laughs. "You know what a pedicure is."

We hit the drive-through for lattes and breakfast sandwiches. I order two, a spinach wrap and a bacon/egg/cheese situation, then we head to the nail salon, a place I've never been inside. It's like entering a different dimension. Did you know there are these giant massage chairs where you sit while you sink your feet into a tub of water?

We don't have to wait long. Miraculously, they have availability for both of us, which Tess assures me is not usual since it's a Saturday and always busy. But the people who were supposed to be here were no-shows, so here I am, ass firmly planted in a burgundy massage chair.

"This is nice." I try to make myself comfortable, calves soaking in the hottest fucking water I've ever stuck my legs in. The woman on the little bench in front of me is smiling up at me in such a way that I didn't have the heart to tell her it's scalding me. "I could get used to this."

"Are you doing a color?" the little woman asks.

I glance over at Tess. "Uh."

"He'll just get them buffed," she supplies for me, taking charge. "No color."

"What about you?"

Tess riffles through these weird little plastic sticks that have fingernails glued to the end of them, and each one is painted a different color. Her toenails are painted hot-pink, and she glances over at me, holding one of the plastic sticks toward me.

"What do you think of this pink?"

"It's cute."

"Or I could do white?" She shows me the white one.

Uh. "Do the pink?"

She seems to be mulling this over, biting the inside of her cheek as she does, sipping her latte, totally in her element.

Meanwhile, my feet are getting tickled.

No, not tickled. She's buffing them with some rock thing, sweeping it back and forth across the bottom of my feet, driving me insane 'cause I yell out, "FUCK. THAT TICKLES!"

All heads turn.

All of them.

Everyone in the place is staring.

Shit.

Did I say that out loud?

But fuck, that tickles.

I stuff the rest of the spinach wrap in my mouth so I shut the fuck up even as this lady tortures me. I thought this was supposed to be relaxing!

I press a button on the massage chair, and it powers up, a hard ball pressing into the small of my back, moving upward as it vibrates. My entire body is rumbling and shaking.

"How do you paint someone's toes when their entire body is shaking?" I ask the woman still going to town on my feet.

"Practice." She grins at me.

I shut the chair off and watch the woman as she grabs a metal cheese grater from her bucket and scrapes it across my heel, back and forth, back and forth.

Interesting.

"You have lots of calluses."

Yeah, which is a good thing because if I didn't, my shoes would hurt like hell, and I'd have blisters.

"Don't shave them off. I should probably keep 'em." I grimace 'cause that just sounds *so* beyond idiotic. "Sorry. Um, I'm an athlete and, um, don't want my feet to get blisters."

She plonks the cheese grater thingy into a jar of blue liquid.

I can't tell if she's annoyed as she plunges my leg back into the water and begins scrubbing my legs with grainy, sandy goo.

"What is that?"

"Sugar scrub," Tess explains. "It's exfoliating so your legs are soft."

I glance down at her legs, which are soft and smooth and tan and long. She has them sunk into the water the same way mine are as the woman doing her pedicure rubs them up and down with the palms of her hands.

I look a little too long.

Clear my throat.

The technician takes both my feet out of the water then, patting them dry with a towel before filing my toenails. That tickles too—though not as much as that rock thing did on the pads of my feet.

My nails get filed. My legs get rubbed. Maybe this isn't all torture.

Tess's get painted the light pink color she'd picked out. It wasn't the color she'd shown me but pink all the same. Cute toes.

Cute feet.

I'm not a feet guy but hers are pretty fucking adorable.

She wiggles them when she catches me looking.

CHAPTER 10
TESS

I'M SO USED TO BEING SINGLE THAT I DON'T EVEN KNOW WHAT I'D DO WITH A BOYFRIEND. DO I WALK IT? DOES IT NEED TO BE FED? I'M NOT READY.

AM I IMAGINING IT, or is Drew checking me out?

No.

He can't be, not possible.

But why isn't it possible? Miranda's voice chimes in like my conscience, whispering in my ear. *You're freaking hot and a good catch.*

I wiggle my toes when I catch him watching my feet, and he quickly looks away as if caught staring at my ass—which I honestly wish he would do. Depending on the dude, I don't mind being sexually objectified a little, ha ha.

Once his feet are done, he waits for me on the couches in the lobby. When my toes finish drying, he rises when I walk over, heading to the cashier at a makeshift counter at the front with his wallet out.

He hands the lady his credit card before I can so much as dig in my crossbody bag, and I put my hand on his forearm to protest.

"What are you doing? I was going to pay."

"You don't have to pay because I just did."

"But I'm the one who forced you to come here."

"You didn't force me to get my feet done." He taps the card

on the counter when the woman hands it back before sliding it back into his black leather wallet.

We can't stand here arguing, but I feel like an asshole having him pay for my feet. I had gel put on them, which is more expensive than regular polish. If I'd had known…

"Stop worrying about it and just say thank you."

"I…" I swallow. "Thank you."

I can't very well admit that no guy has ever paid for my nails before, nor can I admit that I've never sat side by side with one to get them done, and it was an oddly satisfying experience.

"You're welcome." He pushes through the front door, holding it open for me and the two women just arriving.

I feel self-conscious walking in front of him to my car, brain racking over where to go from here. We've only killed two hours with more in the day to spare before our friends get home from work and the bachelor party festivities begin. So what next?

What now?

What is there to do in this town?

The beer garden? Eh, no, we'll be drinking enough tonight. There's no need to start so early in the day.

The zoo? Eh.

Lunch? Possibly.

Shopping? Absolutely not.

I don't want him to think of me as a girl who shops on a weekend instead of doing something practical with my time even though I'm totally the girl who likes to shop on the weekends. I also enjoy going to the library, but we won't get into that. Let's just say I have a lot of free time on my hands…

Miniature golfing?

Hmm, that could work. It would certainly keep us busy, and we'll probably laugh.

"Fancy a Putt-Putt?" I ask with a little laugh, climbing into the car and strapping myself in.

"Putt-Putt?"

I can see by the look on his face that he has no clue what I'm talking about. Or at least, it's not registering in his brain.

"Miniature golf?"

"Ohhh, mini golf. I was confused for a second." He pulls a face. "My brain wasn't thinking golf when you said putt-putt. Don't know why."

I hang a right out of the nail salon parking lot, driving toward the outskirts of town where a well-known miniature golf course lives.

I put my blinker on and take another right at the next intersection. Another three miles down the road and we're there, pulling into the parking lot and assessing the crowd.

Not bad.

It's not crowded in the least, which is perfect.

We make quick work out of paying-which I beat him to this time- and selecting our equipment.

"Would they have clubs long enough for you?"

"Clubs? They're called putters." He laughs, watching me. "You don't golf at all, do you?"

"Um, no. But I do enjoy the occasional mini session."

I choose a lime-green ball, and he chooses neon orange.

"Game on," he says at the first hole—a par 2—tossing his ball to the artificial grass beneath our feet. "Ladies first."

I nod my head, stepping forward. My ball thuds onto the ground next to his, and I spread my feet shoulder-width apart as if I were about to tee off on a world-renowned golf course.

I wiggle my ass for good measure as if that would help me get a hole-in-one.

It doesn't.

My ball flies down the fairway and bounces off the concrete wall, rolling back in my direction in a decadently undignified fashion.

"Fuck," I utter, hoping he doesn't hear me.

"Cursing already, Tess? It's been three minutes."

My nose turns up, and I ignore him, walking toward my ball

once it stops rolling and lining up my tap again. It gets close to the hole but doesn't go in.

One more tap.

Then another.

"Shit."

"That's two."

"No, that was four." I pause. "Oh, you were counting my swear words."

He laughs, moving into position to take his swing, his ball rolling ever so steadily toward the hole in the ground, stopping at the rim of it.

"Damn."

"That was one." I'm smugly enjoying this new game.

Two taps and his neon ball sinks in. I can't help admiring his smooth, tan biceps when he leans over to retrieve it.

We move on to the next hole, and I don't sink this one quickly, either. I'm aware this might have been a bad idea, considering I suck at miniature golf.

"I don't remember being this bad at Putt-Putt," I tell him as we walk to the fourth hole, crossing a tiny bridge over a man-made babbling brook. I can see balls on the bottom, lolling around, waiting to be recovered.

Drew lifts his putter to his lips and blows on it as if it were a smoking gun.

"We can't all be good at everything. I'm sure you have other talents."

I roll my eyes, but secretly, I mentally begin listing my other talents.

Dancing.

Baking—I make killer cakes and can decorate like a pro.

Um.

I can roller-skate.

I used to play soccer.

I'm not afraid of heights or spiders.

Shit, those aren't talents, but raise your hand if you think they should be!

"Besides football, what else do you do?" I wonder out loud.

"I like science. I'm fascinated with the solar system."

My brows go up. "That's certainly a fun fact." And unexpected. "If you weren't playing football, what would you be doing with your life?"

"I'd still be in college, obviously—majoring in science. Maybe I'd be an engineer? It's hard to imagine, though, since I wasn't really allowed to think for myself."

He says it so offhandedly it doesn't sink in, but when it does, I pause over the ball I'm about to putt and look up at him.

"What does that mean?"

"It means…" He isn't sure how to respond. "Never mind."

Now my hands are on my hips, and my foot is propped up on the concrete curb, the putter being used like a walking stick.

"You were going to say something, so say it. What did you mean when you said you weren't allowed to think for yourself?"

"You knew my dad."

Four words.

Small words that pack a punch.

I nod slowly.

I did know of his dad but hadn't ever met the man in person. If I had, I'd probably have wet my shorts. He was a shrewd asshole of a guy, according to Grady, who spent the most time at the Colter household.

"I don't want to disrespect his spirit by speaking ill of him, but…" He shrugs. "My dad wanted us to play ball. So we played ball, end of story. He wasn't even around much, but if he caught wind that we were doin' something else with our time?" He whistles low. "There was hell to pay."

You know. You see people like Drew Colter…and his brothers playing the same sport. And you never wonder what it's like behind closed doors. All you see are four good-looking (like, seriously good-looking) brothers who grew up in a wealthy family with a famous father and a beautiful mother—and you never stop to think about the emotional toll the pressure may have put on them.

All of them.

Imagine not having a choice.

We *all* have choices, of course—but imagine thinking you didn't. What must that be like?

"I'm sorry."

He shakes it off with that pleasant, handsome grin. "Don't you worry your pretty head. Everything worked out."

I'm still stuck in one place, frozen like a statue. "But…"

He cocks his head to the side, waiting for my next words.

"Do you even want to play football?"

A second goes by.

Then another, then twenty.

"Sure."

That's not really an answer—not actually—especially not when it took him so long to respond to the question. But I'm only his best friend's little sister. We are not friends in the literal sense, and I am not his confidant. Who am I to pry into his personal business?

His response makes me sad.

I smile, though.

Then I bite my bottom lip and set to sinking this ball.

CHAPTER 11
DREW

MY DATING LIFE CAN BE SUMMED UP IN ONE SENTENCE: WELL. THAT DIDN'T FUCKING GO AS PLANNED.

"DO YOU EVEN WANT TO PLAY?"

I hesitated.

"Sure."

Now why did I go and say a thing like that?

Sure.

The better answer would have been: Yes, of course! Yeah.

Yup = all better replies than *"Sure."*

I'm an idiot, but she's making me nervous. Her intense stare has me fidgeting with the putter in my hand.

"Do you even want to play?"

"Sure."

Ugh.

"Of course I want to play ball. I wouldn't be doin' it if I didn't want to."

Tess doesn't look convinced, but she shrugs and goes to put her little green ball toward the next hole. Technically, it should've been an easy dunk, but she misses because she's swinging too hard, and it bounces off the back wall. She's not that great at miniature golf, but I reckon it's because she isn't competitive and, therefore, isn't concentrating or trying to beat me.

Seems like she'd rather make conversation than play this game.

My eyes stray to the backs of her skirt and those ass cheeks that seem to want to flirt.

When it's my turn again, I miraculously sink the ball in one stroke—as if mini Putt-Putt were my second skill.

I fist pump for no reason, peacocking around the fake grass to irritate Tess.

She doesn't bite.

Only smiles.

I realize then that she's not shy. She's simply good-natured and a genuinely nice person—unlike her brother, who can be a massive asshole. One who has occasionally given my asshole brothers a run for their money.

"So you like football well enough, but you're not passionate about it. You enjoy science." Tess taps her ball toward the hole. "Are you dating anyone?" She laughs. "Is that too personal?"

I laugh because it's not personal at all. In fact, it's a question I get asked a lot, especially by the media. People are curious about my personal life, Dallas's personal life, and Drake's personal life. You name it, we've been asked it.

"It's not too personal, and no, I'm not." Still single as a goddamn pringle.

It drove me nuts not having a girlfriend last semester. Don't know why it bothered me so damn bad, but here we are. I'm jerking off alone in my bedroom at night, sometimes in the morning, sometimes on the toilet, and occasionally in the shower.

I see movies alone. I eat out alone.

And the last person on earth who wanted a girlfriend—i.e my twin—now has one, and he did it right under my nose.

"What about you?" I ask in kind, though I am curious about her relationship status. I wouldn't have been able to picture the younger version of Tess having a boyfriend or a girlfriend, but I can visualize this one.

Tall. Sexy.

Sweet.

She seems like a real catch.

"Not currently. Last year, I was seeing someone, but he was in a fraternity, and well, you know how those guys can be—not to stereotype."

"I cannot see you with a frat brother."

This makes her giggle. "You can't see me with a frat guy? You barely know me. How do you know I'm not a wild party girl? Or a heavy drinker? Or a sorority girl who only dates Kappas?"

My brows rise. "Are you?"

"No. But you don't know that. You haven't seen me in…how many years?" Tess drags her putter to the next hole. "I had braces the last time we were in the same room, and you didn't even spare me two glances."

"When was that?"

"Remember that time Grady had you guys over when we got that new ATV? And y'all took turns driving it around the property? I had my hand elbow deep in the potato chips, and none of you even noticed I was there."

I stop playing and look at her, leaning against my putter, and matter-of-factly say, "I mean. You're Grady's little sister."

Tess rolls her eyes. "No, I get it. I was mousy and quiet. Of course, you wouldn't have noticed me."

Wait.

I'm confused. "What are you sayin'?"

"I'm not sayin' nothin'." She flounces off toward the last hole —a small replica of a Danish windmill with the spinning wheels.

I don't know a whole helluva lot about women, but I know when one has her panties in a twist, and for whatever reason, Tess is suddenly being salty.

"Are you sayin' you wanted us to notice you?"

And by us, I mean me, but I'm not gonna come outright and say it. I'm not gonna assume she…you know, wanted me to notice her. Nah, that's crazy talk.

She didn't.

Instead, Tess shrugs. "Whatever, I was young."

"Sooo…is that a yes?"

For real, spell it out for me because I'm a guy and kind of an idiot sometimes. Unless it's black or white, I don't see gray very often. Most guys don't.

Isn't it easier to just say what's on your mind, rather than beating around the bush?

"I don't know. Probably." She's got her back to me, trying to act all casual. "Like I said, I was young."

"Fair enough." It answers my question, but not really. Like I said, I'm curious, but it's not my personality to pry deeper. I barely know Tess.

Well maybe you should get *to know her. That's how friendships form, numbnuts.*

Friendship? Really, dude, that's where your head is at?

My head—my eyes—do that traveling thing where they soak in her backside, enjoying the view of those smooth legs I sat so close to and know were freshly shaved.

No, friendship is not where my head is at, but Tess is Grady's sister. We've never technically talked about Tess being off-limits to date, but I've heard him tell other guys to leave her alone, and *that* conversation is not something I want any part of.

I don't think.

Do I?

No.

CHAPTER 12
TESS

MY BOYFRIEND IS SO HANDSOME AND SEXY, LOOKING ALL INVISIBLE AND SHIT.

"ARE YOU SAYIN' *you wanted us to notice you?*"

Do you have any idea how hard it was to answer that honestly? Or at least, imply that I had, in fact, wanted him to notice me.

Yes, my response was wussy, but it's not like I'll come right out and admit to his face that I had a crush on him when I was young.

He's not much older than I am, but it always felt like lightyears. In reality, it's two. I'm two years younger than Drew and three years younger than Grady.

I should have flat-out said yes.

I should have flat-out been like, "*Yes, I wanted you to notice me.*"

But I didn't, and I was vague, and now he's not going to know I had a hard-on for him while I was still that brace-faced kid.

No, not a kid.

A teenager with good taste.

Drew has always been a good catch and, from what I've seen and heard, a good boyfriend.

To my knowledge, he hasn't had many girlfriends, but those he did have never had anything nasty to say about him after their breakups. And Grady has certainly never talked shit about him. Plus, he's adorable.

If you can call someone over six foot two *adorable*.

Which I do.

If I thought Drew was cute when we were teenagers, he could only be described as hot now. Prime grade A hot man meat.

Stop it. You did not just call him that.

I'm sorry, but HELLO, have you seen his arms in that shirt?

He was supposed to get off that plane looking like a scrub or a slob, and he was supposed to do me a favor by being a bit of a douche. But he's none of those things. If anything, he's gotten better looking because he's more of a man now than a child.

What would he do if I…

…flirted with him?

Just a little?

Not that I'm good at flirting, but…

Just once.

Or twice.

It couldn't hurt, right? Plus, he's leaving tomorrow, and I won't see him again for who knows how long. He isn't invited to Lucas's wedding, just the bachelor party tonight, so the odds are favorable. He and his brother play in the Bowl game during the holidays, so he's usually not home then, either.

"I was young," I repeat. "But I'm not young anymore."

I flip my hair over my shoulder, then glance over it, giving him the most coy smile I can muster.

Shit.

Alcohol would help.

But you're not a day drinker, Tess.

No time like the present to become one. Ha!

Drew is watching me, his expression unwavering and hard to read.

Serious.

Always so serious…

It's his turn to put his ball through the little Dutch windmill, and I saunter up behind him as he bends to swing, tapping him on the ass with my putting stick or racket or club or whatever this is called.

I tap him right in the butt crack, pleased when he startles, and his ball flies off course. It ricochets off the spinning wheel, then flies to the right, bounces, and rolls to a stop back at his feet.

I smirk.

"What'd you do that for?" he grumbles.

"I was teasing you." Duh. "Had to see how unflappable you are."

"Unflappable? What's that mean?"

I'm not sure what the definition is, but I'm pretty sure it means unfazed. That sounds about right.

"It means you're cool." I wink at him.

Yeah, that's right, I winked at Drew Colter.

Then I widen my eyes at him. "Aren't you going to hit the ball?"

His mouth opens at my nerve, then closes as if he wants to say more things but can't decide what, and my stomach flutters. Honest to God flutters.

He hesitates before gently hitting the ball toward the hole beneath the windmill. It narrowly misses the slowly turning blades, disappearing into the dark.

I do the same.

Well. I miss, obviously, because I suck.

It takes at least four tries before I can get the ball into the base of the windmill, and just like that, it's gone.

Game over.

Or is it game on?

DEAR DIARY...

Me again. Went to the mall today with Tosh, Bev and our new friend Madison, and then to the see the 3rd Barbie movie.

I got a new bra today at the mall when I was there with my friends—it's pink and lacey and so freaking cute, I can't wait to wear it even though no one is going to see it. Brandon Tyson asked me to Winter formal but I haven't told him yes yet. I'm worried that if I say yes, Drew will find out and think I'm dating someone else, which could ruin my chances with him—just in case he's thinking of asking me on a date. Tosha said he looked in my direction during the basketball pep rally so THERE'S ALWAYS A CHANCE.

Xx Tess

CHAPTER 13
DREW

CURRENT RELATIONSHIP STATUS: MADE DINNER FOR TWO. ATE BOTH.

> Drake: Bro, what are you up to?

> Drew: Nothing. Just took a shower, and I'm getting ready for this bachelor party. Why?

> Drake: I'm calling.

MY PHONE RINGS, and I see my brother calling, wasting no time in video chatting me because it's not possible for him to be anything other than obnoxious.

I prop the phone on the bathroom counter, on top of a bottle of men's daily vitamins, and hit Accept.

"What?"

"Can't I call to see how you're doing?"

I guess so, but it's still weird.

I roll my eyes at my twin, who appears to be lounging on his bed.

"Are you that miserable?"

I grab the deodorant and pluck the top off, rubbing under one armpit, then the other.

"No, I'm not miserable. I just got done playin' golf with Tess."

Drake's eyebrows go up curiously. "Playin' golf with Tess? Since when do either of you play golf?"

"Miniature golf," I amend.

"With Tess," my brother deadpans. "Who is Tess?"

Is he being serious? "Grady's sister?" I say it like a question because duh, how does he not remember Tess Donahue? Then again, I barely remembered much about her, but still.

"Why were you spendin' the morning with Tess and not Grady? What's that dumb bastard been up to?"

My brother certainly has a way with words. "Workin'."

"All the time or some of the time?"

"All the time."

Drake cocks his head, then scratches it. "Now, why the hell would he convince you to fly all the way there—on your dime—then not be around?"

"'Cause he's a guy and invited me here for the bachelor party. He never promised we were gonna hold hands and have a picnic in the park."

"What? He just sticks you with his sister and expects you'll be cool with it?"

I nod, dampening my face so I can shave it. "That sums it up."

"Who picked you up from the airport?"

"She did."

Drake is quiet for a few seconds. "And now you're spendin' all your time with her?"

"Yeah, pretty much." I take the shaving cream off the counter, spray a dollop in my hand, and spread it out over my face. Cheeks. Chin. Neck.

"So…aren't you gonna tell me what she's like?"

I shrug, getting out the razor. "She's cool."

My brother looks unsatisfied. "And?"

"And…" I pull the razor down over my cheek, then tap it against the sink beneath the water to rinse the blade. "She's not what I remember. Like. At all."

His brows go up again. "Oh? Tell me more."

I might as well confess what he'll probably find out when I get home. "When he told me his sister was pickin' me up from the airport, I was picturing the Tess I remember from when we were young; braces, messy hair. Kind of short."

Drake is already hanging on my every word.

"And she looks nothing like she looked when she was a kid." I chuckle, running the razor blade down my throat. "Like nothing like how I remember her."

"What does that mean? How does she look?"

"She's tall and…really cute."

"*Cute.*"

I sigh.

He's so exhausting. "Yes, cute. Hot, pretty, gorgeous, take your pick, dude."

"Aw, I bet she'd be so flattered."

"Fuck you. I said she was cute. You're the one who forced me to say those other adjectives."

Drake lets out a burst of laughter. "Calm your tits, bro. I was kidding."

I continue shaving my face, trying to ignore him.

He does love egging me on and getting me worked up, not that it's hard.

"What else?"

I shrug. "I don't know. You called me, so why am I the one havin' to make conversation? I'm shaving."

"What's the plan for later?"

"Don't know. Drinkin', barhoppin', the honky-tonk."

"Ugh, the honky-tonk!" Drake whines. "I wanna come. Why didn't anyone invite me?"

"Because you wouldn't have come."

He nods. "That's true. I wouldn't have. But I still like bein' invited."

My brother loves telling people no.

He's such a dick.

"Go back to the Tess Donahue stuff."

"What more do you want to know?"

He gives me a look that says, '*are you fucking kidding me right now? What do you think I want to know, idiot.*'

"Is she into you?" Drake pauses. "Better yet, are you into her?"

I sigh again. "Fine. If you really must know, yeah. I think so."

He pulls a face. "Uh. Which is it?"

"Both?" *Actually,* "I don't know."

"Dude, this is why you're single."

"No, I'm single because you're dating my girlfriend." I laugh, bringing up the fact that he hand-selected a girl for me and then fell in love with her. But I don't like bringing up the past, and I didn't actually know about Daisy when he was courting her and just like to give him shit about it 'cause that's what brothers do.

"Ouch. That hurt me, kind of."

He l*ooooves* saying that.

"I don't know if Tess is into me or not." I go back to the original subject. "Does it count that she poked me in the ass crack with a golf club?"

Drake considers this information, slowly nodding. "Like, how far up the crack did it go?"

I think for a second. "Eh, between the legs, I would say."

He nods. "She was definitely flirting. Did she say anything?"

"Yeah, I asked her what she did that for and she said, 'I'm teasing to see how unflappable you are.'"

"What does unflappable mean?" my twin asks.

"That's exactly what I said!"

"So what does it mean?"

I stop shaving my neck to respond to him. "She said it means I'm cool. Then she winked at me."

"Winked at you?"

"Yeah."

"Hmm. That's a tough one. She can still tease you and not be into you."

That's true.

"Has she flirted with you any other time?"

"Not really? I don't think."

Drake watches me through the phone. "Actually, that was a stupid question for me to ask because you wouldn't know a chick was flirtin' with you if she poked you up the butt with a golf putter."

He's not wrong.

"Dude, this is not helping."

He shrugs. "Well are you tryin to make a move on her or what?"

Make a move on Tess?

"That's not a good idea," I tell him.

"Why?"

"'Cause she's Grady's sister."

Drake snorts, real loud and obnoxious like. "First of all, fuck Grady. Second, he's not even around, you said so yourself. If he gave a shit, he wouldn't be stickin' you with her, would he?"

I can't help but nod along.

"Third, it's a free fucking country. If you're into a girl, you're allowed to be into her. You of all people? Please, you're the last person to bag and tag."

Bag and tag?

What the hell is he talking about?

He rolls his eyes so hard at me. "I mean sleep with someone and not call them back. Catch and release. One-night stand." He's clearly disgusted with my lack of awareness. "Dude. Come on."

He's right of course, one-night stands aren't my style but neither is breaking bro code. Normally reserved for ex-girlfriends of your buddies, or women your buddies have banged, moms, or anyone your friend is crushing on or trying to bone.

I've added Tess to this list, out of respect.

"Grady has no respect for you, dude. If he did, he'd be

hanging out with you. He knows your time is valuable, and you get no time off, so where the fuck is he?"

I couldn't care less about that.

I needed a break anyway.

I needed to get away from school, the girls next door, my brother, our teammates, the endless rotation of the same shit, day after day after day. So who cares if my friend isn't around. He's keeping me occupied, isn't he?

"So Tess isn't your type?"

"No…she is."

My type: low maintenance, kind, funny, great personality. I love brunettes and long hair. I'm a leg man and a boob guy. Love someone who's outgoing but not loud and obnoxious.

"Then tell me what the problem is."

"The problem is she's giving me mixed signals."

Now it's Drake that's sighing heavily. "And you're too chickenshit to make a move?"

I guess. "I'm not going to see her after this weekend, so what would be the point?"

My brother grins. "That's exactly the point."

CHAPTER 14
DREW

SINGLE FOR SO LONG I FORGOT HOW TO SPELL RELATESINGLESHIP.

IF I WAS CONFUSED EARLIER, I'm more fucking confused now.

The honky-tonk is loud and crowded, but there is no mistaking Tess when she appears with a large group of young women. The scene they cause when they walk through the doors is enough to draw all the eyes in the room despite the music blasting from the speakers.

The bride-to-be leads the way, wearing all white and a sash that says "BRIDE" while her bridesmaids wear sashes that say "BRIDESMAID" or "MAID OF HONOR." The entire gaggle of them sports coordinating outfits.

White.

The theme is white.

I glance down at my shirt, wishing I'd packed dressier clothes 'cause suddenly this shirt feels all wrong. And too small, the short sleeves squeezing my biceps 'cause it don't fit right.

It's a polo shirt but still.

Too small.

It pulls across my chest in an uncomfortable way, or maybe I'm just feeling self-conscious after my day date with Tess.

She smacked me on the ass and winked at me.

Now what the hell could that mean?

Had she been flirting?

No way.

She's not…

She couldn't be into me.

Grady shoves a bottle of beer in my hand, slaps me on the back, and makes a beeline for the mass of bridesmaids, but it's not to greet the bride.

Great.

I get to lay on the couch listening to him fucking, er, one of these chicks, *whoever she ends up being*.

I take a swig of the beer, averting my eyes so I'm not caught staring at the group of girls—or unintentionally make eye contact with Tess 'cause, for real, I can't take them off her.

If she wasn't Grady's sister, I wouldn't have guessed she was a little sister. Does that make any sense at all?

She doesn't look like anyone's baby sister…

She looks mature and sexy, and I tug at the collar of this damn shirt that's choking me and making it impossible to breathe.

White dress.

Thin straps.

I don't see anyone but Tess standing among that group of girls. Her smile is big, she's laughing with her head tipped back, and she hasn't stopped scanning the room as if she were searching for someone.

Dude, stop. Look away.

I glance away toward the dance floor, watching the line dancing there, the Boot Scootin Boogie, the actual name of the hall we're in. They play the song that's the namesake of the place several times a night—always have, probably always will. The crowd loves it, and it energizes the place.

There's cheering as people line up on the floor to kick, step, hop.

Suddenly, a hand wraps around my lower arm, and I'm being pulled.

"Come on, let's go dance."

I don't dance, and I don't have cowboy boots on. Line dancing in Texas without them is sacrilegious. I'm one thousand percent sure about that.

Even Tess has them on with her strappy, sexy dress. Hot-pink metallic ones that wink at me from her feet.

Damn, she's cute.

Still, I let her pull me.

She has a drink in her hand, and I wonder if she's drunk. Probably since it's eleven and they started their bachelorette party at the same time we started ours—seven o'clock with dinner, drinking, and the honky-tonk.

Lucas and his fiancée wanted to end the night together, so here we all are.

Tess leads me to the middle of the floor, yanking at me until we're part of the masses, bumping my hip to get me into a position. She laughs.

"You should see your face," she shouts over the music.

"What about my face?"

"You look horrified."

She must mean that I look horrified to be out on the dance floor.

Which I'm not?

Not really.

"I haven't danced in years."

I wasn't big into dancing when I was younger, but we would come here in high school to watch the crowds. Tourists. The mechanical bull riding—of course we did, there wasn't much to do in the small town we grew up in, where Friday nights centered around football and not much else.

The honky-tonk on the edge of town is a staple in this state we live in, and even when we were under the drinking age, we'd show up to watch, standing along the split rails surrounding the hardwood dance floor.

Tess bellows out the starting lyrics to the country song we

grew up singing, wiggling her hips as she moves, signing and attempting to get me to sing, too. She warbles it off-key, and off-tempo, which I find absolutely fucking adorable.

I relent.

Why the hell not?

"There's a honky-tonk," I shout with the rest of the crowd 'cause that's what we do. We shout. We drink. We dance.

Just like riding a bike, the moves come back to me, and my body steps into place, my long legs tapping and stepping sideways, back, forward—in sync with the tide.

Across the room, I see a blonde with her arms wrapped around Grady's shoulders, her face tilted up, listening to whatever he's saying to her.

"Damn, he moves fast," I mutter, feet moving on autopilot to the beat of the music as if I do this regularly.

These feet were always meant to be on the playing field, but somehow, this feels right, too.

Weird, isn't it?

How coming home makes things better?

I feel relaxed, and it's not because of the beer, which I've barely touched.

It's cold, though, so I take another swig, relishing the way it hits my throat, then my belly, warming me from the inside out.

When the song ends, another immediately begins—but it's slow. I don't want to make things weird by asking Tess to dance again. It's too intimate, and we're not in that place, despite the fact that she dragged me out here.

I tip my imaginary hat to her before walking off the dance floor, leaving her behind.

Or at least I think that's what I'm doing.

She's on my heels, weaving through the crowded dance floor behind me, cocktail still in her hand.

I take a long pull from my beer bottle to empty it, then toss it in a nearby trash can.

Damn, that was tasty.

Cold.

Hit right.

"I hate when they play slow songs," Tess grumbles to one of her friends—a brunette I don't recognize. "Brianne, this is Drew. Drew, this is Brianne, one of Morgan's bridesmaids."

Another girl walks up to us. "And this is Sissy."

I nod to them both, a Southern gentleman at heart, once again tipping that imaginary cowboy hat in their direction. "Ladies."

"Drew Colter, as I live and breathe." Sissy—whom I've never met and have only heard about—looks as if she belongs on a college campus in a sorority house, the kind of Southern girl you see screaming into the Rush Tok video and the kind of girl you stereotypically see dating athletes.

Any athlete 'cause that's the only kind of guy a girl like her wants to date, and I can smell a cleat chaser from a mile away.

Drew Colter, as I live and breathe. We haven't even met, so what is this girl going on about?

"I'm sorry," I apologize. "Have we met?"

She giggles, shaking her head. "Not yet, but I've heard so many things about you."

I'll just bet she has, and they are, in no particular order:

1. I have a famous family
2. My father was inducted into the Football Hall of Fame
3. My brothers are rich and play football
4. My twin plays football
5. I play football
6. My twin will probably play professional football
7. I will probably play professional football

There's no possible way she could have heard anything else, certainly nothing personal, as if my public persona were the only things that matter knowing.

Unfortunately for Sissy, she is only one of many who have tried hard—and failed—to impress me.

I could give a shit if she's pretty.

I did not come home to be inundated with women like her,

not in my backyard, where most people know me—the real me—and know better than to fangirl.

I channel my twin brother, who's always been better at feigning off clingers-on than I am. I'm always too nice, and too polite, and worry too much about what people think.

But tonight, I'm not in the mood.

Not with Tess looking on with those wide doe eyes and pink metallic cowboy boots.

"So many things?" I tilt my head. "Like what?"

For real, tell me all about myself.

"I just heard you're super good at football."

I snort. "Okay."

Sissy reaches forward to do that thing girls do when they think flirting and touching will have you melting at their feet and chasing after them simply because she giggled and ran a nail down your arm.

I pull away, stuffing my hand in my pocket. "It was nice meeting you. I'm gonna grab another drink."

The three of them are left staring after me, and I let out a puff of air. Holy shit, I can't believe I just did that! It felt so rude!

"Sorry about her." Tess sidles up to me and sets her perspiring cocktail glass on the bar top. "She's always like that."

Yeah, she seems like the type.

I nod. "S'fine."

"Are you having fun?"

"I think so."

That makes her laugh. "You think so?"

"Yes," I amend. "I'm having fun. Lucas looks happy, and his bride seems cool."

"She is pretty cool." Tess puts her arms across the bar, waggling her fingertips until the bartender walks over.

He smiles, wiping down the counter with a white dish rag as he leans forward, grinning widely, wearing a plaid shirt with cut-off sleeves. I feel like a limp dick in my polo shirt compared to this guy.

"Hey, darlin', what can I get you?"

"Yes, please." She tosses her hair. "I'll have a vodka tonic, and my friend here will have…" She waits for me to fill in the blank with my drink order.

"A lite beer."

"And my friend here will have a lite beer." Tess winks at me, and I wonder if she's in the habit of winking a lot or if she's decided it's fun to make me squirm.

"Vodka tonic and a lite beer comin right up." The guy goes to fetch our drinks but pauses, doubling back and squinting across the bar at me. "Hey. Ain't you one of the Colter boys?"

I nod. "I'm Drew." I put my hand across the bar to shake his. "Good to meet you."

"I'm Dillon. Huge fan of your brothers—and yours of course. You one of the twins?"

I nod again. "Yup, one of the twins."

"That's so fucking cool! What are you doing in town? Don't you boys play for Wisconsin?"

"Wedding party."

His eyes go over my head and search the floor until he sees the gaggle of girls wearing bridesmaid sashes, dressed in white, but then again, there are other bachelorette parties here tonight, so ours is no different.

"Gotcha." He taps the bar top with three fingers. "I'll grab your drinks."

Tess's lips move, and I can't hear what she's saying, so I lean in. "What was that now?"

"I said, must be nice to get recognized."

My shoulders move up and down in a shrug. "Eh. Sometimes but not always." I pause. "Did you not see how that chick Sissy reacted to me? That's the shit that happens most days, and in those cases, it's not cool being recognized."

"She didn't recognize you. She's just a maneater." Tess laughs. "She's like that with everyone, no offense."

Dillon brings back two drinks and sets them on the bar. "It's on the house."

"Now is it nice that you get recognized?" She stirs her cocktail with the thin black straw bobbing up and down in her drink, poking the lime inside with the end of it.

"Guess so." I fish a ten dollar bill out of my wallet and slap it on the counter as a tip. "Thanks, man." I hold the beer bottle up, tipping it toward him in salute, then tap it against Tess's glass. "Here's a toast."

"A toast to what?" She sips her drink.

"A toast to…shit, I dunno. Lettin' loose and havin' fun?"

"I'll toast to that, but it doesn't seem like you're letting loose at all or havin' fun." She laughs, looking me up and down and judging me a bit boring.

"What's it gonna take for me to look like I'm havin' fun?"

"I don't know. We could go back on the dance floor, and you can show me what you got."

"Show you what I've got? Darlin', I don't have nothin'."

Tess is giggling, I'm sure of it. I can't hear it, but I can see it in the way her eyes are lighting up.

"Oh, I wouldn't say you've got nothin'. You have plenty." She grabs my arm again the way she had before, pulling at me and tugging me toward the damn dance floor. Making me wonder why I opened my dumb big mouth.

A song about fishing in the dark comes on—a song that's as old as dirt but a country classic—and arms are thrown in the air as people shout and stomp their feet to the tune, yelling the words of the chorus, most of them off-key.

So fucking fun.

I feel like a giant clod pole among short people, towering over most of them as I dance and sing, chugging my beer to loosen up even more.

And let me be clear: two beers isn't going to get me buzzed, let alone drunk, especially not when I'm sweating it off.

This time when the song tempo changes, I don't walk off the dance floor.

I look down at Tess as she looks up at me, putting my hand on her hip as she slides her free hand to my shoulder.

Welp. Guess we're committed.

CHAPTER 15
TESS

"HOW ARE YOU STILL SINGLE?"
LMAO YOU'RE ABOUT TO FIND
OUT, SIT TIGHT BUDDY.

"THIS FEELS LIKE PROM." I smile at Drew so as not to make this awkward and joke about how odd this feels, though it doesn't feel odd at all.

"Prom? So formal."

"Okay, maybe homecoming?"

"Still too formal."

I squint at him through narrowed eyes. "Did you even go to dances in high school?"

"No." He laughs. "Well, nope. That's not entirely true. Our mama made us get dressed up a few times so she could know what it was like to take pictures for a dance. She didn't have girls and always felt like she was missin' out."

"Aw, your poor mama, stuck with you four monsters."

He lets out a low whistle. "Yup, we sure didn't make things easy, but if I'm bein honest, I never gave her much trouble. Dallas and Drake were the worst."

I'd heard about the trouble they'd caused as teenagers. Dallas Colter, his second oldest brother, was a legend in our town for causing mischief. There's a country song about painting on a water tower, and Dallas Colter went and did the same as a senior prank, spray painting his football number on it like some kind of idiot.

"Seriously. Who spray paints their own damn number on a water tower and expects not to get caught?"

Drew knows exactly what I'm talking about. "Do you know how pissed our daddy was? Jesus Christ, he was damn lucky he didn't get expelled, and they only let him graduate 'cause they were headed to the state championship and didn't want to lose."

I purse my lips.

That's the thing I hate about this town: football players are treated like damn royalty and like saints even when they act like dicks and assholes and do shit like spray paint government property. In this day and age, should they still be getting away with that shit?

No, ma'am.

"What's your mom doin' this weekend?"

Drew shrugs. "Probably traveling. My brother is in training, and his fiancée is looking at houses in the suburbs, so I think she's spending the weekend in Dallas. She didn't know I was comin' home. I didn't fancy being shacked up under her roof since she would have given me a curfew."

"Ugh, that's literally the same reason I didn't want to spend the weekend at home. I'm stayin' with Miranda, who's gone missing."

His eyes go wide. "Seriously?"

"No, she's probably banging her boyfriend in the bed of his pickup truck."

"For serious?"

"Yes, for serious." I laugh at his choice of words. He sounds so Southern and Texan sometimes. Other times, he doesn't sound it at all.

Guess you can't take the South out of the boy…one of his brothers plays for Texas, and I wonder if he'll end up living here when he's done with school, too, or if he'll be out East like his other older brother.

Sooo many Colter boys!

And all but one are taken, and he's the cutest one of all…

HEY DIARY, IT'S ME

Not to always keep talking about guys and stuff—I P R O M I S E I'll talk about other stuff soon, k, but Diary. Drew Colter was at the house today ALONE and I almost died. Like, I came out of my bedroom and he was sitting at the counter literally alone and no one told me he was going to be there. I was in PAJAMAS and a sweatshirt. He was on his phone waiting for Grady to get done doing whatever and I just stood there coz I didn't know what else to say, and then looked up and went "hey" and I went "hey" and then he went back to doing whatever on his phone.

It was so awkward.

They went into the den after that to watch movies and that's where mom put the pizza we were having for dinner but there was NO WAY I was going in there after HUMILIATING myself.

XO Tess

CHAPTER 16
DREW

I'M INDEPENDENTLY OWNED AND OPERATED.

I'M SWEATY AS HELL.

Almost as sweaty as I am running five miles in the heat to make weight for my position, or as hot as I am when I've had to wear a literal sweat suit to lose water weight.

'Cause I've been dancing.

Line dancing, the Watermelon Crawl, the Electric Slide, the Hoedown Throwdown, and the Cotton Eye Joe. You know, the usual, mixed in with a few melon tunes and whatever's current on the Top Ten Country charts.

Sweat may be dripping down my forehead cause it's definitely dripping into my ass crack.

Tess looks just as hot—in both the literal and metaphorical sense. Her long, wavy hair has been pulled back and braided to stay off her neck, the pink metallic cowboy boots removed and set to the side.

We've been drinking water, but I still feel lightheaded, gesturing to her that I'm going to bounce from the dance floor in favor of the less crowded area where people are socializing and not dancing.

Grady is nowhere to be seen.

Hell, I don't even know if the bastard is still in the room or if he's back at his place with that girl he was making out with during the cha-cha-cha.

I need something cold.

I need the wind on my face.

I need a shower.

"You wantin' to leave?"

Tess is next to me, locating a water pitcher that someone has set down on a nearby table, filling our cups to the brim and pushing one in my direction.

"Drink this."

"I've drunk enough."

"Well, drink more. I don't need you fallin' over from heatstroke."

Not one to argue with a lady, I drink more.

It pleases her that I'm listening, and she smiles, taking a drink from her own cup before saying, "I think my brother is gone."

"Yup, I think he's gone."

"Pretty sure he went home with Tarryn. Or she went home with him."

Probably.

"Do guys do that often? Leave each other hanging so they can get laid?"

My brows go up. "Is that what you think he's doin'?"

She laughs. "That's exactly what he's doin'."

I lean my elbow on the table as I regard her. "Where's your friend? That one you introduced me to who was trying to play matchmaker?" I can't remember her name to save my soul. "She's dating that guy with the strange drummer name."

"Um, she's getting laid. Duh."

She's cute.

And funny.

And the sweat glistening between her tits isn't bad, either.

"You want a ride? 'Cause I don't think any of these idiots are in any condition to give you one, and do you actually want to be stuck in an Uber with them?"

I clear my throat. "I'd be an idiot to refuse a ride from a pretty girl."

"Girl." She scoffs. "Ha."

CHAPTER 17
TESS

SINGLE. DON'T WANNA MINGLE...

MY BROTHER IS GONE.

He's gone, and he left Drew without a ride.

It's not late. It's not even midnight. But if Grady has gone home—with a female—then he's probably at his place fucking, and Drew will have to hear it the entire night, and that's gross and annoying.

"I'd be an idiot to refuse a ride from a pretty girl."

"Girl." I make a noise in my throat. "Ha."

He used to make me feel like a girl, but tonight, I've felt like a woman. Even though it didn't feel…romantic or…overly flirty, I get the feeling that Drew is holding back for some reason.

"Give me your keys, and I'll drive," he offers, holding out his hand.

I stare at that massive palm; the calloused fingers, his thumb.

Shiver.

"Alright." Yeah. He can drive. I'll give him that.

If Drew was a sexist prick, I'd refuse him my keys, but he's not. He lets me lead, and he lets me boss him around, but at the same time, he's a gentleman and treats me like a sexy female.

He hasn't made any moves. He's way too polite for that.

But if he thinks I didn't just catch him checking out my boobs, think again, buddy.

He's good at hiding it, but he's not *that* good.

And when he puts his hands at the small of my back, guiding me through the exit door and out into the huge, crowded parking lot, I shiver again.

He leaves it there while we walk the long row to my car.

He opens the passenger side door for me, then closes it while I buckle my seat belt.

We don't have much to say while he's navigating through the parking lot and turning right onto the main road. He knows the way back to my brother's house, but something nags at me.

I'm not ready for him to leave.

I'm not ready for him to go back to Grady's place.

I'm not ready for him to go to the airport tomorrow.

Shit.

It's not as if we're drunk; we danced and sweated most of the alcohol out of our systems until we were as sober(ish) as we were at the beginning of the afternoon, so what's my excuse for what I'm about to say?

He doesn't need to come home with me.

We weren't pawing at each other. We weren't making out (like Grady was). We weren't dry humping each other on the dance floor, much as I would have loved to.

Ha!

Fuck it.

I'm just gonna do it.

Don't be a wuss, Tess.

Shoot your shot.

It's not your place, it's Miranda's.

She isn't going to care. It's not like you're sleeping on her couch the way Drew is sleeping on Grady's; you're in the spare bedroom.

I wring my hands in my lap, debating.

Wine.

Miranda has wine. I can invite him in for some of that?

You don't drink wine, and neither does he.

Ugh.

"If you'd rather not go back to my brother's place and listen to him having honky-tonk sex, you're more than welcome to come to Miranda's with me, where it's quiet," I blurt out.

Drew bursts out into laughter. "Honky-tonk sex?" he repeats. "What the hell is that?"

"You know—finding someone at the dance hall and bangin' 'em."

"She's part of the wedding party, yeah?" He has his eyes on the road, and the oncoming headlights are doing wonders for the color of his eyes and the dark slashes of his eyebrow. He looks mysterious and sexy.

"So...wedding party sex?"

"That's more like it," he amends. "That blonde, don't know what her name is."

"Chelsea," I supply.

"Ahh. There's always a Chelsea, isn't there?" Drew studies the road, and I appreciate the fact that safety is his primary concern. He's not flirting with me, but a stolen glance at my rack would be nice. "Sure, I wouldn't mind the peace and quiet." His hands grip my steering wheel. "And maybe rinsing off in the shower?"

My face gets red. "Doesn't a shower sound amazing? I think Miranda's rock drummer wannabe boyfriend has probably left some clothes behind."

"That dude?" Drew laughs. "He's tiny, man. He's like half my size."

"I'm just trying to be helpful. You aren't gonna wanna lie around in that stinky gross polo shirt after you've rinsed off."

He pulls at the collar. "What? You think I'm stinky and gross?"

"I haven't gotten a proper whiff of you," I tease. "I'll smell you when we get to my place."

I catch his smile and study his profile.

So handsome.

"At the light, turn right."

He nods. "Gotcha."

CHAPTER 18
DREW

WOULD YOU BELIEVE ME IF I TOLD YOU I'M SINGLE BECAUSE NO ONE BELIEVES I'M SINGLE?

I BARELY FIT beneath the showerhead, but I manage, only needing to rinse my lower half anyway and dipping my head to wet my hair. I told myself this was going to be quick, not wanting to make it weird with a full-on shower. Water sluices down my body and pools at my feet before disappearing down the drain.

I stare at my limp cock.

"Sorry, dude. We're not goin' to have any privacy tonight."

My dick doesn't respond, only continues to rest against my thigh, pouting.

Neglected little bastard.

Tess was able to scrounge up a pair of clean boxer shorts, and beggars can't be choosers so when I'm toweled off, I lift them from the bathroom counter and give them a once-over.

"These are not going to fit me," I grumble. "Is she high?"

No shirt, just the shorts, which is fine. I walk around the gym sometimes with no shirt on, and this is far less public than that.

And not to like, humblebrag, but I've got a great physique and have nothing to be ashamed of.

She's on the spare bedroom bed when I walk through the bathroom door, steam billowing around me like a smoke machine. And when she sits up—remote for the TV in her hand

—her stare has me rethinking the wisdom of not throwing on a tee shirt.

"Sorry that I'm wearing this," she starts. "But it's all I had and I wasn't expecting company."

I swallow, my feet inching forward on the carpet toward the bed, eyes daring around for oh, I don't know—a chair or a table or a desk. Something other than the bed while she's sitting there in that… That…

Is that lingerie?

No, can't be. She wouldn't be traveling with that, would she?

But it's thin, and it's a tank top, and those shorts leave little to the imagination. Lavender silk bottoms that barely cover her ass.

Shirt dipping low.

She's apologetic, *but I'm not sure if I believe her.*

Nothing about those pajamas is sweet.

Her tits are bigger than I thought they were—and let's be fucking honest, I've been thinking about what they look like. And I'd be fucking lying if I hadn't imagined what she looks like naked, but now I'm trapped in a room with her wearing nothing but these goddamn boxers that are squeezing the life out of my nutsack.

Chill, bro.

It's peaceful and quiet and it's not like she has an ulterior motive.

Neither do you.

Liar.

My god, I'm such a liar…

CHAPTER 19
TESS

MAYBE I CAN SEDUCE HIM WITH MY AWKWARDNESS...

MY HEART BEATS out of my chest.

What possessed me to wear this in front of him? It's not like I didn't have a choice—last night, I wore a tee shirt to bed that was three sizes too large, my father's XXL, and a pair of sweatpants I stole from Miranda. So this little barely-there number I had thrown in my overnight bag could have stayed retired.

Drew looks like an animal backed into a corner, terrified to take another step toward me.

"So you watching something already?"

He's at the edge of the bed, knees hitting the mattress, and my eyes stray south to the waistband of those ill-fitting boxer shorts he was brave enough to put on.

My mouth waters, damned if it doesn't, as my eyes travel lower still.

I can literally see the outline of his dick.

Drool.

I touch the corner of my mouth, hoping I don't look like a sex crazed maniac but how would you feel if you were sharing a bedroom with your childhood crush?

You'd be drooling at the sight of him, too.

The fact that he's being so polite only makes me want to push those boxers down his hips, shove him onto the mattress, and—

"I love this show too. I binged seasons one and two already. Which season are you on?"

He plops onto the far side of the bed, watching the TV screen, looking at the reality show about sex and dating I've pulled up. Hot singles "stranded" on an island and they're not allowed to bang, kiss, touch, or get each other off.

"Um. Season four."

Drew nods his approval. "Who's that?"

"Chelsea." I laugh.

"See! There's always a Chelsea…"

I settle in. Drew settles in.

The ceiling fan is on, so it's not too hot and not cold enough to be beneath the blankets, but I'm not sure if I can lay here like this. I feel like I'm on the beach in a bikini and have no idea how to behave or move my body.

Shit.

I'm an idiot. I should have worn the tee shirt.

"Uh. I think I'm going to grab a water from the kitchen. You want anything?"

"Sure, if you're doing water, I'll do one too."

I roll off the bed, pulling the door closed behind me before walking to the small, galley kitchen, and when I bend over to take two water bottles out, Miranda walks through the front door.

"Hey, roomie, home so—" She stops in her tracks. "Whoa. You little hoebag." She makes a twirling motion with her hand. "Spin around for me once."

I shake my head.

"Oh my god." Her eyes go to the two water bottles. "Are you with someone?" she whispers. "Did you bring someone home?"

"Shhh, lower your voice," I hiss.

"Lower my voice? I'm literally whispering." She's grinning from ear to ear. "So who is it in the bedroom? Have you had sex yet? Wait. Please don't tell me it's the best man, Billy."

I roll my eyes as if I'd bring that idiot Billy back to her place.

"It's not Billy. It's…" I move my mouth, but no sound comes out. "Drew."

"Who?"

"Drew."

"Oh my god, talk louder."

"My brother has a girl at his place, and I invited him here so he would have peace and quiet."

"Dude. WHO is in the bedroom?"

"Drew." I mouth the word as clearly as I can so I'm not forced to say the name out loud. Miranda is being so damn loud.

"Wait. Back the fuck up. You have Drew Colter in your room, and you're wearing that?!" Her eyes roam my body. "If you're wearing *that*, what the hell is *he* wearing?"

I shrug, water bottles in my hands beginning to condensate. "Boxers?"

"Oh my god, whose boxers?"

I shrug again. "I don't know, Zero's?"

"Are you fucking serious? He put on Zero's shorts?" Her head shakes in disbelief. "I have to see this."

I grab her arm when she tries to stalk toward the bedroom. "Don't you dare!"

"Please. I have to look. There is no way that guy fits in my boyfriend's boxer shorts. No fucking way."

"You're right, he doesn't fit in Zero's boxers," I hurriedly say. "And I doubt he'd want you to stick your nose in there."

"But this is my place, and what kind of hostess would I be if I didn't say hello?"

"Um, you're drunk, and I doubt he wants you oogling his naked body."

"HE'S NAKED?" she shouts. "SHUT UP."

I shush her again. "Shhh, oh my god, he's wearing boxers. We just talked about this. We're just watching TV, okay? Calm down. Nothing is going to happen."

"Are you insane? Seriously, are you literally insane? You

should see your tits in that shirt. I'm straight, but I'd go gay for you in that shirt."

She reaches out to touch one, but I slap her hand away with a laugh.

"Nothing is going to happen."

"Tess, I love you." Her hand goes to my lower arm somberly. "So hear what I'm about to say 'cause I'm only going to say it once. If you do not fuck that guy, it's over between us."

CHAPTER 20
DREW

MY LEVEL OF FLIRTING IS FINDING SOMEONE ATTRACTIVE AND PRAYING THAT THEY'RE BRAVER THAN I AM.

I HEAR LAUGHING from the kitchen which means the roommate is home—but it doesn't sound like that boyfriend of hers is with her and if he is, he hasn't uttered a peep.

"HE'S NAKED? SHUT UP!"

I stifle a smile, reclining against the headboard, waiting patiently for Tess to come back with our water.

I strain my ears to hear what they're saying, and they do not disappoint.

"Shhh, oh my god, he's wearing boxers. We just talked about this. We're just watching TV, okay? Calm down. Nothing is going to happen."

"Are you insane? Seriously, are you literally insane? You should see your tits in that shirt. I'm straight, but I'd go gay for you in that shirt."

Miranda isn't wrong. Tess and her tits look hot in that shirt, and I'd go gay for her too if I wasn't already straight.

Wait.

That makes no sense…

"Nothing is going to happen."

"Tess, I love you. So hear what I'm about to say coz I'm only going to say it once. If you do not fuck that guy, it's over between us."

Welp. At least they didn't have the decency to whisper. And

if anything was said after that last part, I didn't catch it because Tess comes through the door breathlessly, as if she's run a marathon, back leaning against the door after she closes it behind her.

"Um. Hey. Sorry that took so long."

"If you do not fuck that guy, it's over between us."

I can see her nipples through the shirt. The silhouette of color, the hard nubs, the outline of her areolas.

Shit.

I'm a boob guy.

I'm a leg guy.

I'm an ass guy.

"Nothing is going to happen."

"If you do not fuck that guy…"

"Hey, I'm back!" Tess is cheery in the doorway, her eyes betraying nothing of the conversation she was having in the kitchen.

How is she able to act normal?

I'd be blushing, red from head to toe.

But Tess just stands in the doorway watching me with two bottles of water, one in each hand, before strolling in and closing the door behind her.

"Miranda stopped by. She's spending the night at her boyfriend's and wanted to grab her skin care stuff."

Oh.

Skin care stuff…

I half expect her to tell me she's going to move to her friend's room and give me my privacy, but instead, she hands me a water bottle, crosses the room, and sinks to the bed on the other side.

The mattress dips.

The door flies open, and Miranda sticks her head in. "Oh my god, I am soooo sorry." Not. Her eyes are darting around the room. "I'm heading out now, but I wanted you kids to have this."

She tosses a book at us, and it hits my calf.

"Whoops. Don't do anything I wouldn't do." Her head disappears, then pops back in. "Actually, do some things I wouldn't do. Live a little, go crazy."

The door slams.

Tess sits frozen on the bed, water bottle halfway to her parted lips, eyes wide as if she were petrified. Or horrified, both different and the same.

"*Oh my god,*" she whispers. "*Literally shoot me now.*"

Her expression has me laughing and reaching for the book. "Sexy and Thought Provoking Questions to Ask the Person You're Dating."

Um. Okay.

"Apparently, she doesn't want us to be bored."

"Apparently, she wants a lot of things that are never going to happen." Tess forces out a laugh, taking the book from my hand and leaning against the headboard before cracking it open and perusing some of the pages.

"*If you do not fuck that guy, I will never forgive you…*"

Tess isn't reading anything out loud, so I give her a nudge. "What's the book say?"

"Um. Hmm." She flips a page. "What is the last sexual thought you had about your partner?" Her brows are raised. "See, we can't play this because you're not my partner."

"Maybe not. But I can answer the question," I blurt out.

Tess looks surprised. "You can? How?"

I snort. "Easy. The last sexual thought I had was about your legs." *And your tits, because I can see your nipples and if I look at them again my dick will get hard, so please stop wiggling around on the beg, your tits are jiggling.*

"My legs." She moves her legs, crossing them at the ankles. "Huh."

Yeah, huh.

Her nose goes back into the book. "What do you normally sleep in?"

"Pajamas." I pause. "What about you?"

"Nothing."

She doesn't look at me when she answers.

"You sleep naked?" I blink. "Even in the winter or just in the summer?"

"Yes." Tess laughs. "And you sleep in pajamas? What kind of pajamas?"

Oh, Christ. The dorky kind. "Flannel bottoms and a tee shirt." That my mom probably got at Costco.

"Flannel bottoms? Even in the summer or just in the winter."

"Yes." I laugh, mimicking her answer since she mimicked mine.

"Fair enough." She goes back to the book. "What characteristic do you find attractive in another person?"

"Male or female?"

She bites down on her bottom lip. "Female."

Now we're getting somewhere. "I'm attracted to funny people. And brunettes with long hair." Tess is a brunette, and she has long hair. She touches it now as I continue, running her fingers through it like a comb. "A nice smile is a bonus. I also like freckles. And short girls are cute, but I like someone a bit taller."

It's not lost on me that I just described my best friend's younger sister.

"What about you?"

She snuggles into the pillow, book on her chest. "Um. I like someone tall. Uh." Her eyes slide to my side of the bed, skimming down the front of my body before meeting my eyes. "Tall, dark. Handsome."

I roll my eyes. "So you like a walking cliché."

"You're a walking cliché." She scoffs before she can catch herself. "Here, you take this. Unless you want to watch TV."

I could give a shit about the TV.

I take the book. Start from the beginning and read through some of the pages:

- French kiss your partner.
- Give your partner oral for 30 seconds

- Would you rather: Play would you rather, or answer intimate questions?
- If you could change one thing about yourself, what would it be?

"What's taking you so long, read one." Tess is impatient. "Read exactly the question your eyes are on right now. Go."

"It says 'Whisper a compliment into your partner's ear.'"

Easy enough but somehow too familiar.

"Oh, I get a compliment? Yay me!" Tess tilts her neck, lending me her ear so I can lean over and whisper something into it.

I have to think a few moments before I'm ready, not wanting to say anything too revealing, too perverted, or too personal.

I schooch over so I'm closer; close enough that I can easily lean down and speak into her ear.

The first thing I notice is that she smells fucking amazing. Like sweet perfume, but nothing overpowering. Perfect.

Her hair smells good too.

"Did you just smell my hair?"

I mean. "It's right there."

Her low laugh sends a small tingle down my stomach and into my groin.

"Let's see," I say in a quiet voice, into her ear, right below her lobe. "If I..." I gulp down my next words. "If I..."

Tess goes still. "If you..."

"If I lived closer, I think I would...like very much to date you."

Shit.

That was more of a confession than a compliment. Definitely not a compliment.

I pull back.

"Sorry. I don't think that complied with the rules."

She looks as stunned as I feel, having said the words out loud; the words I've been thinking since I climbed into her car two days ago at the airport. And the confession has nothing at all to do with her long brown hair, or her perky tits, or her smooth, long legs.

No, it has everything to do with how sweet she is. And patient. And kind. And how she's always smiling and hasn't said anything unkind since the minute I saw her.

She's a nice person; pretty inside and out.

I pick the book back up, dragging my eyes away from the low-dipping neckline of her top and the swell of those sweet tits. "What's, uh, one secret you have never told the person sitting across from you?"

"Is that a trick? That could be anything. You and I have barely spoken."

"Answer it however you want to answer it."

I am all ears.

I am still tingling from whispering in her ear, my own nipples hardening from the smell of her perfume. And then she leans toward me so she can lie on her side, I get a full view of her breasts, the edge of her areola peeking out from the sheer fabric.

"Hmm. One secret I've never told you…" She brings a finger up and taps it on her chin. "Promise you won't hold it against me, and things won't get weird?"

Oh shit.

Where is she going with this?

I force out a laugh. "Now I'm scared."

"Ha. Don't be. Just promise you won't be weird."

"You know my brothers and I weren't allowed to be Boy Scouts, right? I can't do that whole Scout's Honor bullshit, but I can pinky swear."

I hold my hand out so she can loop her pinky around mine.

She doesn't.

She just smiles, grabbing hold of a nearby throw pillow, hugging it to her chest, and blowing out a puff of air.

She squeezes her eyes shut for good measure. As if she can't dare say anything while she looks directly at me.

"I've had a crush on you since I was a teenager."

Wait.

What?

"Say again?"

"I said, I've had a crush on you since I was—"

"No, I heard you, I just…" I pause. "What?"

How did I not know this?

And.

Would it have mattered if I had?

Probably not when she was younger. I wasn't interested in dating as a kid, certainly not when our dad was alive—he would never have allowed it. We didn't even go to prom or homecoming—not with girls, anyway. Drake had gone with a girl, but she was just a friend.

Our father never would have allowed us to be serious with anyone. In fact, none of us dated anyone until after he'd died. How fucking sad is that? It took him having a heart attack and dying for us to have personal lives and to fall in love.

Well. Not me.

But my brothers.

"You know how it is when you're young."

"No, I don't know how it is when you're young," I find myself saying even though as soon as the words are out of my mouth, I know it's the wrong thing to say.

Tess struggles to explain herself—not that she has to. "We don't know any better."

My brows go up into my hairline.

"That's not what I meant." She laughs. "But it's rough on someone's self-esteem when you're young and the person you have a crush on doesn't know you're alive."

"You…you're Grady's sister."

I sound like an idiot.

I am well aware of this fact.

I feel like that is enough of an explanation. At least in my brain, it makes sense.

"I'm more than just Grady's sister," she says quietly. "I'm your friend, too."

She's right, of course, but that didn't stop me from having a one-track mind for all these years. I don't think a single dude in our friend group ever looked at Tess Donahue in a romantic way, not even this weekend when she had her tits out and was wearing a sexy dress at the bachelorette party. And if they were thinking it, no one said a word.

"You are my friend, too," I repeat dumbly.

The pillow is suddenly gone, and her hand is in the center of the bed, tracing one of the embroidered flowers on the comforter, the pink nail of her index finger going round and round.

She reaches forward and takes the book back, sliding it across the bedspread, pressing her hand into the pages to hold it open before reading out loud.

"When's the last time you had sex?"

"Can't remember," I answer robotically and honestly because I literally cannot remember.

She frowns. "What do you mean you can't remember?"

"I mean—it's been a while." I adjust myself on the bed uncomfortably; her eyes go to my rock-hard abs. "You can't be asking me all those personal questions without answering them yourself, Little Miss Nosy."

"Sure I can."

As she teases me, the fluttering butterflies in the pit of my stomach make me slightly ill.

"Uh, no, you can't."

Tess considers the question. "I've only done it a few times, and the last time I dated anyone was..." She squints at the ceiling. "Maybe six months ago, and he was a douchey frat guy, remember."

CHAPTER 21
TESS

MY BEST FLIRT: I DISLIKE A LOT OF PEOPLE...BUT I DON'T DISLIKE YOU.

HE CAN'T REMEMBER the last time he had sex?

How is that even possible?

Drew is the sexiest guy I've ever seen up close—his twin brother doesn't count even though they're identical because Drake has a gap between his teeth, and gaps are not my thing.

So, in my opinion, Drew is way hotter.

By a landslide.

Miranda's words continue echoing in my brain, on a loop: *"Tess, I love you. So hear what I'm about to say coz I'm only going to say it once. If you do not fuck that guy, it's over between us."*

If I do not fuck Drew Colter…

Who says shit like that?

And better yet, who lays in a bed with a guy considering seducing him to save face with their girlfriend in the morning? Cause Miranda is going to come home and she's going to ask, and what will my brother have to say about it if he found out?

Scratch that. Fuck my brother, he's the reason half these guys refused to ask me on dates.

He's the reason Drew never took me seriously.

But he's not here now, and we have the apartment to ourselves. No one to hear us but the walls.

Drew continues keeping his distance, an invisible wall built between my body and his. He doesn't so much as roll forward an inch, even when I move my hand to the middle of the mattress to gauge his interest.

He is stone.

Ugh.

This is torture. I want to climb on top of him, rub my boobs in his face, make him want me.

What is it going to take to get this guy to touch me?

An engraved invitation?

Yes, dipshit.

It's called consent and he isn't the type of guy who is just going to make a move without a flashing green light.

"I've…got to use the bathroom," I blurt out, moving off the bed. Walking around it to the door, which is closer to his side of the small bedroom.

The bedroom feels even smaller now that there are two of us in it; when it was just me in here, it felt roomy—and when I make it to the bathroom and catch sight of myself in the mirror…

Whoa.

Holy hell, Miranda was right, my tits do look fantastic in this top! I had no idea how sheer it was, but oh my god!!

I turn this way and that, puffing out my chest like a peacock, admiring my boobs, not actually needing to pee but needing a second of privacy so I can regroup mentally.

What am I supposed to do now that I admitted I had a crush on him and he barely reacted to it?

"You're Grady's sister."

No shit, I'd wanted to say. Big fucking deal.

But I didn't because I'm a lady and I wasn't raised like that.

Pfft.

Grady's little sister, my ass.

I'm wearing a thong under these short, *barely there shorts*, for god knows what reason, turning my back toward the mirror and staring over my shoulder so I can also admire my own ass.

Slap it for good measure, ramping myself up to go back inside that room and put the moves on Drew Colter.

This is my one and only chance.

One night.

One chance.

When am I ever going to have him alone in a bedroom again, wearing only boxers and no other clothing?

The worst thing that can happen is he says no, he's not interested, and we both lay on our own sides of the bed and go to sleep, but I caught him watching me at the honky-tonk and there was no mistaking the look in his eyes. The only thing holding Drew back is Grady and he's not here to police the situation, now, is he?

And sure, I'll be humiliated if he rejects me but then again, maybe I won't be rejected at all.

"You're sexy. You're single. You're…" I search for a rhyming word. "Ready to mingle."

Oh jeez.

"You got this."

Take off your shorts and walk in there with your thong, my lusty little brain shouts. "Go in there and show him you're dressed for the job you want."

I push the silky shorts down my hips, kicking them to the floor.

Now it's just me and my skimpy thong and this skimpier top…

I count to three.

Pull open the bathroom door and step out into the hall.

Immediately regret taking off my bottoms.

"Shit."

Um.

Now what?

One foot in front of the other, that's what. You are seducing the guy you've had a crush on since you were eleven.

I'm also pep talking myself in the hall, but that's not exactly the point, is it. *If I have to pep talk myself, should I even be doing this?*

Yes, you idiot—you're only pep talking yourself because you've never seduced anyone before. It takes practice!

If this skimpy situation doesn't get his attention, I don't know what will. It's sending a clear message: touch my ass. Touch my tits. Touch my thighs…

Touch *me*.

Me.

Anywhere.

I put one foot in front of the other and walk through the door, holding my head as high as I can without faltering on my steps, almost tripping on the carpet in true Tess fashion.

Only I would trip and almost fall on my way to a seduction.

Only me…

I'm in the doorway. Not hovering but close to it, waiting for Drew to notice me.

He has a remote in his hand and he's pointing it at the television from a sitting position at the foot of the bed and I'm pleased to see that he hasn't abandoned the bedroom for the couch—because if Miranda isn't spending the night in her own apartment, there's technically no need for us to be sharing this bed.

But he hasn't moved.

And he's still not wearing a shirt and now my mouth is watering…

That chest.

Those muscles.

The thick thighs.

Have I mentioned those?

Guh. Thick thighs are my literal weakness, the most underrated part of a guy's body, in my professional opinion.

It takes him several seconds to look away from the TV. It's not that he hasn't noticed my presence, it's that he hasn't noticed I'm no longer wearing shorts—and I'm standing here in my thong.

Now what?

I close the door behind me on the off chance Miranda makes an appearance again, strolling into the bedroom casually as you please, as if I hadn't just stripped down out of my shorts.

It's easy to watch the play of expressions on his face. They go from neutral to 'what the fuck is happening' to 'what the hell do I do?' as I slowly stride up to where he's sitting, needing to get past…

DIARY...

It's Tess.

Do you think it's weird that every time I write to you, I say Dear Diary? LOL

Since this is my book and I'm the only one who sees it?? I suspect that SOMEONE might have found this because I had it STRATEGICALLY placed on the shelf, positioned at an exact angle and it was moved slightly. So GRADY IF YOU'RE READING THIS I AM LITERALLY GOING TO KILL YOU HOW DARE YOU GO THROUGH MY PERSONAL PRIVATE THINGS. I cannot stress this enough, I will MURDER you.

I know mom would tell me not to choose violence but seriously, Grady, reading my diary??? I know the cleaning ladies weren't even at the house today so it had to have been you.

Okay. Now that we have that business out of the way, something major happened and its not what you think—it's worse. I repeat: positioned at an exact angle and it was moved slightly!!!!

Who can you trust if you can't trust your own FAMILY.
#Betrayed

CHAPTER 22
DREW

YOUR NUDES ARE SAFE WITH ME.

WHAT THE FUCK IS HAPPENING…

Is it just me or is Tess half naked?

Ass cheeks out, tits right there, Tess is standing in front of me as if she has to get past, when all she'd have to do is flop down on the bed to claim her spot back.

I'm only at the edge of it because I had wanted to adjust the television set; it's sitting atop the dresser but at an odd angle and I just thought…

I thought…

I…

Tess tries to skirt around me but somehow, my hands end up on her hips. To assist her? To stop her?

No idea.

Legs spread, I pull her close.

I must have had more alcohol than I realized or maybe she had more alcohol than she'd planned or maybe…

She bends her head. Leans in, pressing her pelvis against the apex of my spread thighs, tentatively kissing the tip of my nose. Featherlight kisses on my cheekbones.

My eyes briefly flutter closed, palms spread, running up and down her bare ass. It's smooth and fits perfectly in my hands.

Tess Donahue.

Little Tess Donahue…

…is kissing me on the mouth and when I open mine to kiss her back, a jolt of electricity runs down the back of my spine. A totally unexpected jolt. It zaps my dick, too, and he comes to life. Twitches in these boxer shorts that aren't mine so there's barely room for him to grow, but somehow, he manages.

I open my mouth.

She opens hers.

Tongue.

So much slow tongue. I never knew I liked French kissing this much, and it spurns me on. My hands move north, traveling from her bare butt cheeks to her rib cage.

Tess has her hands on my shoulders. Those move, too, until they're behind my head, nails lightly scratching the back of my neck as she kisses me.

I pull her closer, still.

Fingers flirting with the hem of her thin camisole or tank top or whatever this excuse for a shirt is, the fabric as silky as her skin, and I run my hands beneath it—tentatively at first.

It doesn't take long for the tips of my fingers to brush the underside of her tits. Trail along her smooth flesh. Thumbs grazing.

Then my hands cover her tits.

They fill my palms perfectly, just as those few times I'd imagined what they look like, feel like, taste like. Damn, it's been an age since I've felt boobs—and all the reasons I had tried to date with intention last year rushed back, sex being one of them.

Sex.

Affection.

Physical touch.

All the same thing, basically just marketed differently.

I groan when her nails scratch my scalp. Fuck, that feels good…

She groans when I pinch her nipple, and now I want to see

what her boobs look like, reaching to lift the hem of her 'barely there' shirt over her head.

Damn.

The view does not disappoint and neither does the weight of her breasts in my hands.

For real.

Best tits ever.

Or am I buzzed?

Either way, she feels amazing pressed against me, letting me run my hands over her body though my palms are calloused from football and the gym.

"That feels so good," she mutters before our lips lock again.

I tug so she's on me; straddling me, my hands gripping her ass now.

Tess moves in slow motions over my dick as if she were giving me a lap dance, hips gyrating, the fingers on her rear now perilously close to her crack.

She moans.

Lowering my head, I lick one of her gorgeous nipples. In my mind, they're perfect; the perfect color, the perfect size, the perfect perfect.

I lick.

Suck.

Tess moans again, letting me know she's into it.

I mean, not that her appearing in the bedroom almost naked wasn't her telling me she was into it, but this verbal signal is more than enough to get me rock hard.

Tess continues to give me a lap dance as if it were her job, moving on top of me still. A vision of Grady flashes through my mind, but I quickly blink it away, trying to focus on how she feels on top of me.

No one—*and I mean no one*—wants the brother of the girl riding him cockblocking him, even invisibly.

I can no longer stand it.

As much as I love the way it feels, I can no longer sit here and let her torture me this way.

I stand, bringing her along for the ride, hefting her up, and turning toward the bed. I dump her onto the mattress and look down at her, watching as her chest heaves up and down breathlessly.

No bra.

Skimpy underwear.

Long hair that fans around her.

She's fucking gorgeous, have I mentioned that?

Tess spreads her legs, and I climb onto the bed toward her, dick throbbing, face going to the center of her core. My hands are already at her inner thighs, fingers already hooking her panties.

I haven't gone down on a girl in ages.

What if I can't remember how?

What if she doesn't like it?

Her hips wiggle as if she were impatient, and I'm more than happy to bury my face there. Pull aside her thong completely. Kiss her inner thighs; they're smooth and she smells like baby powder and perfume and the right amount of female.

I want to devour her.

I do devour her, spreading her with two fingers, lavishing my tongue on her.

My lips, my hands, my finger.

Above me, Tess pushes her hands through my hair. It probably needs a haircut, *but who's thinking about that shit?*

Her pussy tastes fucking amazing, and I'm not embarrassed to say it, and I'd say it out loud too if my mouth wasn't sucking her clit right now.

Fucking delicious.

Tess pushes at my shoulders now.

No, she's tugging.

Pulling at my shoulders, she's trying to hook beneath my armpits so I'll climb back up her body.

I war with myself: on one hand, I want to make her come. I'm *desperate* to make her come… On the other hand, what does she need me up there for? I'm perfectly content licking her pussy, trying to push her over the brink.

So for real, what does she need me up there for?

To dry hump her? To rub my cock between her legs so she can see how it feels?

I'm not and wasn't planning on having sex with her so shouldn't I just stay down here where I want to be, where it's nice and cozy and warm and pleasure her until she's crying out my name?

Tess has other ideas.

I remove my mouth—so sad to go—and let her boss me around. I follow her lead and move up her body 'cause she wants me to until we're face-to-face again, my mouth instantly seeking hers.

God, her lips are perfect.

This fucking mouth…

The tongue.

Her hands roam up and down my back, pushing at the waistband of these tight underwear.

She wants them off.

Fuck.

Shit, she feels good…

Too good.

So warm.

Hot.

Her perfect tits are in my hands again, and I'm caressing them even as I begin to move my pelvis, letting my hips roll, dick like a heat seeking missile into the apex of her legs.

"So fucking good…" she groans. "Take off your underwear," she moans.

Take off your underwear.

Play with fire.

Make her feel good.

Let her make *you* feel good.

The battle rages on inside me, her hands at my ass, nails scraping my skin, lips sucking the side of my neck.

I wonder if I'll have a hickey.

"You feel so good…" I murmur.

"Take off your underwear," she says again, more demanding.

"Why, so you can fuck me?" I joke, our tongues meeting between the words.

"Yes, so I can fuck you."

CHAPTER 23
TESS

ONLINE DATING HACK: LET YOUR FRIENDS IN RELATIONSHIPS SWIPE FOR YOU WITH THEIR PARTNER. IT'S FUN FOR THEM AND LESS WORK FOR YOU.

I WANT HIM REAL BAD, and I don't care if I'm being forward.

The weight of Drew on top of me is intoxicating, and I could get drunk on this feeling every single day of the damn week.

"Yes, so I can fuck you…"

His dick has no such hesitation as it presses into my pussy, wanting to slide inside me, in and out, hot, wet, and hard.

Do it, Drew.

Do it.

Stop being the nice guy.

Be bad for once.

Forget my dumb, stupid brother, and fuck me.

Your cock wants to fuck me, so why won't you listen to him?

He's a smart boy.

A very smart boy.

I pout when Drew hesitates, taking his time to decide what he's going to do. He pulls back, and I can see the debate behind his eyes—is it my brother holding him back, or does he actually not want to have sex with me? Because I want him. I've wanted this boy for ten years, and if it's only for one night, I'll take it.

"Are you sure?" he finally drawls, looking me in the eye and asking for my consent even though I've already given it.

"Yes."

He raises his lower half, and I reach between our bodies to help push down his boxer briefs. They're so fucking tight, and it's a bit of a challenge to get them down his hips, and we find ourselves laughing.

God, his dick is beautiful.

I'm not one of those girls who finds dicks attractive—not even remotely—but this one?

This one makes my mouth water.

"Wait," I tell him, pushing at the center of his chest to move him on his back.

I want his dick in my mouth if only for a few seconds. A minute.

Okay, two.

CHAPTER 24
DREW

DATE SOMEONE WHO GIVES YOU THE SAME FEELING AS YOU FEEL WHEN YOU CATCH SIGHT OF YOUR FOOD BEING CARRIED OVER AT A RESTAURANT.

TESS HAS me on my back, briefs around my ankles.

I lie flat on my back, waiting with bated breath to see what she'll do next.

Suck my dick, apparently…

"Oh fuck," I groan loudly, drinking in air as her warm, wet mouth comes down over my cock. Her head bobs up and down—not all the way, my dick doesn't seem to fit all the way in—but she begins working it with both her hand and her mouth, and I'm here for the show.

I'm enjoying this turn of events.

Fuck…

God, this feels fantastic. Holy shit.

Holy fuck.

I'm here for the show, wanting to sink my hands into her hair, tug at a ponytail, push her mouth farther onto my dick—all things I resist the primal urge to do. Watching is enough. The sight of her sucking me off feels like my version of a porn. Not that I watch porn, but if I did, this is what I'd see, and this is what would get me off.

Sexy.

Hot.

Wet.

Ugh.

My head hits the pillow, and if I don't get her off my dick, I'll dump my load into her throat when I'd rather be coming inside her, and this is what she seems to want…

And whatever she wants, I want to give her.

My fingers brush through her hair. Gently. Tenderly?

Tess looks up at me, cock in my mouth, eyes wide.

She pulls back, letting me fall out, licking at her lips with a slow smile.

Crawls up my body.

I assist—'cause I'm a gentleman like that—taking her by the waist and helping to steady her as she lowers herself on top of my body, adjusting so she can slide on. Since she's already slick and wet and I'm hard as a fucking rock, it's easy. Only for a moment do I wonder *"Is she on the pill? Is she on any form of birth control? Do we have a condom?"* but my brain and my mouth aren't working in conjunction.

Cause goddamn is she tight.

So tight I don't know how long I'll last. It feels like she's got a clamp on the base of my cock, and it feels out of this world fucking fantastic. I swear, if my eyes roll into the back of my goddamn skull, it would be a miracle.

I moan loudly, head tipping back.

Tess fucks me, moving back and forth, back and forth, *back and forth* in a rhythm that has the headboard banging against the wall, the sound a turn-on itself.

My balls get tight.

Tingle.

I squeeze my eyes shut to refocus, concentrating on not coming—I want her to be the first one since she obviously wanted to get laid. God, what if I blow my load, and she's pissed. That happens to my brother sometimes if he comes before his girlfriend. I can hear them arguing through the walls about it.

Do not fucking come, do not fucking come, do not fucking come….

"Oh my god," Tess gasps with a low, breathy whine. "You're so deep."

She leans down to kiss me, brushing her tits against my chest. She moans again into my ear, which makes me harder, swear to fucking god if it doesn't.

I grip her ass, pulling her deeper still.

She groans again, louder.

Louder still.

"Oh fuck…oh Drew… oh my god…"

"You feel so fucking good, baby," I grunt out despite myself even though she's not my baby, and I have no idea how to talk dirty.

You feel so fucking good, baby, is as dirty as it gets.

I give her ass a slap, and she whimpers.

"I'm gonna come," she moans. "Oh god, it feels so goodddd…"

Her hands grip the headboard and she pushes faster, faster, moving back and forth. "Don't stop," she begs. "I'm so close… right there…right there in that spot, oh god…"

Oh god is right.

Right there.

That spot.

Fuck yes…

Fuck yeah…

My brain isn't functioning right now. I can't think. Brain dumb. What's my name?

What's hers?

Oh shit, this feels fucking great.

So good.

She's moaning again, loudly, hands braced on my shoulders as her orgasm hits, lost entirely in her own pleasure—and I follow shortly after. I can't wait a single second longer, or I'll fucking die. Surely, I will.

I grip her hips as I come, moans coming from my chest, lower body wracking with quivers as I dump my load into Tess Donahue.

CHAPTER 25
TESS

PERKS OF DATING ME: I'LL LET
YOU TOUCH MY BOOBS.

WE'RE STILL NAKED.

Fell asleep that way, and neither of us in is a rush to put clothes back on. I was surprisingly relaxed after we finished; not even a little bashful or embarrassed, and Drew wasn't either.

Honestly, I'm surprised.

I thought maybe he would do that guy thing you hear about where they make excuses and list all the reasons they shouldn't have fucked you or kissed you or apologized for having had sex with you because they just want to be friends.

But he didn't do that.

Instead, he reached over to hit the lights, pulled the covers up over us, and kissed me.

We kissed in the dark, not saying much of anything but not needing to, holding hands beneath the covers until both of us drifted off to sleep.

It felt good.

Not as good as my orgasm, but…

You get what I'm saying.

I can't tell what time it is, but today is the day Drew goes back to the airport—this time, though, I'm not the one taking him. My brother is.

Grady, who Drew has barely spent any time with or seen, my

asshole brother working the entire weekend or sleeping with some random girl at his house instead of being a decent friend to his buddy who flew all the way here.

Oh well.

My gain.

Chilly, I roll toward the heat.

Drew's large body, sheets around his waist, beautiful chest slowly rising and falling.

My eyelids are heavy, but I can make that much out in the dim light as it struggles to peek through the blackout curtains.

Mmm, so cozy…

He's so warm.

I turn so my ass is pressed against his hip, hugging my share of the blankets when he rolls, pulling me into his big spoon, resting his large hand on my hip. At least that's where it starts—on my hip. Palm heating my skin.

My eyes stay closed, the late night keeping me from fully waking up. So drowsy.

So comfortable.

So warm.

Mmm.

Obviously we all know what happens next as I get settled into his big body, his hands big into roam because I've stirred him. Was it intentional? The world may never know, but there's nothing better than a warm body—correction, a warm *naked* body—pressed against the back of yours, especially one attached to a beautiful dick that's been inside you.

I can feel it moving, that dick of his, and smile into the sheets I've got clutched to my chest.

I move a little to let him know that I'm not entirely asleep but I'm not entirely awake, pushing the bedsheets down my body a little bit on the off chance he wants to begin playing with my chest. My breasts. Actually, he can play with anything he wants—nothing feels better than lazy, middle of the night, early morning sex. At least not in my opinion, and it's too early for me to be thinking of other things that could be better.

My brain isn't exactly functioning right now. I haven't had my latte and all I want is him inside me again.

Do you blame me?

Lord, even in my sleep, I'm babbling…

Drew groans.

I can feel the rumble deep in his chest against my back. I don't know if it's because he's dreaming or if it's because he is waking up; both good things I suppose, the latter would be better.

I give my hips a little wiggle, feeling a bit bossy, even in our sleep.

A little wiggle, sheesh!

I'm not a total jerk and don't want to completely wake him up if he's passed out and dead to the world, but I also wouldn't mind accidentally poking the bear.

It's amazing how one small movement can get a man awake—in more ways than one—Drew's entire body does a small stretch as he tries to figure out what's happening, his erection getting bigger, his hand moving from my hip to my stomach.

His thumb begins a slow circle around my belly button.

Delicious sleepy sex…

I crave it.

Crave this closeness all the while cursing the distance that is about to be between us.

I like Drew so much.

How terrible is it that these past two days did not help this attachment I've always felt to him; this crush. This affection?

And today he is leaving.

I mean, *I'm leaving for school too*, but the point is that once again he'll be hundreds of miles away, and he has no idea how I actually feel because up until Friday, he had only seen me as Grady Donahue's annoying little sister.

Well I'm not so annoying now, am I?

Ha.

Drew's hand is on my breast, and I arch my back, *loving, loving, loving* the boob play. Ugh, it's been ages since I've been felt up, and I have the nicest boobs—they should be worshipped.

"You awake?" his gravelly whisper is in my ear and sends a shiver down my entire body.

I try to moan in a sexy, sleepy way. "Mm-hmm."

His mouth is on the back of my neck, kissing the column, brushing my hair to the side so his lips have better access.

Oh goodness...

It's easy to get me wet, apparently.

He kisses the back of my neck as his palms skims my stomach, up to caress my breasts, then back down… skims my belly button… grazes the spot between my legs, middle finger—at least I'm assuming that's the finger he's using—presses into my body.

I spread my legs ever so slightly…

He fingers me gently as his cock presses into my backside, hard and needy, my pussy getting wetter and wetter and wetter.

His thumb moves in small circles over my clit.

Oh…

Yes…

I reach behind me and move his head closer, my nails scratching the back of his scalp.

Our lips meet in the dark.

Then.

I move.

On to all fours on the mattress, my back arching, and Drew follows my lead, moving so he's behind me. He pulls my pelvis closer, sliding his dick inside me from behind.

I have to help him—he doesn't find the spot on the first try, but when he does…

Oh.

My.

God.

It takes a few seconds to adjust to him; he's not massive but from this position, I feel…full…like he's huge even though he's not—the height and weight and cock are all proportionate—but even so, I have to take a second.

"Wait a sec," I tell him, groggy and tired but horny, reaching for the bedside table.

I'd put a vibrator there when I arrived, hiding it in the drawer so Miranda wouldn't give me shit about it despite the fact that she has an entire drawer full of this shit, too. I know for a fact she has at least nine vibrators and dildos because I've been to the sex store, shopping for them with her.

Where do you think this pink one came from?

"I'm gonna use this," I whisper since it's still early and still mostly dark. Mostly awake but still sort of asleep.

I press the little hidden power button until it begins a slow hum.

Leaning forward with my ass in the air, I let my cheek rest against the mattress as Drew kneels behind me, fucking me doggy style.

Is that what it's called? Doggy style? And can you tell I've never had sex in this position before? I'm just assuming Drew has—not to make assumptions or stereotype him, but even though he told me he can't remember the last time he had sex, that cannot possibly be true, can it?

He's popular.

He's gorgeous.

He's one of the most well-known figures in football simply because of his last name, if not for his skill.

So surely, he's fucked plenty of women this way…

Jesus, Tess, get your head in the game.

Sorry, I'm tired.

Mmm.

He's gripping my hips to steady me, not exactly pounding into me but not exactly gentle, either.

It's fine.

I love it.

I focus on the buzzing, humming, and pulsing between my legs. I concentrate on holding the pink vibrator on my clit, biting my bottom lip as the tension inside me builds.

"Uh…" I moan into the pillow.

"How does that feel?" he mutters, his voice deep from sleep. A low and sexy baritone, deeper than usual because it's so early.

"So good." So good, baby, don't stop.

Keep going.

I pull the vibrator off my pussy so I don't come so soon—I want to drag it out. Tease myself.

If I keep it there I'll come before he does and I want us to come at the same time if I can help it…please let us come at the same time, I want it so bad.

I want to feel connected to Drew—I want him to feel connected to me too, although that's a long shot, isn't it? Considering he barely knew I existed until Friday.

I lose myself in Drew.

In having him inside me—this may be the one and only time I'll get to have sex with him or spend the weekend with him, or share a bed with him, and I plan on cherishing it.

I like him so much…

I want him so much.

I stop moving and look over my shoulder, watching him a few heartbeats before telling him to, "Stop."

He stops.

"Pull out. I want you on top of me."

Rolling to my back, we reposition ourselves. I spread my legs so he can fit himself between my thighs. Drew's hands reach down and caress my breasts, gently toying with my nipples.

I close my eyes, imprinting this moment in my mind where I plan to save it so I can think about it later. It will come in handy when I'm alone again and pleasuring myself…

DIARY...

I GOT BRACES today. Yes, braces. How am I supposed to look Drew Colter in the eye EVER AGAIN????????? Okay fine. We both know I don't actually look him in the eye but you know what I mean, this is humiliating, he's going to think I'm a brace face and if he EVER thought about kissing me, what if he's worried about the metal in my mouth? UGH.

Mom says I'll only have them for year—I don't have them because my teeth are crooked, it's because of my jaw but WHO CARES THE REASON WHY, he isn't gonna know that!!!!

I'm literally crying, this is my tear —> *tear drop*

I can't even talk to you right now that's how upset I am.

Bye for now.

T

CHAPTER 26
DREW

> I'M AT THE STAGE IN MY LIFE WHERE I'M LIKE, "ARE WE DOING THIS OR NOT, CAUSE I HAVE SHIT TO DO."

I WOULD KILL to have a girlfriend who looks at me the way Tess looks at me now.

As if she were...

As if...

As if she were in love with me.

Crazy, right?

Tess Donahue isn't in love with me.

But for a few seconds, I imagine it. I let myself believe it. I let myself drink in the way her eyes soften as I push my dick into her; let myself drink in the way her lips part. The way her palm reaches up to brush the hair back across my forehead.

I want to call her babe and baby and whisper other words of endearment to her but bite back my words, knowing she isn't interested in hearing them.

Tess wants sex from me and nothing more.

She's not using me, but...maybe just a little.

"You're so handsome," she whispers, making those doe eyes at me again—the eyes that will probably haunt my dreams tonight. How could they not?

No one has ever looked at me this way before.

No one.

Not that I've slept with a ton of people, but I haven't slept with anyone who genuinely gave a shit about me.

The girl who lives next door, for one. Gold diggers, cleat and jersey chasers—a trio that have almost ruined more than one of my brother's chances at love with their scheming.

Tess isn't like that.

Fucking her doesn't feel like fucking. It feels like something else entirely that I can't quite name…

"I love watching your face," I tell her. "You're so beautiful, Tess."

In reply she leans up and presses a kiss to my shoulder.

My neck.

My lips.

I kiss her as I fuck her, and the vibrator in her hand hums against the mattress.

She moves her arm, fitting it between our bodies, and I give it room. Lean back so she can place it on her pussy, all the while thrusting in and out of her.

"Can you feel that?" she wants to know as the pink thing buzzes faster.

"Sort of." I don't think vibrators have the same effect on a man as a woman, but now isn't the time to tell her that.

Her nod is sexy.

Tess licks her lips; they're pouty and wet, which is so fucking hot.

Oh shit…

Looking down at her while I pump into her is such a turn-on. If my dick weren't already hard and buried inside her, I'd have the biggest hard-on for her.

Is there anything sexier than a pair of beautiful tits jiggling with the rhythm of thrusting?

Yeah, no.

There isn't.

It doesn't take long for us both to come—we do it at the same time, Tess loudly moaning and wriggling and making a ton of noise as her orgasm hits.

When I come, it's so intense that at first no sound comes out of my throat; I bury my face in her neck. Groan. And groan.

Her hands are on my ass, fingers kneading my glutes causing goose bumps to cover my flesh.

I shiver.

So sexy….

CHAPTER
TWENTY-SEVEN

Drew: Hey, uh—lol. I just wanted to shoot you a note and tell you I had a good time this past weekend. Sorry it took so long to text you.

Tess: Hi! I was wondering if I was going to hear from you. I didn't want to assume...

Tess: How have you been?

Drew: Good. The same, you know how it is. Practice, training, studying, more practice...

Tess: But your season hasn't started yet...

Drew: No, but we're either always getting ready for it to start, or knee deep in the season. So it never fucking ends even when we have time off. As soon as I got back on Sunday I went to the gym to work off that beer.

Tess: You went to the gym? Damn. I took a nap.

Drew: LOL, I didn't have a choice. My damn brother was waiting for me when I walked in the door with my bag. He's such a pain in the ass.

Tess: He always was kind of, wasn't he? Haven't seen him in years, so obviously, I don't know if he's changed.

Drew: He hasn't. Still butts into my business, he's still loud as hell, he's still a psycho when it comes to football. He lives and breathes it. Thank god he has a girlfriend now, she keeps him grounded.

Tess: Does she?

Drew: No, not really. LOL

Tess: He was never the modest type was he?

Drew: Not even a little…

Tess: And what about you?

Drew: I'm definitely the modest type.

Tess: I wouldn't argue with that. You're such a nice guy. I can't see you being anything but humble…

Drew: Ugh, "a nice guy." Is that the kiss of death?

Tess: NO! I meant it as a compliment…

Drew: 'Cause you know what they say about nice guys

Tess: What? That they're the freakiest, and you have to watch out for them? Ha.

Drew: Nah. They say nice guys finish last.

Tess: Do they? Hmm, I hadn't heard ;)

Drew: You're funny.

Tess: Just teasing you...

Drew: So. Speaking of being freaky—should we talk about what happened this weekend?

Tess: What happened this weekend?!

Drew: You're cute, do you know that?

Tess: **fluffs hair** I try

Drew: I'm being serious. Should we talk about this weekend?

Tess: I mean, we can if you want to, but I'm scared to.

Drew: Scared? Why?

Tess: I'm scared you're going to tell me to forget it, it was just fun, no hard feelings, let's be friends, don't make it weird.

Drew: Want to know something?

Tess: What

Drew: That's exactly what I was worried YOU were going to tell me.

Tess: Seriously? Or are you messing with me?

Drew: Why would I mess with you? I'm being serious. Just because I'm a guy doesn't mean I want to be rejected.

Tess: You're not just a guy. You're Drew freaking Colter

Drew: Drew FREAKING Colter? LOLOL

Tess: Quit acting like you're normal, and you grew up normal around here—everyone treated y'all like gods, and you know it.

Drew: Not me. My brothers, yes. Me, no.

Tess: I'm rolling my eyes so hard. You are all one and the same. No offense, but...

Drew: Fine. I'm stuck with the Colter last name, and you're right, it comes with certain...stigmas.

Tess: Stigmas? You say it as if it were a bad thing.

Drew: Long story that we don't have to get in to right now, but honestly, there are days I wish I'd been born into a normal family that didn't come with such high expectations.

Tess: I'm sure it's been a lot of pressure.

Drew: Yeah.

Drew: There is no such thing as taking a day off from it.

Tess: I'm sorry.

Drew: Hey, don't be. It is what it is

Tess: It sounds so depressing when you put it like that. "It is what it is."

Drew: Okay but it is LOL

Tess: I KNOW but you don't have to SAY it like that!

Drew: Blah. Change the subject, then.

Tess: Let's get back to the original subject: the one where you were scared I was going to tell you this weekend was just fun, no let's be friends, don't make it weird.

Drew: You forgot the bit about "Don't tell Grady."

Tess: Why on earth would I tell my BROTHER? Wait. Didn't he ask where you'd gone off to when you didn't show back up at his place Saturday night?

Drew: No actually he did not. He just assumed I went back to someone's place and banged her.

Tess: I mean...you did.

Drew: He doesn't have to know that. I don't need my ass kicked.

Tess: Don't make me laugh. Grady could not kick your ass. You're like twice his size.

Drew: It doesn't matter how big he is. If he's pissed enough, he could probably take me LOL

Tess: Eh, I doubt it.

Drew: You get my point, though. The last thing I need is my best friend from high school knowing I slept with his sister.

Tess: Hey. Let's get one thing straight: I banged YOU, okay?

Drew: UM, THAT SOUNDS EVEN WORSE.

CHAPTER
TWENTY-EIGHT

A MORNING TEXT DOESN'T JUST MEAN "GOOD MORNING." IT ALSO MEANS, "I THOUGHT ABOUT YOU WHEN I WOKE UP."

Drew: Good morning…

Tess: Oh, hello. Good morning to YOU!

Drew: You're up early. Do you usually get up at 7?

Tess: Um no, but my phone was vibrating, and I was curious to see who was texting me at 7 IN THE MORNING.

Drew: What time is your first class?

Tess: 8

Drew: See, you would have been awake soon anyway…

Tess: True…

Sixteen hours later.

Drew: Back from my night class. What are y'all up to?

Tess: Getting unpacked from being gone. My roommate is grocery shopping. She went home for break, too.

Drew: It's weird knowing you have roommates, and shit I haven't met yet.

Tess: Yes LOL this whole life at school the same way you do. So crazy.

Drew: That's not what I mean. A part of me has to constantly remind myself that you're Grady's sister, while the other part of me likes learning all the shit about you I hadn't known before.

Tess: Well, that's kind of sweet

Drew: Is it?

Tess: I said 'kind of' LOL

Drew: Brat

Tess: I am a brat, yes. Thanks for noticing.

Drew: So you're unpacking—at ten o'clock.

Tess: I felt lazy when I got back and ended up on the couch scrolling and watching TV, and now I want to go to bed, but I have a pile on my bed and have to put everything away.

Drew: You're not the "sweep it onto the floor and forget about it" kind of person?

Tess: Omg, no. Grady is like that, and it used to drive me nuts. Remember how we had to share a room until we were in like, middle school?

Drew: Yeah, I remember that.

Tess: He was such a slob it turned me into a neat freak, so here I am at 10:00 putting shit away. What are YOU up to right now?

Drew: Lying in bed talking to you.

Tess: What were you doing before that?

Drew: Gym. Eating. Shower

Tess: Long day?

Drew: Not anymore 😌

Tess: Are you FLIRTING with me? 'Cause that would be awesome.

Drew: Do you WANT me to flirt with you?

Tess: Kind of.... Is that bad?

Drew: Not bad. I'm just BAD at it.

Tess: How are you bad at flirting?

Drew: I don't know how to do it. All I know how to do is chat with people and make conversation. How does a guy flirt?

Tess: I don't know. Let's google it.

Tess: Okay. I found this article

Tess: ** Sends Link **

Drew: "Ten Ways to Flirt with Your Crush That Will Get You Noticed In No Time?" LOLOL stop it. Be yourself? That's not a way to flirt.

Drew: Suggest hanging out in a group? Oh, SO SEXY. LOL this list is trash.

Tess: I'm trying to be helpful.

HOW TO SCORE OFF FIELD

Drew: None of that is helpful.

Tess: If you can do better, have at it.

Drew: **Sends Link**

Tess: 5 Ways to Become the Master of Flirting! Okay, this better be good...

Drew: I'm partial to Number 1

Tess: Head tilting?? How is that flirting?

Drew: It shows that you're engaged in the conversation and also shows me if you have a long, sexy neck.

Tess: Oh lord... long sexy neck? Stop it.

Drew: Number 3: Lean in.

Tess: So you can see my boobs? Noted.

Drew: Yes, ma'am.

Tess: What about Number 4? Touching... Did you touch me when we were together? Eh, barely.

Drew: Right, but I wasn't flirting. I was trying to keep my hands off you out of respect.

Tess: Okay, but did you WANT to touch me?

Drew: Obviously.

Tess: When?

Drew: When we were playing miniature golf— did you not see me staring at your ass in those short shorts?

Tess: Those were NOT short shorts LOL they were regular jean shorts.

Drew: If you say so.

Tess: I'm saying so.

Drew: Well, I still wanted to touch your ass in those. Or slap it.

Tess: See, now that's what I'm talking about. Look away.

Drew: For real?

Tess: Yes, for real. And maybe I also wished you'd have put your hands on me. Like an accidental brush against my boobs or brushed past me when it was your turn to Putt-Putt.

Drew: I thought I did accidentally brush past you.

Tess: Uh, once—and it was actually an accident so I don't think that counts.

Drew: Wait. I'm confused. You say accident, but you mean...on purpose?

Tess: Now you're getting it...

Drew: Huh. I never would have known. You have a good poker face.

Tess: No one likes rejection, Drew.

Drew: I guess I can't say what I would have done if you'd have said something when we were eating or playing golf.

Tess: Guess it all worked out the way it was supposed to.

Drew: When is the next time you're going to be home?

Tess: Mmm, Thanksgiving? You?

Drew: Good question. Don't know. We have a Bowl Tournament usually Thanksgiving Day, which sucks, but that's how it is.

Tess: Yeah that does suck. It would be nice to see you.

CHAPTER 29
DREW

"IF A DUDE REMEMBERS THE COLOR OF YOUR EYES AFTER A FIRST DATE—YOU HAVE SMALL BOOBS." – DRAKE COLTER

"I HAVE A CONFESSION TO MAKE."

I'm sitting in the kitchen, at the table with my brother, picking at a rotisserie chicken, too lazy to have cooked us an actual meal.

Our other brother's girlfriend—and our roommate, Ryann—isn't home tonight, so it's just the two of us to fend for ourselves, not that Ryann makes us food.

We normally rotate the responsibility.

But when Ryann isn't home, we don't bother making anything at all. Sometimes, I even eat dinner out of a can.

"What's the confession? That you took a piss with the toilet seat down?"

"Ha ha, very funny." I pop a piece of meat into my mouth and chew. "No."

"Is your confession that you forgot to transpose your typed notes into written notes in your Trapper Keeper?"

I wipe my fingers and stare at him. "Seriously? You think I'm only capable of nerdy shit? Gee, thanks."

Drake laughs, stealing a piece of chicken from my plate that I'd painstakingly carved from the bones and putting it in his mouth before I can steal it back from him.

"Sorry. Those are the only things I could think of off the top of my head."

My mouth is set into a serious line. "I slept with someone while I was back home."

Drake blinks at me.

He sets down the water bottle he was taking a drag off and blinks again.

"You got laid?"

I nod, although I wouldn't call it getting laid—sounds too… too…casual. And like I slept with someone I don't give a shit about or someone I don't care to remember.

"With who? Did you even get her name?"

"Yeah." I'm a little insulted he thinks I'd sleep with someone without knowing her name but whatever. "Tess Donahue."

Drake begins coughing, almost choking on air, face turning red as he slaps at the table with his palm.

"What?"

I hand him his bottle of water, and he takes a sip from it. "Tess Donahu—"

"I heard you." He wipes his mouth. "You have got to be fucking kidding me."

"Then why did yo—"

"Goddammit, Drew," he interrupts. "You're not supposed to shit where you eat!"

Shit where I eat?

Talk about being melodramatic.

"Having sex with Tess is not shitting where I eat." I pick at my food. "And since when do *you* care whether or not someone is related to our friends or not. It doesn't matter."

Before he was in a relationship, Drake was a bit of a manwhore, sleeping with the girl next door and any good-looking girl who caught his eye. Swore off being tied down in favor of playing matchmaker for me, which he found way more interesting—until he fell in love with his girlfriend.

Bastard.

My twin brother laughs sardonically. "Okay. *You* be the one to tell that to Grady Donahue once he finds out you boned his sister and then left town."

"It wasn't like that at all." I pause, choosing my next words. "She's the one who seduced me."

Drake's eyes go wide. "That's…that's literally going to get you punched in your pretty face. You don't say shit like that."

"Grady is not going to find out." At least, I'm not going to be the one to tell him.

My brother snorts. "He'll find out. Trust me."

He'll find out? From who.

I highly doubt Tess is going to tell her brother. She'll tell Miranda, no doubt about that. Don't girls tell each other everything?

But her brother?

Nah.

Don't think so.

Still, the idea plagues me all night. And as I'm climbing into bed it's on my mind. Even when I open my book to read, it's on my mind. I try to stay distracted, trying not to grab my phone and immediately message Tess.

We've been talking quite a bit the past few days, which is idiotic considering we're hundreds of miles away, and when do long-distance relationships ever work out?

Especially with a guy like me, who's busy all the time and has real-world commitments on top of going to class and maintaining the house we live in, basically busting my ass and not having fun.

Well, this weekend was fun.

I had more fun tagging along with Tess and spending time with her than I did with my best friend, whom I rarely saw, which turned out for the best. Grady got the credit for dragging me home, and I had a blast hanging with his little sister, plus I got laid.

But the only problem I'm having now?

I can't stop thinking about her.

If we continue talking, wouldn't it make sense that we develop feelings for each other?

I thumb through my phone—at the dating apps my brother Drake installed for me—poking open the one where I have the most matches and scroll through the faces of my matches, none of whom I've met in person since Drake announced he'd been pretending to be me online.

Just haven't had the energy, though I've always had the intention.

Chatting isn't hard. What's stopping you?

Tess Donahue is stopping you…

But she's halfway across the United States, and these girls are here, some of them less than one-hundred feet away.

Closer.

But Tess is from your hometown. She'll be there when you finish with school.

You don't know what you're doing once you graduate, asshole—you might end up in New York. Or Washington.

Or Seattle.

Why is that thought so depressing?

Because your heart isn't in it anymore. Now that Dad is gone, there's no one pushing you to stay in the game.

But what the hell else are you qualified to do?

I shrug off the thought, blankly staring at the open pages of my book.

> Tess: Quick, tell me one thing you just got done thinking about.

> Drew: Shit. Um. What I'm doing after I graduate.

If I graduate and don't enter the draft instead.

> Tess: Dang, Colter, why so serious?

> Drew: Just where my mind wandered—no reason.

Except that I'd been thinking of her and dating and that's why my mind wandered to what I would be doing with my life post-college.

> Drew: What about you?

> Tess: Um, nothing as philosophical—I was thinking about whether or not I actually want to take a shower or if I just want to put my pajamas on right away. A shower feels like too much work.

> Drew: Are you admitting to me that you don't like showering?

> Tess: That's literally not what I meant at all. I SHOWER! I'm just lazy… plus I still smell good.

> Drew: You do smell good.

> Tess: LOL how would you know?

> Drew: 1. You just told me and 2. I remember

> Tess: Is the memory burned in your brain?

> Drew: Yes. A lot of things are burned in my brain.

> Tess: Mm, like what else?

She's fishing for compliments, and I don't mind at all. I'm willing to humor her. What's the harm?
I like her.
She's cute, she's funny, she's smart.
She's long-distance.

> Drew: Like…the way your voice goes up an octave when you're pretending to be excited when you're not. And your laugh. And how soft your hands are.

Her hands are soft and gentle, running up my chest, finger trailing up my sternum. I remember it making me shiver, and the tingles shooting to my cock.

> Tess: Wow, that…

> Tess: I wasn't expecting you to say all that.

SHIT. SHE WASN'T?

> Drew: Sorry

> Tess: Drew, don't apologize! It's nice. It's…you know, been a while. When we were talking about flirting the other day, I realized I don't know how to do it either, despite my best efforts.

> Drew: You tried flirting with me?

> Tess: Um, yeah—at the Boot Scoot Boogie, I decided I was going to get drunk and flirt with you, but it turns out I wound up doing neither. If you don't count me dragging you onto the dance floor.

> Drew: I think it counts?

> Tess: Good. Because A: I wanted to dance and B: I was trying to flirt

> Drew: Mission accomplished…

> Drew: I don't want to make shit awkward but…

> Tess: Oh god. What? Just say it.

Drew: How long exactly have you had the hots for me?

Tess: The HOTS for you?! Oh brother, you're starting to sound like Drake.

Drew: I mean, we are identical.

Tess: Ha.

Tess: And. I don't know. I had a tiny crush on you in middle school.

Tess: And high school. But it was harmless.

Drew: I'm sorry, I had no idea.

Tess: Why would you be sorry? You were busy, and you barely even looked at girls.

Drew: That's true. I don't think I went on an actual date until I came to college, and you see how well that's working out for me.

Tess: I think people expect you to be a certain way, and you're just not, so girls have these expectations, and if you don't meet that, that is NOT your problem. It's their problem.

Drew: What do you mean, expectations…?

Tess: You're this big, good-looking dude who's in the spotlight (for lack of a better term, right?), and they expect you to be cocky (like your brother) and self-assured, but in reality, you're a bit shy and a bit reserved and not in everyone's face, and you certainly don't put the moves on everyone.

Tess: Like MY brother. Who even did he go home with the other night??

Drew: No idea. Some redhead…

Tess: Chelsea something or other, I think that's her name, but she's friends of the bride. There are so many bridesmaids I can't keep them straight.

Drew: Ahh. That would explain why she didn't look familiar...

Tess: You've been gone a while.

Drew: Yeah. Sometimes I wonder if that was a good idea or not

Tess: What do you mean?

Drew: Sometimes I think maybe I should have gone to a state school and played ball for fun—like D2 or D3—and just had fucking fun instead of a place where I feel all this pressure. I might have been able to sustain a relationship and done more normal shit...

Tess: You don't think you do normal shit?

Drew: Eh, not really. I mean, yes—but being part of the Colter Duo doesn't make us inconspicuous. Even people who don't watch football and aren't fans know who we are. I can't even run into Walgreens without someone saying something or looking into my basket.

Tess: At your rash cream?

Drew: Exactly.

Tess: So sexy.

Drew: You think so?

Tess: Ha ha, yes. I think everything you do is sexy, Drew Colter...

CHAPTER 30
TESS

THE FIRST TIME I SAW HIM, I KNEW I WAS GOING TO GIVE HIM THE WRONG PHONE NUMBER...

Tess: I have a crazy idea.

IT'S LATE, I know, but I'm not tired—not in the least. And I haven't seen Drew's face since he left and wouldn't it be nice to talk, face-to-face.

Drew: What's your crazy idea?

Tess: Want to video chat?

With bated breath, I wait for him to reply, not sure if he's going to jump at the chance to see me in person.

I mean, is it weird that I...*miss* him?

Nah, I don't miss him. That's not what this is.

Is it?

Can't be.

I'm totally not the type of girl who assigns physical intimacy as *actual* intimacy or thinks that having sex with a guy makes us closer. And I'm certainly not foolish enough to think Drew might feel connected to me because we screwed.

I see the three tiny dots from his phone as he replies.

Drew: ...

> Drew: Sure. Let's do it.

"Eek!" I squeal because I cannot stop myself, kicking my feet and blankets at the foot of the bed, giddy that we'll see one another for the first time in over a week.

"Oh shit."

I scramble, leaping from the bed and going to the mirror above my desk, fussing with my hair and the collar of my tank top.

"Not the best but not the worst."

The invitation to chat was spontaneous, so I'm not dressed for a cute video date. My fingers tuck the stray strands of hair behind my ear and pick up the gold hoop earrings on my desk.

I put them in, one by one.

My stomach flutters.

Knots up nervously.

The recognizable sound of my phone going off startles me. Even though I'm expecting it, I wasn't expecting him to call me first.

I jump onto the bed, throw myself down, head on a pillow. Take a few deep breaths and hit Accept.

"Hi." I sound as if I sprinted a mile or had to run from a wild animal.

"Hey there." He raises a hand to wave, and I take note of everything: what he's wearing, his hair, the palm of the hand he has lifted in greeting.

White tee shirt with a blue ringer collar.

His dark hair is swept off to the side as if he ran his hand through it moments earlier.

I remember how that hand felt on my body, calloused and rough.

I liked it…

"Don't you look cute," he says. "What were you up to just now?"

Literally nothing.

Absolutely nothing.

"Chatting with you mostly."

"Same." He smiles at me.

Oh god…

This.

This is the reason I like him so much. Not only is he crazy good-looking but he's so freaking nice and kind and caring and ugh, that smile! Not to sound cheesy, but it could literally light up a room, and the fact that it's directed at me?

Mind blowing.

Drew watches me through the camera, and I smile back, feeling somewhat shy.

What's going on in his brain?

What's he thinking?

"Are you a night owl?" he asks, breaking the silence.

"Usually, yes. I've always been like this. What about you?"

He shrugs. "No, not really. I'm normally sleepin' way earlier but got distracted by you."

"Aw," I simper.

"Do you always sleep in tank tops? What else are you wearing?"

I cast a glance down my body at the white ribbed shirt. He can't see what I can see, which is my nipples through the fabric, and I know that if I move the phone south, he would get a glimpse. And I want him to, so I move the phone slowly so that his gaze can skim my body even though we are not together in the same room.

"Sometimes I don't sleep in anything, sometimes I sleep in pajamas. My mom is always buying me cute pj's. It's kind of her thing." I pause. "I have this one pair of red bottoms that have little white snowflakes embroidered on them. I've worn them so much that there are literal holes in the knees and the ass."

He smiles widely. "Guess I'll have to see them for myself sometime."

"Guess you might."

Is this flirting?

"Are you home alone?"

"No, my brother is here, and I thought I heard Ryann rootin around in her room. She's across the hallway but doesn't come out much, though." He moves his pillow, putting one arm behind his head. "Spends a lot of time chatting with my brother. She graduates soon so we don't see her much."

"I'm really looking forward to graduating," I tell him without him asking. "I don't know if I want to stay in Texas. I guess I'll see what kind of job offers I get."

"What did you say your major was?"

"I didn't. It's boring—English."

"What made you major in English instead of something like, oh, I don't know, teachin'?"

"Good question. It's something I ask myself almost on the daily." I blow out a puff of air. "I read a lot when I was growin' up—total book nerd. So I thought majorin' in English was an extension of that, but it turns out, it's not. Not sure what I'm gonna do, but I have a little time to figure it out."

"You could definitely be a teacher."

I pull a face. "I cannot imagine myself molding minds."

"Why not? You'd be the sexiest teacher in school."

I laugh. "Oh right, 'cause that's what they look for when they're hirin' folks. Sexy teachers."

Not.

He laughs, low and deep.

I hunker down lower on my pillow, hair fanning out around me, trying to look cute and glamorous.

Drew's eyes stray, and I imagine that if he were here, he'd be staring at my chest.

"So your brother is home, your roommate is home." I toy with the strap of my tank top. "My roommates are both gone. They aren't here much since both of them work."

"What do they do?"

"One is a nanny for a professor, and the other one works in a diner. Second shift when all the bars close."

"Ryann was a server at a place like that. Pretty much how she met my brother."

"Oh?" I can feel my brows rise with interest. "I don't think I know the story."

"You know how Dallas is. Kind of a hardass, never dated."

"Um, sounds like literally all you Colter boys."

He nods. "Yeah, so. There was this dumbass on his team—can't remember the guy's name, but he was datin Ryann and wanted to dump her. So he paid my brother to do the dumpin'—and Dallas showed up at her job and ambushed her after her shift or something like that."

"Showed up at her *job*?"

"Yup. Like I said, he's a dumbass."

"No, you called the guy on his team a dumbass."

"Oh, well. Dallas is a dumbass too, but it all worked out 'cause now they're in love and all that shit. Movin' in together as soon as she graduates, which is why she's so busy and tryin' to get done with school." He rolls his eyes. "You should hear them carryin' on."

I bet it's nice. "Well, I'm happy for them, even if you're disgusted by it."

Drew shakes his head. "No, no, I'm not disgusted by it." He clears his throat. "'It's what made me want to date. Them and Duke—he's livin' with his girlfriend too. That whole story is a doozy too. Makes me feel like the sane one."

Ha.

"I think I read about Duke and his girlfriend—wasn't she his roommate or something?"

He nods. "He needed a place to crash and rented her place, but she was there the whole time, and well, now they're living in Dallas and shit."

"So that makes what, three out of four?"

"Yup." Drew pops the "P" when he says the word, intense eyes studying me through the camera. "You know, Tess, I wanna apologize."

"For what?"

"For...not seein' you."

I blink, replaying the words in my brain. *For not seeing you.*

"What do you mean?"

Drew shifts on the bed, taking his arm out from behind his head. My eyes can't stay off the biceps that bulge slightly, flexing.

"I don't know how to put this without soundin' like a complete douche, but you know." He looks uncomfortable as he struggles to find the words. "I'm sorry I didn't see you for you, and that I was seein' you as Grady's sister. And not as a woman."

A woman.

Literally no one has ever called me a woman.

Young lady, sure, but that's strange too.

Woman?

That's a term I would categorize to my mother, but I understand what he's trying to tell me. He's telling me that he sees me as my own person—someone sexual, with her own mind and own opinions and not just a girl who's in the background to be ignored and passed over.

He sees me.

"I don't blame you." Everyone my brother hangs around used to look through me, and it didn't help that my mother would say things like, *"Tess, leave your brother and his friends alone,"* as if I were a pest and not around their same age. "My brother always acted like I was in the way." I snort. "He's only three years older, not thirty."

There is no reason I couldn't have hung out with them as friends. Other girls were around, so why wasn't I good enough to be among them?

"Well, anyway. I'm sorry and…I'm glad I got to know you over the weekend."

"Got to know me?" I giggle. "I'd say you more than got to know me."

"You know what I mean."

"Are you blushin'?" I pull the phone closer to my face as if I'd be able to see him closer. "Drew Colter. Are you blushin'?"

"I don't know. My face feels hot. Does that count?"

"Oh my god, you are too cute."

"Cute." He scoffs. "No one has ever called me that."

"Um. Pretty sure I have."

"Speakin' of pretty, did I tell you how pretty I think you are?"

I…

Um…

He thinks I'm pretty?

"Stop. Now you're going to make *me* blush."

"I've already seen you blush."

He has?

"When?"

"When you got naked and came into the bedroom. You had a red rash on your chest right here." He swipes his hand over his pec muscles, indicating the spot on my body where I'd been blushing.

"Yes, I tend to get a rash across my chest when I'm dying of embarrassment."

"You were embarrassed?" He looks surprised. "Couldn't tell."

"Do you think I seduce guys on a regular basis? Please, give me some credit. I wanted to pee my pants I was so nervous." Pee my pants, throw up, toss my cookies. Barf.

You name it.

"That's not what I was getting at." He smiles. "You're cute when you get riled up."

"Am I riled up?" Or just embarrassed again 'cause he's

calling me out on seducing him? "And that was my very first seduction, okay?"

"I personally thought it went pretty well. Ten out of ten would recommend."

"Go write me a Yelp review," I tease, biting down on my bottom lip, enjoying this part of the conversation that's turned flirty and fun. "I appreciate the feedback."

It's easy.

And comfortable.

"Do you want more feedback? 'Cause I can provide it."

"Oh yeah?"

He nods.

"Okay. Hit me with your highlights."

"You've got great tits."

Oh my god. I was not expecting him to say that.

"And." He goes on. "A smackable ass. I wasn't sure if you were into that, so I didn't want to, you know, smack it."

Is my mouth hanging open right now? Drew isn't talking dirty, but it's the first time he's ever spoken to me this way, so all the thoughts are clogging my brain.

"Can we get back to the part where you like my great tits?"

He laughs. "Sure."

"What part do you like about them?"

"All of it. They fit in my hand." He holds up his hand to demonstrate as if he were cupping one of my boobs. "And my mouth."

Is it hot in here?

Am I sweating?

"Did the temperature just rise a few notches?" I tease, hiding my face.

"I don't think so." He grins. "Let me tell you, though. The second I saw you at the airport." Drew lets out a low whistle. "All bets were off."

"All bets were off?" What does that mean?

"I knew I wasn't going to be able to stop myself from, you know. Thinkin' about you."

"So what I'm hearin' is that it was a good thing you scored the night before you left."

He scored.

I scored.

Everyone wins.

Funny how that works, innit?

"So you like my boobs, and you like my ass. I guess I should give you a few compliments, hey?"

Drew watches me through the phone intently. No, he is hanging on my every word, waiting for what I'll say next. The truth is what don't I like about him? How do I compliment him without going overboard?

Oh God, does that make me sound like a stalker?

"A compliment? I like the sound of that."

"Oh gosh, the list is endless," I tease, and in all seriousness, it is. Where do I start?

"Let me see…" I tap my chin as if I have to think about this. "I love your smile and hmm."

"Just my smile? It's the same as my brother's."

"That's not true." I shake my head. "He has that gap in his teeth."

When we were younger, it was well and truly the only way to tell them apart.

"True." He laughs. "Proceed."

He waves an airy hand around, so I continue.

"You have a great chest."

A great chest? Ugh, that sounds so dumb.

Regardless, he puffs his out in pride. "Thanks."

"I could seriously rub my boobs on those pecs all day long." *Damn, girl.*

I give myself a mental pat on the back for sounding so confident and sexy.

"Whoa. That escalated quickly."

"Well, it's true." I laugh. "When you squeezed yourself into Zero's boxers, I knew immediately they had to come off."

"Come off, eh?" He's lounging back on his bed, lazy and sexy, his eyelids suddenly become hooded. "I feel like I need a reminder about how that whole night went down. I have a terrible memory."

DEAR DIARY...

No boys like me.
To be clear: NOT THAT I CARE because I am in LOVE with Drew Colter but wouldn't it be nice if like, someone had a crush on me for a change?? Is that too much to ask, NOT that I would reciprocate? But it would be nice. I've had a crush on that stupid idiot for three years and he looks right through me like I'm invisible and every time he's at my dumb house it's like I'm not even here and like he's only here to see his friend.
X Tess

PS: I am SO SO SO sorry I called him a stupid idiot. I take that back. Omg I shouldn't have said it, what if I jinxed myself and he was about to ask me out but #KARMA

CHAPTER 31
DREW

PRO TIP: IF EVERY GIRL WOULD ARGUE WITH THEIR BOYFRIEND TOPLESS, THEY WOULD WIN THE ARGUMENT EVERY TIME.

I CAN'T THINK of a single time I have ever had phone sex with a woman. I know for a fact Dallas and Duke have, since at one time or another they were in long-distance relationships. Drake and I've heard Ryann in her room talking to my brother on a video chat, and I'm not an idiot; I know that they were sexting. I just don't know how to do it myself.

Tess looks gorgeous as usual, and in the mood to flirt, if her teasing is any indication. I can't quite see through her white tank top, but her nipples get hard, and I can see the little indent of the hard points through the fabric.

That's enough for me.

"Why are you looking at me that way?" she asks, gazing back at me.

"Honestly, you're just so beautiful. I just keep kicking myself for not seeing it sooner."

"It's not your fault, Drew. Everybody forgot that I was around if Grady was around, and nobody was going to mess with his little sister."

"The funny thing is he never warned us away from you. I think it was just naturally understood, right? Like bro code. Like dating somebody's ex-girlfriend or whatever. You just don't do it."

"Well. Too late for that." She laughs. "We did it."

"It *is* too late for that now," I concur. "So we might as well have fun, yeah?"

"Indeed." Tess hesitates. She seems to gather her courage enough to say, "What next? Should I take off my top?"

She laughs, but I also think she's serious.

"If you want to show me your beautiful boobs, who am I to object?"

"I'll take off mine if you take off yours," she negotiates, one hand disappearing from view to pull at the hem of her white tank.

Shit, that's an easy one.

I scramble to yank my tee shirt off, tossing it to the end of the bed in a heap, and when I go back to my phone—back to looking at Tess—I draw in a breath.

"Damn, you're hot."

Fire.

Beautiful.

I can't see her entire chest but don't have to—the tease she's giving me is getting me hard. The tease she's giving me makes me want to see the entire thing again in person. Up close.

This is me wanting to fuck her again.

Instead, I have to settle for the only thing I can get right now, which is ogling her through the phone. I'll take what I can get, and right now, that is a peep show of her goods. Of all her best parts…

She quickly lowers her phone to give me a glimpse of her tits, but raises it so fast it's a blur.

"Oh, come on now!" I practically shout. "Not fair."

"Gotta be quick, and don't take your eyes off the prize."

Prize? She sure is.

In reply, I flex my pec muscles, making her laugh.

"I wouldn't have pegged you as the type who could do that."

I flex them again, making them dance up and down. "So douchey, I know. Can't help it, though. I'm showin' off."

Tess laughs, then flashes me again at a moment when I'm not looking.

"Dammit, knock it off!"

And that's when my fucking brother barges into my room, door slamming open as he fills the space.

"What are you doing?" He eyeballs me but doesn't come all the way inside, thank fucking god.

"Nothin'."

"Pfft." He leans against the doorframe and crosses his arms. "Are you on the phone with someone?"

"Yes."

"Why are you half naked?"

"I'm not half naked."

He snorts. "Dude, you're only wearing underwear, and I can tell you had your hand on your cock."

I do not have my hand on my fucking dick.

"How the hell can you tell if I have my hand on my cock or not? What are you, psychic?"

"No, I'm a twin." He rolls his eyes, still planted in the same spot. "Are you having phone sex?"

"No. And even if I were, it would be none of your damn business."

My brother laughs. "Yes, you are. Don't lie."

"I'm not."

He stands in the doorway, and I curse myself for not having the foresight to lock the damn door.

"Dude, it's not a big deal. Daisy and I do it all the time, and we're not even long-distance."

How does he know I'm talking to someone long-distance? For all he knows, this is someone I met on the dumb dating app he installed on my phone.

That I deleted last week.

"Did you barge in here to tell me something, or are you just being nosy?"

"Just being nosy. I heard voices, so naturally, I had to see who you were talkin' to." He pauses. "Who are you talkin' to?"

I give him a look that says "you know who I'm talking to," but he doesn't get the hint to shut his yap.

"That's Tess Donahue? 'Cause what did I tell you about shittin' where you eat?"

Oh my god…

"Well. If you're gonna bone your best friend's sister and then fuck her via video chat, you might as well make the best of it." He uncrosses his arms to salute me. "Godspeed, my friend."

He walks out, pulling the door closed behind him, but it doesn't click into place.

"CLOSE THE FRIGGIN' DOOR!" I shout after him, and thank Christ he comes back to properly shut it.

"Sorry." Another salute and he's gone.

I breathe in and out, winded from the stress of it all.

God, he's obnoxious.

Tess clears her throat in the background.

"Wow," she finally allows, and I catch her nibbling at her bottom lip, a move I find sexy as hell. She looks innocent, but I know she's not.

"Now, what was he saying about phone sex? I think it's a lovely idea, don't you?"

"Yes, but I don't know how I feel about it when he's lurking in the hallway."

"Is his bedroom upstairs by yours?"

"No, Ryann's is, though. He was probably taking a shit in my bathroom because he's an asshole. His bedroom is downstairs by the kitchen."

That makes Tess laugh. She's always doing that, laughing at the dumb things I say.

"It sounds like Drake is really into phone sex."

"I think he's into sex in general. He's way hornier than I am."

Tess tilts her head. "Is that because you aren't into casual sex or because you just don't think about it? 'Cause I know you don't have a lack of opportunity."

She's not wrong. I don't have a lack of opportunity. "I don't like casual sex." I've tried it, and I'm not into it.

I can't do it.

"Neither do I."

My brows go up. I can't help it. Was it not casual when the two of us had sex? How could she consider it anything but when we're not dating, and we're not in the same state the majority of the time? Up until last weekend, I hadn't thought about Tess at all. She wasn't on my radar.

"You don't count," she supplies before I can ask. "I've had a crush on you since forever."

"I can confidently say had I not had my head firmly planted up my ass, I probably would have had a crush on you, too."

"Now you're just bein' nice," Tess demurs.

"I'm not like my brother, but I'm also not in the habit of blowin' smoke up someone's ass just to make them feel good."

She grins into the camera—into the phone.

"I think that earns you a little reward, don't you?" Tess lowers the phone again, tilting it so I can check out her body. My eyes follow along, drinking in the sight of her beautiful breasts.

I swallow.

"Like what you see?"

Did she ask me that already, or is my brain completely dead? "Yes."

My dick goes instantly hard—how could it not?

"I swear your tits are perfect."

And they are.

Round. Full.

Topped with the most gorgeous, dark areolas. Like two cherries on a sundae, my mouth waters at the memory of licking and sucking them.

My dick grows harder still…

My hand makes its way south, stopping at my boxer shorts

as I debate my options: start touching myself and make things weird or not touch myself and suffer having a rock-hard cock.

"Do it," she says as if reading my mind.

"Do what?"

"Touch yourself."

"I'll touch mine if you touch yours," I challenge, not wanting to jerk off over the phone all by myself.

"Let me get my vibrator."

"The pink one?"

"No. One that's not as intense. I don't want to come so fast…"

CHAPTER 32
TESS

THERE'S NOTHING MORE DANGEROUS THAN A GOOD-LOOKING NICE GUY...

NEVER IN MY life have I spoken to a guy like this.

So freely, without considering how he'll take my words first.

Because I know Drew isn't judging me. It's not his personality—he's literally the best.

And the sexiest.

His eyes are hooded as his hand disappears from view, and I visualize it sliding over his stomach, down over his belly button, over his pelvis, and into the waistband of his boxers.

"What color are your shorts?" I ask him.

He moves the camera so I can see: navy blue with a dark blue band.

Tight.

And with a hand down the front.

Oh god…

So sexy…

"You should maybe push them down your hips. Yeah?"

Drew nods. "I should. Good idea."

I can't watch him doing it since he hasn't shown me, but the simple fact that I'm aware of him doing it…

Drool.

"This feels super porny," I mutter.

"Does it?"

"Ha. In my dreams…"

"Like. What kind of porn?" Drew wonders, voice low and gravelly.

I shrug my bare shoulders. "I don't know. Probably one where the guy is lying in bed jerking off, and the door opens, and one of his female roommates catches him in the act and joins him."

He nods. "What else?"

"That female roommate is me. And I'm not usually home, and everyone else is out of the house for a party. I come into the room looking for you because I need help."

"Help with what?"

"Getting my dress off. You've always been so good with your hands…" I softly tell him, enjoying the look on his face as the fantasy plays out in his mind.

"Mm-hmm. You need help with your dress, and I'm on the bed. Am I naked?"

"You just have your boxers on—like you do now. And I don't know what to do when I walk in because I'm so startled."

He nods. "Yeah."

Licks his pouty lips.

"Are you stroking yourself?" I ask him quietly.

"Yes." He pauses. "Did you get your vibrator?"

"Yes," I whisper, pressing the button to power it on, moving it down my body. "I'm wearing a beige-colored thong. It looks like I'm naked," I tell him so he can get a visual. "Do you like me in a thong?"

Drew licks his lips again. "I do."

Good.

"What do you do when I accidentally walk into the room?"

"I apologize."

"You do? What are you sorry for?"

He isn't sure and takes a few seconds to come up with an answer. Clearly, I'm better at porn scenarios than he is.

He backtracks, changing his story.

"When you accidentally walk into the room, I continue stroking my cock and look you dead in the eye to see what you'll do about it. Just see if you're embarrassed and if you'll run away. Or maybe you'll join me."

"Are we those kinds of roommates?"

"Not yet." He laughs.

But his laughter is strangled because he is so turned on he can barely talk.

"I see." And I do. I can easily picture this scenario because it's so similar to what happened over the past weekend. "I close the door behind me just in case someone happens to come home—and lock it. You watch as I put my back to the door and continue watching you. I still don't know what I should do."

"You know what you should do."

"And what's that?"

"You should walk over to the bed, stand at the foot of it, and slowly pull my boxers down my hips."

"Oh, that's hot…"

I close my eyes to imagine it. Taking the small vibrating toy, I place it between my legs, positioning it over my clit and letting it *hum hum* ever so softly.

My eyes are still closed as Drew softly tells me what happens once the boxers are down over his hips, and I can see it so clearly.

Me, pulling the blue shorts down. Watching as his beautiful dick springs free. Wanting it in my mouth, eyeing it hungrily.

I had no idea I was such a dick enthusiast, but here we are.

The vibrator continues humming, making me purr.

Drew is silent.

His phone moves to a rhythm I can only identify as his body to the tempo of his arm.

He groans.

"So I stand at the foot of the bed and slowly pull down your boxers?"

I lied when I said he wasn't good at role-playing. He's very good.

We should do it in person sometime.

Oh, a girl can dream.

"Yeah, you pull them down, and your mouth begins to water."

"Not literally, I hope."

Drew laughs. "God, I hope not."

"I would never drool while I was standin' over you like that. Now, if it was in my mouth, that would be another story."

"Now there's a thought."

He strokes.

Strokes.

My pussy vibrates.

"So what next?"

This is his fantasy now.

"You start peeling your clothes off. First, you take off your shirt, so you're only in a bra. And then you reach beneath your skirt and take off your panties."

I'm in a skirt?

"Then you climb on the bed on all fours, crawl toward my dick, and lick it up the base."

So hot.

So sexy.

"For a few minutes, you suck me off, and I take a handful of your hair and work your head up and down my cock, pushing it deeper into your throat."

Yikes.

Good thing this is only a fantasy 'cause I'd probably choke.

Wouldn't be the worst way to die…

"I can feel my balls tighten because I'm close to coming, so I make you stop."

I nod, the tingling in my lower half getting stronger as the neon blue vibrator works every nerve in my body, flirting with an orgasm before pulling back again.

It's such a tease.

"I know what happens next," I whisper. "I climb on top and raise my skirt and sink down on top of you."

"Good girl…" he breathes. "Such a good girl."

Am I?

Not really.

"And I ride you nice and slow because I want to come too. I want you to come inside me, and I don't want it to be quick. I want to drag it out. I want to fuck the shit out of you, but at the same time, it has to be slow." I whimper. "Uh, it would feel so, so good…"

"So good." He moans, the furrowed brow is deep. His groan is long and drawn out. "Oh fuck, it would feel good."

"Better than before when I was riding you and the headboard was banging against the wall."

"God, I loved hearing that. So fucking hot."

"That was hot."

I wonder what Miranda's neighbors might have been thinking. I would have been so freaking irritated if I were trying to sleep in the apartment next door and had to listen to someone having sex through the wall.

I turn up the volume on my vibrator, and it buzzes a bit faster.

"How close are you?" Drew asks.

I swear I catch a glimpse of perspiration on his upper lip, or am I imagining it?

"Close." I can be closer still with the touch of a button.

"Me too," he replies. "Show me your tits."

I lower the phone so he can see my chest. It's an easy request, and his expression doesn't disappoint.

He looks like he's in pain, eyes fixated on my boobs, arm working faster.

"Oh shit, Tess. God, you have great tits. I want to suck on them."

"Mm-hmm," I muster in reply, memory jogging back to the

moment he had lowered his head to put his lips and mouth on my nipples. Back to the moment I plunged my hand through his hair, watching him suck and lick my breasts, the spot between my legs soaking wet.

"I want to come so bad."

Moan.

Groan.

"Then do it."

I don't know who is making more noise—Drew or I as we simultaneously pleasure ourselves. I don't know if this is going to bring us closer together or draw us further apart.

I don't know if this was a good idea, either.

All I know is that the orgasm that hits me is just as strong as it may have been if he were thrusting in and out of my body.

Drew comes with a moan, his body jerking as he silently orgasms. Way quieter than when we were actually having sex.

Intense.

A first for me.

And hopefully, it's not the last.

We lie there, sated, not uttering another word to one another. Then after about three minutes of silence, Drew finally says,

"I had no idea I was such a boob guy."

My laughter is quiet. "We learn something new about ourselves every day."

CHAPTER 33
TESS
...HE SHOULD HAVE PULLED OUT.

I THINK I'M LATE.

And by late, I don't mean "I showed up to class late," or "I was late with a credit card payment."

I'm talking about my period.

Which is weird because I'm like clockwork most months.

There is no way…

But it's been four days and…

Nothing.

Not a spot.

Not a speck.

Zero sign that a period is forthcoming.

The sun dips below the horizon over the neighboring apartment building, casting a warm golden glow across my apartment. It's pretty this time of day, and I'd normally love the sunset, but I want to puke right now.

I'm nervous.

I sit on the couch, clutching my phone tightly in one hand, the other hand unconsciously rubbing my forehead.

Seriously, thank god my roommates are gone. The last thing I want to tell them is my suspicions before I have proof because what if I'm only imagining it? What if I'm so stressed out it's just late? That happens, yeah?

If I'm being honest, the first few times I had sex, I thought I might be pregnant, ha!

My heart races as I dial Miranda's, my stomach churning with a mix of anxiety and uncertainty.

Her phone rings. And rings. And rings, until FINALLY her sing-songy voice answers.

"Is this an emergency because why are you calling and not texting," she teases, her tone playful and lighthearted. "But for real. Why are you calling?"

I take a deep breath.

I have no idea how to start. Or how to put this.

It could be nothing!

It's been four days…

"Miranda…" I start, already feeling out of control. "I haven't gotten my period, and it's been four days."

There's a brief pause on the other end of the line, and I can hear my best friend's wheels turning.

"Wait, are you saying what I think you're saying?"

I nod even though she can't see me. "What if I'm…?"

I can't even say the actual words. "What if I'm…you know?"

That.

Preggo.

Oh god.

"You're not," she reassures me with almost no information because the idea of it being true is too surreal. "You can't be."

But I could be.

Because we didn't use protection.

"But what if I am?"

A soft exhale of surprise escaped her lips. "Wow, that's… that's…are you sure?"

I lean back against the couch cushions, my mind racing with a million thoughts. "I mean, I haven't taken a test yet, but something's off. My body just…knows, does that make sense? I'm kind of freaking out over here, Miranda."

I stand, pacing around my living room, my heart racing with

anxiety. I need to confide in someone—lord knows I can't tell my brother or my parents, at least, not yet—and Miranda is always the first person I call when I have a problem.

She knows everything.

She also knows I have a very low chance of getting pregnant.

Miranda's soothing voice floats through the phone. "Come on, relax. There's no way, Tess. Remember that time we laughed about the so-called 'pregnancy symptoms' when you had sex with that one guy Paul? It's just your body playing tricks on you."

I sigh. "I know, but it feels different this time."

She chuckles. "Trust me, fate has better timing than this. Let's not jump to conclusions. Remember, we've got a girls' night planned next weekend, and you'll feel normal. We'll laugh about this too, I promise."

Her optimism works; it begins to melt away my worries, and I smile a little. "You always know how to make me feel better, Miranda."

"Of course, that's what best friends are for. Now, go treat yourself to some chocolate, watch a cheesy rom-com, and relax. Everything will be okay." There's some background noise, and it sounds like she's moving around. "Listen, I wish I could come over, but I just walked into the chem lab for my makeup test."

She lowers her voice. "Hey, it's going to be okay. First things first, have you talked to a doctor about this?"

"No," I admit, feeling a twinge of guilt for not seeking professional advice sooner. "Isn't the first thing you do is run out and get a test?"

"Usually." She laughs. "At least that's what I've done, but you've had issues with your lady parts. You should go have an honest conversation about what's going on."

Since when is she so mature all of a sudden?

"You're right. I should definitely do that." At some point.

Just not right now.

Right now, I'm too freaked out.

"In the meantime, let's not jump to conclusions. Remember that time we thought you had that rare tropical disease after we came back from Cancun, and it turned out to be a bad case of food poisoning?"

I grin at the memory despite the situation at hand. "Yeah, I remember. I guess I do have a tendency to overthink things every once in a while."

"Oh, you absolutely do. But that's what I'm here for – to keep you grounded and remind you not to spiral into a frenzy of what-ifs."

My chest squeezes with warm fuzzies. She's such a damn good friend. "Thanks, Miranda. I don't know what I'd do without you."

"You'd probably drive yourself crazy," she quips quietly. "Now, promise me you'll schedule that doctor's appointment. Don't geek out and run and get thirty tests. You're probably just stressed out."

"I promise."

But my fingers are crossed behind my back.

"Good. And hey, even if the worst-case scenario were to happen—which I highly doubt—you wouldn't be alone in this. You've got me and you've got Grady and all our friends."

Grady.

Why did she have to mention my brother?

Not only is he going to freak the hell out but he's going to go postal on Drew.

My stomach is in knots.

The conversation continued, seamlessly transitioning from my worries to lighter topics, and I hear most of them. Mostly.

Eventually, Miranda has to end the call, and when she does, I stand in the middle of the living room with my phone in the palm of my hand. Sure, I'm relieved my bestie has managed to talk me down off the ledge, but that doesn't stop the reality of the situation from sinking in again.

I might *actually* be pregnant.

And no matter how badly I want it not to be true, I can't help but think that it is.

Because my body just knows.

I place a hand on my stomach.

I, the girl who can barely keep a cactus alive, could potentially be responsible for a tiny human being.

Shit.

I let out a theatrical sigh and sprawl out on the couch again, staring at the ceiling.

"Well, this is a fine mess you've gotten yourself into," I mutter to myself. "Why would you have let him bang you without a condom, you idiot? Who does that?"

Just because he's the crush of your life and your childhood fantasy doesn't mean you weren't going to get yourself preggo—or an STD.

Don't even get me started on that…

I roll my eyes at my own melodrama, but deep down, I can't help feeling a flutter of excitement beneath the layers of anxiety.

I was told I might never be able to get pregnant, so I'm not going to lie and say the thought of a little version of me running around is both terrifying and oddly…exciting. I can already picture mini-me demanding bedtime stories and insisting on ice cream for breakfast.

No.

Dude, you're twenty-one.

Your parents are going to freak out.

Speaking of mini-me, I can practically hear my brother's voice in my head, complete with his signature overprotective scowl. Grady is going to flip when he finds out. He's been in big brother mode since we were kids, and the idea of his baby sister becoming an actual mother will make his head explode.

But then there's Drew.

Ah, Drew.

The guy who swept into my life like a whirlwind and turned

everything upside down. What if I'm about to turn his life upside down when all I wanted was one night with him?

Don't be ridiculous. You won't ruin your lives if you find out you're pregnant. Plenty of people who aren't in relationships manage just fine.

I mean, I don't know any, but they're out there.

Ha!

A surge of affection warms my chest as I think about his goofy smile and the way his eyes light up when he talks about his favorite nerdy books and how he admires his older brothers because they're all bonded by football.

I can almost see the disbelief on his face, his expressive eyebrows shooting up to his hairline, his strong jaw clenching.

As I continue to drift in my sea of thoughts, the room around me seems to blur into the background. The possibilities and challenges of the future dance before my eyes, a kaleidoscope of emotions that leave me both exhilarated and overwhelmed.

With a determined grin, I push myself up from the couch and head toward the kitchen.

It's time to face this situation head-on, armed with a healthy dose of humor, so I do what any modern girl would do. I take my phone, poke on the Door Delivery app, and swipe it open.

Add a pregnancy test to the cart.

One.

No, two, just in case.

Fine. Better make it three.

To be on the safe side…

DEAR DIARY...

Framk Phillips asked me to prom and I didn't know what to say. He asked me in gym class while we were running the mile, which I thought was weird—he had the balls to tell me that if I say yes, he'll do an actual Promposal, but he didn't want to do one first and waste his time and money if I said no.

What the HELL.

On the other hand, he's the only one who's asked me and I want to go to the dance with a guy, all of my friends have dates this year. Tosha said I should tell him to piss off and that telling me he didn't want to spend money to ask me out was tacky and gross and he doesn't deserve me. I guess she's right? I was telling Mom about it and she said "Guys are idiots, you've seen how your brother and his friends act, this shouldn't surprise you."

Which she's right about—doesn't make it any easy. I told Frank I had to think about it. Been dress shopping all night HAHAHAHAHAH

Will keep you posted
xx Tess

CHAPTER 34
DREW

GETS GHOSTED ME: THANK YOU FOR THE FREE 15 DAY TRIAL BUT I'D RATHER HEAR FROM YOU.

I HAVEN'T HEARD from Tess in at least two weeks.

Which is weird because we had been talking every day; almost all day, since I got back from visiting home and can we not forget that night we had phone sex?

Why would she ghost me like this?

It's not as if I were a stranger, and if I'd done something wrong, wouldn't she have said something?

I feel like we're at that point—becoming friends and being open and honest with one another. At least, that's my perspective on it. I could be wrong, but I felt like we were…getting to a place where we might become something more?

In the past four weeks, we'd discussed it all: Family. School. Careers. Goals. What we want to do once we graduate, where we want to live. Places we want to travel. Food. Hobbies.

Tess is funny. We spent most of our time laughing.

Definitely becoming a better flirt.

We've video chatted a lot too, and at one point, she'd flashed me her boobs. I might be overly optimistic here, but I think we were approaching the point of phone sex…again. I think we were approaching a point where…I feel comfortable asking her to fly out and see me.

I'd buy the plane ticket, of course, since I'd be the one asking her to drop everything to come see me, and flights these days aren't cheap.

But I haven't gotten the chance because out of the blue—out of nowhere—Tess Donahue up and stopped chatting with me.

Grady, too.

Can't get ahold of him either, and now I'm starting to worry that something serious may have happened. Did one of them get sick? Did something happen to their mom? Their dad? Is one of them hospitalized?

Jesus, I can't stop worrying, and I wish one of them would answer my fucking text messages or answer my calls.

"She stopped respondin' to my messages," I tell my brother as I set my phone down on the coffee table, eager to forget that I was stupid enough to shoot off yet another text.

"Dude, she probably started seein someone else and didn't have the heart to tell you."

"Gee, thanks." I pause. "And we weren't seein' each other. We were talkin'."

Drake shrugs his big shoulders. "Is there a difference? You like her, don't you?"

"Yes."

"So you're seeing each other." He jams a handful of potato chips in his mouth. "Have you talked about, you know—not datin' other people?"

"No."

He shrugs again. "Well, that's the problem, then. Chicks ain't mind readers. How was she supposed to know she isn't supposed to go out with other dudes? It's not like you're in the Army; she shouldn't be expected to wait for you."

"I don't expect her to wait for me. All's I said was she hasn't responded to my messages. Grady, either."

This time, Drake pulls a face. "Huh. That is weird. That dude loves texting. He texts back embarrassingly fast."

"Obviously, she doesn't."

My brother puts down his chips and faces me. "How soon after you phone fucked her did she stop responding to you?"

I shrug. "I don't know—a few days?"

"She's probably embarrassed. Some girls do impulsive shit and then they feel guilty about it. Maybe that's the problem."

"Thanks, Einstein, I am aware." But Tess isn't apologetic; she is a take-charge kind of girl who knows what she wants. She wanted me, and she went for it. So there's no way in hell she's ashamed of a bit of masturbating together over the phone.

"Too bad you can't ask her what the problem is." His arm is back in the bag of chips, and when he stuffs more in his face, he crunches loudly.

I want to smack him.

"You're an asshole."

"What! It's the truth."

"You don't think I texted her to see if there's an issue? Hell, do you know how hard it was to text Grady? He's going to see right through it and know something was going on between us."

I nudge my brother. "You text him. Ask him if everything is alright with his sister."

Drakes rolls his eyes but takes his phone off the table, thumbs through it, and taps out a message to our friend.

He talks out loud as he types. "Hey, Grady. Is. Everything. All. Right. With. You. And. Your. Sister. Question mark." He glances up at me. "Send."

He plunks the phone back on the coffee table.

"He told me to piss off."

Fuck. "He did?"

Drake grins, leaning back on the couch. "Hey, you're the one asking your big bro for dating advice. Now you're coming off as desperate."

"Desperate? Fuck you. All I did was ask what you thought the problem might be."

Drake puts a hand over his heart. "Ah, the trials and tribulations of the modern long-distance text-based romance. *How tragic.*"

I laugh, feeling the tension from earlier melt away. "Yeah, yeah, mock all you want. Just remember, when you need help deciphering Daisy's love for cat memes, I'll be here with my world-renowned meme expertise."

Drake raises his hands in mock surrender. "Fair enough. Now, let's get serious. What's your plan for getting Tess to text you back? I mean, dude, maybe you should just let it go. Find someone here. Wasn't that the original plan?"

No, that was *his* original plan, and that plan failed miserably.

Case in point: he's dating the one decent prospect he found for me.

I chuckle, shaking my head. "I think I'll start by sending her a bouquet of eggplant emoji. Subtle yet profound."

Drake snorts. "Ah, the language of love. You're a true poet, bro."

As we continue to roast each other I realize how lucky I am to have a brother like Drake. Someone who can always make me laugh, even in the midst of romantic turmoil.

"Know who we should call for advice?"

"Who?"

"Duke."

"No. Hell no." I laugh because the idea sounds hideous. "Over my dead body."

"That can be arranged."

"Dude. All I want is for some closure—if she truly wants nothin' to do with me, I want to know so I can move on."

But with any luck, Tess and I will be back to texting and flirting and—dare I hope, naked video chatting—like our usual goofy selves in no time.

CHAPTER 35
TESS

GHOSTED IN OCTOBER? HOW FESTIVE. BOO!

> Drew: Hey, Tess! Long time no hear. Are you ghosting me, or did your phone decide to take a vacation? Everything alright?

> Drew: Hey. Just checking in again. Did I…do something to offend you?

> Drew: So listen. I don't want to be weird or keep hounding you if you're not interested, but now I'm getting worried everything isn't okay?

I STARE at the text messages Drew has sent me. There are a half dozen of them, and each one he sends has my heart breaking further.

I don't know what to say.

Obviously.

But I can't continue not saying anything at all. I owe it to him to explain why I've been so quiet, but no way can I tell him the truth.

Not all of it.

Not yet.

> Tess: Hey, Drew! Sorry for the silence. No ghosting, I promise! Just got caught up in the chaos of life. You're not getting off the hook that easily. Ha ha.

> Drew: Phew, thought I was about to be the star of a "How to Lose a Friend in 10 Messages" sequel. Life's chaos, huh

> Tess: Ha ha, don't worry, you're not getting rid of me that easily. School has been stupid the past few days, and then my car decided to do a dramatic breakdown on the busiest street in town. So you know, just your typical comedy of errors.

Why am I lying?

God will strike me down for making up bullshit to this caring, sweet guy.

Ugh.

I hate myself, but he's going to hate me more when he finds out the truth.

> Drew: A dramatic car breakdown? Dang, what ended up being the problem???

> Tess: Nothing serious—I, um, ran out of gas? Miranda came to my rescue, but it took hours, and the whole thing was a nightmare.

> Drew: As long as you're not mad at me

> Tess: Nah, you're in the clear, Drew. No secret grudges being held here. Just life being its usual unpredictable self.

I sound like a robot giving him scripted answers.

> Drew: Glad to hear that! I was starting to think I accidentally offended you with my bare chest or something. So when can we officially declare war on the chaos and grab a coffee?

> Tess: Ha. How are we going to grab coffee when I'm here and you're there? Were you planning on coming home this weekend?

> Drew: I wish. No, I was thinking it might be fun if we had a date—like an actual date. We could both go to a coffee shop, get something to drink, and sit and talk while we video chat?

WHY IS HE SO NICE?

> Tess: That is such a cute idea. I'll let you know. I've been crazy busy.

> Drew: Ahh, gotcha. Well. Let me know.

I feel like I just kicked a puppy.

> Tess: I will. I'd love to catch up, Drew. Thanks for understanding and being your awesome self.

> Drew: Thanks for understanding and being my awesome self? Um, are you sure you're alright? Nothing else is bothering you?

Yes, something else is bothering me but telling him in a text message is not the way to do it.

I have to find a way, but I also know I should wait.

I'm not far enough along to be confident that it will stick; everything I've read said to wait until you're at least ten to twelve weeks, so that's what I plan to do—no matter how hard it will be.

CHAPTER 36
DREW

I'M FULLY COMMITTED TO OUR RELATIONSHIP OR REPEATED ONE-NIGHT STANDS.

MY HEART RACES as I stare at my phone.

Fuck.

Grady Donahue is calling me, his name flashing on the screen. He never calls.

I mean, who even does that in this day and age? If you need something and it's important, everyone knows you're supposed to text that shit.

Relax, I remind myself. Drake texted him to see if everything was okay. That's probably what this is about.

Granted, he did reply and tell Drake to piss off, but that's how they've always been.

I answer the call, trying to sound casual even though my damn heart is pounding.

"Hey, Grady, what's up?"

"Don't 'hey, Grady, what's up?' me," he practically growls through the phone. "I just got an earful from Tess about what happened during that damn bachelor party weekend. I had to drag the details out of her, though."

"Whoa. Back up. What do you mean?"

I know what he means. I'm just too chickenshit to admit it. I want to know what he knows first.

"You slept with my sister, motherfucker."

My heart drops to my stomach, and I legit want to barf.

"Look, Grady, I can explain—"

"Explain?" he interrupts, his voice incredulous. He lets out a sardonic laugh. "I think the words you're looking for is 'Gee Grady, it must have slipped my mind that I forgot to tell you I slept with your sister.'" He pauses. "You *slept* with my sister, Drew."

He doesn't have to keep saying it.

It's not like I don't already know.

I was there.

"Yeah, I know, but—"

"How long has this been going on, huh?" he demands, cutting me off again. "How long have you been sneaking around with Tess behind my back?"

I take a deep breath. "It was just that one time, dude. The weekend of the bachelor party was the first and last, I swear."

If you don't count phone sex where we jerked off at the same time?

Oops.

"Like hell it was just one time, there is no way," he snarls. "Tess is hurt, man. She's been acting strange lately, and I finally got it out of her that the two of you… fucked." He goes silent again. "Jesus, I can't believe I'm saying those words. I want to puke."

And I don't?

"I understand, Grady, I really do. I'm sorry," I admit, my voice heavy with regret. It's on the tip of my tongue to say something stupid like, "I messed up," and "I regret it," but the truth is, *I mostly don't.*

Sure, I regret ruining this friendship.

"I care about Tess, a lot. And I never meant for this to happen the way it did."

"Things guilty assholes say."

"Dude. Why are you so mad? It was her choice. And it's not like it was a random hookup, we care about each other."

There. I said it.

I care about Tess.

Too bad the first person I'm admitting it to is her pitbull of a brother, who hadn't even bothered to spend time with me over the weekend I was home.

Barely saw the dude.

Of course I was going to bond with his sister.

"Oh, you 'care about Tess, a lot'? That's rich." He's being so sarcastic. "Did you 'care' about her while you were fucking her in my place, behind my back?"

"It wasn't at your house—it was at hers." I make the mistake of saying.

"Fuck you."

"Okay, I deserve that." But I'm frustrated as hell and this conversation is going nowhere productive. "Grady. Brother. I'm being honest with you. It was a mistake, a stupid one, and I take full responsibility for it."

"You're damn right you take responsibility," he snaps. "But that doesn't change the fact that you betrayed my trust, Drew. I thought we were friends."

"We *are* friends, Grady," I insist. "I never wanted to hurt you or Tess—but with all due respect, this wasn't about you. This is about her and I."

"Excuse me?"

"This is about Tess and I."

Grady laughs. "I swear to god, I always thought Drake was the cocky one between the two of you. Turns out all along, you're the one we can't trust."

"Why are you getting all bent out of shape?" I blurt out. "It's sex. And we care about each other. It wasn't a one-night stand. Did she not explain that to you?"

I can literally hear him breathing in and out. "All I know is that she's been crying a lot lately, and it has something to do with you."

"That makes no sense," I utter, almost to myself. "All I've been tryin' to do lately is get ahold of her. She isn't texting me back. She ghosted me. Check her phone. I've sent so many messages."

He lets out a heavy sigh, the tension in his voice finally giving way to something resembling resignation. "You've got a long way to go to make this right, Drew. Tess is hurt; I have no idea why, but I plan to get to the bottom of it."

I nod even though he can't see me. "Fair enough."

"I don't know if or when she'll be ready to forgive you."

Swallowing hard, I feel my throat tighten. "I understand. I promise to give her the space she needs."

He's silent for a moment, and I can almost hear the cogs turning in his head. Finally, he says, "Fine. Here's what you're gonna do. You're gonna make it up to Tess, and you're gonna do it without screwing up even more. You hurt her, and if you hurt her again, I will fly to Illinois and beat your ass. Understand."

"Uh. How did that work out the last time you tried?"

"Screw you, dude."

I can hear the grin on his face even though he probably wouldn't admit it.

"Just saying. You'd have to take me by surprise if you were going to get a fair fight."

He scoffs. "Listen. I hate that you and my sister…you know. Fucking hate it. But I hate that she's upset even more. I've never seen her like this."

"Like how?"

"Cryin'. Seems miserable. Been sick."

She's been sick?

Weird.

"She didn't say anything to me about being sick. She said she was busy with school, and that night she ran out of gas on the side of the street really stressed her out."

Grady goes quiet, thinking. "Ran out of gas on the side of the street? When was that?"

I shrug. "Don't know, two weeks ago maybe?"

"Huh." He's quiet. "Weird."

"I promise, Grady," I reply earnestly. "I'll do everything in my power to make things right between us—you and I. Me and her."

"Good," he says. "Because Tess deserves better than someone who makes her feel like crap, and you damn well know it."

"I know," I say, my voice heavy with remorse. "I thought I made her feel good. Shit. I don't mean that the way it came out, I meant I thought we made each other laugh. She's funny as hell and a good friend."

"A good friend," he deadpans.

"Again, not what I meant."

Jesus, this guy.

He's coming at me hard.

Not that I don't deserve it, but damn, I *like* her. Why is that a problem?

There's a moment of silence, and I can almost sense the weight of his scrutiny through the phone. "You better. And if you hurt her again, you won't just have to deal with me. You'll have the entire football team on your ass."

I chuckle despite the seriousness of the situation. "Have you already forgotten that you don't play football anymore?"

"I meant the intramural league I play with on the weekends, smartass."

"Uh. Aren't those mostly dads and ex-frat boys?"

"Shut up. I won't hesitate to tackle you harder than any linebacker ever has."

I can't help but laugh at that mental image. "Deal, Grady. You win. No tackling from you or your dad frat football team; I'll be on my best behavior, and I'll do whatever it takes to win Tess back."

"Not sure if I want you winning my sister over but I would love to have my sister back. She's making me sad, dude."

"Understood," I reply with a nod. "Thanks for giving me a chance to make things right, Grady."

"Don't thank me yet," he warns. "I'm dying to pummel your ass."

"Yeah, you've said that like twelve times."

"Fuck you."

"You've said that like twelve times, too."

I'm confused when we hang up.

What the hell is going on, and why isn't she telling me about it? What could she be crying about? And when was she going to tell me she's sick?

Sick.

How?

Does she have Covid and didn't want me to know?

Shit.

Do I need to get tested?

A million things run through my mind, and I can hardly sleep at all when I finally crawl into bed, a conversation I had with Tess flashing through my brain after we'd had sex that night—the first time, not the second.

"I can't get pregnant."

"What do you mean you can't get pregnant?" I'd turned my head to look at her. *"How do you know?"*

"I had endometriosis as a teenager, and I have low progesterone. The doctor told me my chances were slim. Like—super slim."

"But not impossible?"

"I guess not impossible, but according to my research..."

Tess wasn't pregnant.

I would know.

She would tell me.

CHAPTER 37
DREW

ACTUALLY. IT WASN'T A ONE-NIGHT STAND CONSIDERING WE DID IT AGAIN IN THE MORNING.

I'M SPRAWLED across my bed, engrossed in a novel, when the door to my bedroom bursts open. I startle, nearly dropping my book as my brother Drake barges in with his usual flair for dramatic entrances. He's wearing his signature smirk, the one that usually means he's about to rope me into some harebrained scheme or mock my life choices.

"Drew, my man!" he exclaims, plopping down on the edge of my bed and grabbing the remote from my nightstand. "You won't believe what's on TV right now!"

I raise an eyebrow, a wary feeling settling in the pit of my stomach. "What did you do?"

He grins like the Cheshire cat, waving the remote triumphantly. "Oh, nothing much. Just thought you might want to catch up on the latest news. Trust me, it's a story you won't want to miss."

Before I can protest, he presses a button, and the TV springs to life, blaring the all-too-familiar tune of the sports channel. My eyes widen as I watch the screen, my heart pounding in my chest.

"Breaking news: Drew Colter, star quarterback of the college football team, has found himself in the midst of an unexpected scandal," the news anchor announces dramatically, a photo of me plastered on the screen next to a headline that reads, "Drew's Unplanned Touchdown: Girl from Hometown Claims Pregnancy."

My jaw practically hits the floor.

I sit back down on the bed.

Stand.

Sit.

"What the hell?"

Drake chuckles, clearly enjoying my stunned reaction. "Dude. I'm sorry, man, but this has been all over social media. Duke is the one who saw it first and texted me."

I grab the remote from his hand and mute the TV, staring at the screen in disbelief. "How is this even possible? I haven't heard anything from Tess about being pregnant."

"Because it's not real, bro. You know how the media circus is."

That familiar pit settles back into my stomach, and my eyes scan my bedroom for the closest garbage can on the off chance that I need to vomit.

I scramble to grab my phone from the nightstand, fingers fumbling as I dial Tess's number. The phone rings, and I feel a mix of anxiety and confusion swirling inside me.

Voicemail.

Why would she go to the press before even talking to me?

"Are you seeing this, Drake?" I point at the television, my hand shaking. "For real, what the fuck!"

"Oh, I'm definitely seeing it, little bro, by two minutes. And let me tell you, the world is getting yet another eyeful of the Colter family drama."

He isn't taking this seriously at all.

Not that he takes anything seriously. To my brother, everything is a goddamn joke.

First Duke, when he was between teams and hiding out in the suburbs. Then Dallas, taking money to break up with his teammate's girlfriend then bribing her to fake date him. Then

Drake himself, who pretended to be me on dating apps, although the media never caught wind of that little gem.

I shoot him a glare. "It's not funny, Drake. This is serious."

My head is going to fucking explode. The story on television seems to be on repeat with one reporter then another commenting and giving their opinion on the rumor's validity.

"I didn't say that it wasn't, but come on. You know how this goes." He flops onto the bed next to me, finally pinning a somber expression on his face. "You've always been the golden boy, Mr. Perfect—of course, they're going to take one whiff of a scandal and run it. This just adds a little spice to your squeaky-clean image."

"I don't want to add spice to my image." I shake my head, not amused in the slightest. "You have no idea what's going on, do you?"

My twin rolls his eyes. "Enlighten me, oh scandalous one."

I let out a frustrated sigh, running a hand through my hair. "It's Tess, it must be. This is the reason I haven't heard shit from her in days."

Weeks.

Drake's eyes widen in surprise, his smirk fading. "Wait, what? Are you fucking with me right now?"

I nod, my heart heavy with a mix of emotions. "Yeah, her. I can't believe she went to the press with this before even talking to me."

My voice is a whisper now, my throat constricting.

Fuck, I think I'm going to cry.

Actually cry.

Drake's expression shifts from surprise to genuine concern. "Damn, Drew. That's messed up."

I groan, burying my face in my hands. "Tell me about it."

He pats me on the back, a surprisingly comforting gesture. "Look, bro, I get that this is a total curveball, but you can handle it. You've faced tougher challenges on the field, right?"

Now is not the time for his locker room diatribe, feel-good

nonsense. But leave it to Drake to put things into perspective, even if he does it in his own Drake-like way.

"Yeah, you're right. Maybe it wasn't her that went to the press, eh? Maybe it was…"

I pause.

Grady Donahue, that motherfucking bastard.

He couldn't have.

He *wouldn't* have…

It had to have been him.

He was so pissed off on the phone, but dude, he promised me he would let me make this shit right.

"People get paid a lot of money for stories like this," my brother says quietly as if reading my thoughts. "You know that. And if she could use the money…"

"Not her," I whisper. "Him."

"Him who?"

"Fucking Grady."

My brother shrugs. "Hey, drama sells. And clearly, she's looking for her fifteen minutes of fame."

I don't correct him.

For all I know, she was fine with her brother going to the paparazzi and selling the story. If she is actually pregnant, a few hundred thousand dollars probably sounds like a really good deal. Good enough to screw over your friend.

And lover.

And father of your kid.

My kid.

Oh my god, I'm going to be sick to my stomach.

"Drama sells." I give Drake a weak smile, his humor lighting the room's heavy atmosphere. "Yeah, well, she got her fifteen minutes. The whole world knows now."

Drake nudges me playfully. "So what's your game plan, superstar? How are you gonna handle this scandal?" He pauses. "Handle scandal—I made a rhyme."

I flop down on the bed, staring up at the ceiling, running a hand through my hair.

"First, I need to talk to Tess. Figure out why she did this if she did this—and why she didn't tell me about…the pregnancy. Then I guess we'll have to figure out what we're gonna do next."

Drake raises an eyebrow, a mischievous glint in his eyes. "You know, you could always consult our family's resident scandal expert."

I chuckle, shaking my head. "You mean you?"

He grins, clearly pleased with himself. "Who else? Duh. I've navigated my fair share of drama. I've got tips, tricks, and a few creative cover-ups up my sleeve."

I give him a skeptical look. "Are your 'creative cover-ups' legal?"

He waves a dismissive hand. "Details, details. Let's focus on the task at hand. First, call Tess again. Get the facts straight from the source. Then we'll brainstorm some damage control strategies."

Like get a lawyer.

Call Drew's agent.

Call my mother and brothers.

Leave it to Drake to turn a potentially disastrous situation into a slightly less daunting one. "Alright, fine. I'll call her. But no shady cover-ups until we get to the truth, yeah?"

He holds up his hands in mock surrender. "You're the boss. No shady cover-ups. Just a touch of Colter charm."

He winks.

I can barely muster up a smile. "I can't believe I'm actually taking advice from you."

He grins, giving me a playful wink. "Hey, I'm the big brother for a reason, right? And then we can call *SportsCenter*—the world is waiting to hear your side of the story."

As I dial Tess's number, I can't help but feel a strange mix of nerves and determination.

With Drake by my side, armed with his unique brand of

advice and a touch of idiot sense of humor, maybe I can navigate this scandal without throwing up in the garbage can.

I find Tess in my phone.

Hit CALL.

Listen as it rings.

And rings.

And goes back to voicemail.

I give my brother a frantic look when the phone beeps so I can leave a message.

"Uh. Hey, Tess, it's me. Drew. Uh—Colter." I'm an idiot. "I was watching *SportsCenter*, and uh, there's a story about me, and I was wondering if you knew anything about it? About, um, me getting a young woman pregnant? Seriously, Tess, please call me back, I'm kind of freaking out here. Let me know you're okay. We need to talk. If this isn't you they're talking about, then I'm seriously fucked. Okay. Well. Call me. Bye."

"Well, you're not winning any awards for speech writing."

"Screw you."

And that's when my stomach heaves. Clenches.

Empties.

Straight into the garbage can.

CHAPTER 38
TESS

THE HEART WAS MADE TO BE
BROKEN. – OSCAR WILDE

"WHY WOULD you have sold the story? Why, Grady?"
I don't understand.
Plus, I'm not far along, anything could happen between now and…
I told him in confidence because Miranda convinced me it was the right thing to do and what's the first thing my brother does?
Sells the story to the press.
I'm so confused.
"*Uh. Hey, Tess, it's me. Drew. Uh—Colter. I was watching* Sports-Center *and, uh, there's a story about me, and I was wondering if you knew anything about it? About, um, me getting a young woman pregnant? Seriously, Tess, please call me back, I'm kind of freaking out here. Let me know you're okay. We need to talk. If this isn't you they're talking about, then I'm seriously fucked. Okay. Well. Call me. Bye.*"
I watched as my phone rang and saw that it was Drew; watched the NEW VOICEMAIL notification light up my phone, listened in horror as I played it.
His voice.
He sounded so…
Sad.
And confused.

One more thing we have in common.

"He feels betrayed. He thinks I did this to him!" I shout at my brother, who has the gall to sit in my best friend's kitchen, looking not the least bit affected by the shitstorm of drama he created.

"Actions have consequences," Grady states, plucking a banana off the counter and peeling it.

My brother hates bananas, so I know he's only doing it to appear unaffected and bored.

When did he become such a dick?

"This is not what I need right now."

"You clearly don't know what you need," he tells me, eyes scanning down the front of my shirt.

I'm not showing yet, but that doesn't make his intense scrutiny any better. He's judging me.

First, he judged me for sleeping with his friend, who I care deeply for, then he judged me when he heard I had gotten pregnant.

Brother of the year, you can fuck right off.

When did it get like this?

I thought we were good, he and I. Now suddenly, he's angry all the time and went to the press without telling me. It's humiliating and unforgivable.

This isn't the way I wanted Drew to find out.

I planned to fly to Illinois and break the news in person once I knew for sure that I would stay pregnant.

Now that Grady has forced my hand, I have no choice but to do it sooner.

"How much did they pay you?" Miranda asks my brother.

He shrugs, looking a little sheepish. "Enough."

"And I don't suppose you're going to share any of that with your pregnant sister."

"I don't want anything to do with that money," I say through gritted teeth.

Miranda steps between my brother and I before I scratch his eyes out. "You should go."

I watch as my best friend walks him to the door, slamming it behind him.

"He is some piece of work," she starts. "I had no idea what an asshole he is, did you?"

"No." I walk to the couch and sit, staring blankly at the TV.

Miranda sits down next to me and wraps her arm around my shoulders. "You should stay here tonight. I don't want you driving back to school when you're upset. You can sleep in my room with me, mmkay?"

I nod because I don't have the energy to argue and quite honestly would rather not go home to my roommates.

I still haven't told them.

They won't know until I do. They don't follow sports and have no idea who Drew Colter is, and they sure don't know that I had sex with him weeks ago.

Sober sex.

I can't even use alcohol as an excuse….

Drew's usually warm eyes are now ablaze with anger, and the tension in the air could be cut with a knife.

I take a deep breath, mustering the courage to say the words weighing on me…

Lost.

I have to take another breath.

"Drew," I begin, my voice shaky, "there's something you need to know."

He glares at me, his jaw clenched.

Why is he already angry? I haven't told him anything?

"What is it, Tess?"

My mind races, my words stumbling out. "I'm pregnant. And… you're the father."

The color drains from his face. "Pregnant? You've got to be kidding me." He pauses. "Wait. Why are you telling me this?"

"Because it's yours."

"Mine?"

I nod, tears tingling behind my nose. "Yes."

"How."

I roll my eyes. "You know how."

"How far along are you?"

"Ten weeks or so?" That's how long it's been since we were together.

"I don't know what ten weeks means."

"It's like two and a half months."

"There is no fuckin way."

"I'm sorry..."

His voice suddenly becomes laced with bitterness. "How could you keep something like this from me? Do you know what you've done?"

"Drew, I didn't know how to tell you. I was scared of your reaction, and I thought... I thought I could handle it on my own."

He scoffs, his frustration echoing in his voice. "Handle it on your own? By shutting me out completely? And where the hell was your brother, Grady, in all of this? Did he put you up to this?"

I shake my head, desperate to explain. "No, Drew, it wasn't Grady's idea. He didn't even know until recently. Please, try to understand."

"What a lie—he took money to sell a story, didn't he? Stop lying for him." He practically spits out the words. "You've kept me in the dark about something life-altering, something that involves me, and you want me to understand?"

Tears stream down my face as I reach out to him, my voice cracking with emotion. "Drew, I messed up, I know that. But I never wanted things to turn out like this. I never wanted to hurt you."

He steps back, his anger still simmering beneath the surface. "Hurt me? Tess, you've betrayed my trust in the worst way possible. You and your damn brother."

My heart aches at his accusation, and now he's directing his anger toward Grady too. "Drew, please don't blame Grady."

"Don't blame Grady? That's hilarious." He runs a hand through his hair, frustration etched across his features. "I can't believe this, Tess. I trusted you, and you kept something this important from me."

"I'm so sorry," I choke out through my tears. "I know I can't undo what's done, but I want you to be a part of our child's life. I want us to figure this out together."

Drew's anger seems to waver for a moment, replaced by a mix of sadness and confusion. "I don't know if I can do that, Tess. This changes everything."

I take a step toward him, reaching for his hand. "Drew, I know you need time to process all of this. But please, don't shut me out completely. Our baby deserves to have both of us in their life."

"Our baby." He looks at me, his gaze searching mine for some sign of sincerity. "Our baby? Ha. I need time, Tess. This is a lot to take in."

I nod, my heart heavy but hopeful. "Take the time you need, Drew. Just know that I never meant for any of this to happen like this. I never wanted to hurt you."

As I utter those words, the dream begins to fade, slipping through my fingers like sand.

Our baby? Ha.

"Tess, wake up. You're having a dream."

The voice sounds familiar and a lot like Miranda's, and when I finally open my eyes, it's pitch black in her bedroom.

"You were having a dream." There's a cold cloth being laid over my forehead. "Ugh, you're so warm. I'm going to turn the fan on."

The mattress moves when she rises from the bed to cross the room.

I can only nod, slowly falling back asleep.

DEAR DIARY...

Turns out, Frank Phillips was the only guy to ask me to Prom.

Go figure, right?

The last guy on earth I wanted to go with is the only guy who asked and obviously I said yes. It's not like a had a choice. The good news is, I had a decent time and he didn't try anything—I was basically terrified the entire time that Frank was going to kiss me, or worse, try to finger me or whatever. Or maybe I've seen too many movies where all the guy is trying to do at Prom is get laid, but Frank's not like that. I actually think he was afraid to touch me. During pictures, his mom made him put his arm around me and SHE was the one who handed me the bouquet of flowers (that matched my dress, SQUEE) because he was dying inside. It was pretty cute and I forgave him for being an asshole about the Promposal thing—which he did end up doing, although it was lame and cliché and one of those poster boards with a cheesey saying on it **eye roll**

We went to dinner with his group of friends, most of them football players, obviously, all of them in our grade. Diary I have a confession to make that's going to make me sound like the WORST DATE EVER: I looked for Drew Colter all night, thinking maybe he'd be there even though Grady had told me his dad didn't let them go to dances, not even homecoming. God if I had a father like that, ugh. I've heard Dad call Mr Colter a raging prick and heard both my parents blast him for being demanding but never really around? Which makes no sense to me. How can a dad be controlling when he travels for work and doesn't show up for anything? But...it's not my place to judge, you know? Also, I'm GLAD Drew wasn't there because I had a DATE, and who wants a date hanging around when you're trying to get the love of your life to pay attention to you???
Not me.
    Okay diary, time for bed.
    XOXOXO Tess

CHAPTER 39
DREW

THE SADDEST THING ABOUT BETRAYAL IS THAT IT NEVER COMES FROM YOUR ENEMIES.

"SO WHAT ARE you going to do? You have to find out if this is legit or not."

I'm on a weight bench in the gym, staring at myself in the mirror as my brother stands behind me, ready to spot me.

"I don't know."

"Have you talked to Eli about this?"

Eli is his agent. I haven't signed with one yet, but I should. The only thing holding me back is the fact that I'm not sure if playing professionally is what I want to do.

On the other hand, I'm not sure if I'm qualified to do anything else with my life.

"Yes. He told me I need to issue a statement to *SportsCenter* so they can get my side of the story."

Drake shifts his stance on the balls of his feet. "And what is your side of the story?"

I lay on the bench, ready for him to hand me the weights. "My side is that I have *no idea* if any of it is true, as I haven't heard shit from Grady, and the last time I got a text from Tess, she was actin' like everything was fine, and she was just stressed about school."

"So like—he wants you to issue a denial?"

"Basically."

Which I think would be kind of a dick thing to do. Jesus, what if she is pregnant and it's mine, and I speak out in public about it, telling the whole world it couldn't possibly be mine. Wouldn't that embarrass her? And make things worse?

Too bad she isn't contacting me.

She's been sick…

Sick.

Morning sickness?

I sit up again, not ready to do reps and have three hundred pounds of metal bearing down onto my chest. I don't think I can withstand the weight.

Let it crush me.

I don't care.

She's been sick.

Fuck.

Everything in my gut is telling me it's true.

Tess must be pregnant. I don't know if it was her or a friend who sold us out but…

Shit.

"What's wrong?" Drake asks, a frown marring his brow.

"I just…" My head shakes. "Feel a certain way about it."

"Um. I would too if some chick I banged was tellin' people I knocked her up."

I shoot him a sharp gaze. He's being loud, and I don't need my teammates overhearing our conversation.

It's fucking embarrassing.

And private.

Never have I ever felt so exposed.

People are staring; it feels like all the females in the room are watching us, whispering.

Great.

I can imagine what's going through their heads—there is that piece of shit Colter who was dumb enough to be entrapped by a jersey chaser.

Well, little do they know that isn't what Tess is.

But I can't walk around with a sign on my back declaring otherwise. People are going to think what they think.

I push myself off the bench, grab my cell phone from the shelf where we keep towels and water bottles, and head for the hallway where I can make a call.

This time when I dial her, it only rings three times.

"Hello?"

She obviously already knows it's me.

"Hey."

I roll my eyes because I sound like an idiot. Is this seriously a way to start a conversation?

"Hey, Drew." Her voice sounds distant.

Not that I blame her.

Apparently, a shit ton has been going on in her world.

"Hey, Tess." I have no idea where to begin, so I say, "I have no idea what to say right now." Except maybe, "Is it true?"

What follows is the world's longest, most deafening pause.

"Yes," she whispers.

I suck in a breath, damned if I don't.

Fuck.

"Is it…" *Mine.*

"Yes," she whispers even softer.

My mouth guppies over.

Closes.

I clear my throat so I don't start to cry. "Care to explain why I'm finding out about your pregnancy from the news?"

My question comes out harsher than I'd wanted it to, but this isn't something you rehearse or plan for unless you're one of those couples trying to have a baby.

Except we're not a couple, and we weren't fucking trying to have a baby.

There's a long pause on the other end of the line before she finally speaks.

"Look, Drew, I didn't want it to come to this, but I felt like I had no choice."

No choice?

What does that mean?

"Was it *you?* Or did you tell someone who sold the story?" I know how this shit works by now and both things can be true at the same time.

She hesitates, weighing her answer. "Yes."

"Does that mean it was you, or was it someone who sold the story?"

"The second one." Her voice is so quiet I have to strain to hear it over the sound of the gym's echoing chaos. Machines, people grunting, music.

"No choice? What are you talking about?" I demand, my frustration mounting. "We should've talked about this before it went public."

"I know, I know." She sighs, sounding defeated. "But I didn't know how to tell you. And then I told my brother, and he went apeshit, and I panicked."

I run a hand through my hair, trying to process what she's saying. "And that dumb asshole thought going to the press was the best solution?"

"I don't want you to feel trapped or obligated."

Too fucking late for that.

My phone has been blowing up. My brothers have all threatened to hop on the next flight here, and my mother wants to sue the Donahues for defamation, lies, and slander.

Teammates.

My coaches.

Everyone is up my ass, including the media.

I let out a frustrated sigh, torn between anger and a strange sense of understanding.

"Tess," I say calmly. "We're in this together, whether we like it or not. Going to the press without even talking to me first was a shitty thing for Grady to do. Please tell me you didn't know about it."

"I didn't know about it."

"Please tell me you didn't take money for the story."

"I didn't take money for the story."

My sigh of relief is palpable.

Thank god.

"I'm sorry," she replies, her voice sounding small. "I messed up, Drew, and I regret it."

I can see Drake watching me intently through the glass doors of the gym, clearly picking up on the tension in the conversation. His twintuition is probably buzzing.

I give him a pointed look, silently asking for this moment alone with Tess. I do not need him charging out into the hallway to interrupt or give her his opinion on the matter.

"Tess," I say, my tone softening slightly. "We need to figure this out together. This whole thing is a clusterfuck, but...let's talk about our options and come up with a plan."

I hear her soft laughter on the other end. "Why are you always so sensible?"

"Because. I'm the boring Colter, remember?"

The quiet, kind brother who can't keep it in his pants and gets himself in trouble.

She hesitates, and I can practically hear her thinking on the other end of the line. "You're right. We need to talk face-to-face. When can I fly to see you?"

I glance at Drake, who's pretending to be engrossed in a magazine. "I mean, we're still off-season, so things aren't crazy yet. I can come and see you."

Stay with my mom.

Figure shit out.

Hide.

"Tess?"

"Yeah?"

"I'm sorry."

"For what?"

Gee, where do I start?

"Not bein' there when you needed me, not bein' there when

you found out. Not bein' there when you saw the story on the news."

She laughs again, but it's not like a ha-ha funny sort of laugh. "Yeah, it hasn't been great."

"I'll…" I watch my brother through the glass and hold up a finger so he knows I'm almost done. "Figure out when I can come and let you know."

"Okay."

"Alright."

So awkward.

"I'll keep you posted."

"Hey, Tess?"

"Yeah?"

"How are you doin'?"

I should ask that, right? This isn't all about me and how I was fucked over by my buddy, and this isn't about her keeping this pregnancy a secret.

"I'm doing better."

"Like, how did you know?"

"As soon as I didn't get my period, I knew something was off. Then I took a test or five or a billion. I couldn't sleep for days. It was pretty bad. I was freaked out."

"I bet." Now what do I say? "Grady told me you'd been sick."

"Morning sickness," she says. "He didn't know that's what it was, though. I hadn't told him yet."

"What did he say when you told him?"

"He went ballistic. He'd already been mad about us sleepin' together, which he figured out on his own. Don't know how. So the baby thing didn't go over well." She pauses. "I always thought he'd support me no matter what, but it turns out, he hasn't."

"What about your parents?"

"My mom cried, but honestly, she's excited. I wasn't planning on having kids, remember? She sees it as a blessing in disguise."

"That's awesome. I'm glad."

"What about your mom?"

Er.

Uh.

"It's complicated."

I can't come out and say my mother has already demanded a paternity test, lawyers, contracts, nondisclosure agreements, and wants to silence the Donahues with money.

Like, calm down, Mom.

Chill.

Tess isn't a gold digger. I know it deep in my heart.

Tess is silent. "I imagine that to your family, this would be complicated."

"It'll be fine." *I won't let them come after you...*

My brother taps on the glass, shrugging his shoulders and mouthing the words, "Dude, what's going on?" because the moron never wants to be left out of anything. But I might as well end this phone call while we're still on good terms.

This is good. Everything is fine.

"I'll try to get there soon."

"How soon is soon?"

I worry my bottom lip, going over the calendar in my brain.

"Let's see, it's Tuesday? So...I don't know, like this Friday maybe?"

"Oh, that is soon. I thought maybe you'd try to get here by next month."

Next month? Is she nuts? "We have to get this figured out."

And we need to do it face-to-face.

I *wanted* to see her.

And now I *have* to see her.

All the hopes I'd had about possibly dating her, having fun with her—those hopes are gone. But at least we can be friends, yeah?

"Okay. I'll wait to hear from you."

"You don't have to wait to hear from me. You can text or call whenever you want."

"Okay."

"Alright."

"Thanks for calling."

I look over at my twin brother, whose face is pressed against the glass. "I'll talk to you soon."

When I end the call, I stuff the phone in my pocket and go back into the gym. Some of the tension has lifted from my shoulders but not enough to get the scandal out of my mind. *I'll never stop thinking about this, not even for a second.*

"Looks like everything went well?" My brother smacks me on the back, ushering me inside the weight room.

I nod. "Yeah it went well."

"Good. I'm counting on you to keep this family drama from turning into a full-blown circus."

Drake smirks, his eyes sparkling with mischief.

"Don't worry, Drake. I'll be the trusty ringmaster. "I shake my head, a small smile tugging at my lips. "Just make sure to keep the lions and acrobats in check."

"Groan!" he yells, giving me a mock salute. "Aye aye, captain. Lions and acrobats are under control."

Who would've thought that a romantic comedy could take such an unexpected twist?

CHAPTER 40
TESS
I LOVE HIM AND HE HAS FEELINGS FOR ME, SO WHY IS NONE OF THIS SIMPLE?

I THOUGHT my belly was going crazy when I found out I was having a kid, but it's going absolutely bonkers now as I wait for Drew to arrive from the airport.

This whole situation is bonkers, but there's not much to do about it now…

I'm back at Miranda's for the weekend. It's a safe space where we can have privacy. No one knows he's coming—not my parents, not my roommates, not my brother.

Miranda is staying with Zero so Drew and I have the place to ourselves. I'll sleep in her room, and he can sleep in her spare room, so it doesn't have to be awkward.

My emotions are all over the place.

I had dared to hope that we could explore the possibility of something more, a real relationship beyond the secret we kept from Grady—but all that shattered, thanks to my brother's meddling.

I still don't know how to face Drew after this media debacle.

I glare at my phone, which mocks me with its silence.

Drew hasn't responded to my texts in hours. Did he already regret agreeing to visit?

Was he coming to talk about the mess my brother created, or was he planning to cut ties with us altogether?

My heart races, and I sink onto the couch, burying my face in my hands.

And just like clockwork, there's a knock on the door.

I rise, wiping my hands on my leggings.

But when I open the door, it's not Drew standing on the other side like I expect.

It's Grady.

"Hey, Tess." He lounges against the doorway, a smug grin on his lips. "You weren't going to tell your older brother you were coming to town? How rude."

"What do you want, Grady?" I snap, my frustration reaching a boiling point.

He saunters into Miranda's apartment without an invitation, completely unfazed by my obvious annoyance.

"Just checking in on my favorite soon-to-be niece or nephew."

Oh, he's a comedian now?

"You are literally the last person I want to see right now." My hand still grips the door.

I don't want to close it. I don't want to be trapped inside with this asshole. I thought I knew him, but money does crazy shit to people, and my brother has proven he's no exception to that rule. He took the first chance he could to make money off me.

Off his best friend.

"Maybe this wouldn't have happened if you weren't sneaking around. Did you consider that?"

"What I do in the bedroom and who I do it with is none of your business."

He makes a sound like a buzzer. "Wrong. It is my business. I'm your brother. And Drew was my best friend. Don't you think I have a right to know if you're screwing around behind my back?"

"How did this become about *you*?"

Seriously. I'd like to know.

"How does our sleeping together remotely affect your life?"

His eyes rake down my body. Of course they do because he's immature and out to prove a point.

Grady raises his brows.

"Who even are you? Where is my caring brother? Why are you acting like this?"

Our parents are appalled too. It isn't just me. Especially the afternoon they were served with a gag order from the matriarch of the Colter family, Isabelle Colter, so none of my family members speak to the press.

Well, too late for that...

"You fucking ruined everything, Grady. Drew and I had a chance, and now... now I don't even know where we stand."

"Whoa. Language."

I couldn't give a crap about my foul language. "You betrayed me."

Grady meets my eyes.

His expression softens as if he hadn't considered that before.

"You took money and sold a story about your sister not thinkin' for one second about the shitstorm that might follow. And when I say shitstorm, I'm not talking about Drew being pissed. I'm talkin' about haters and trolls sending me messages and emails and driving past my apartment at school. And kids on campus are calling me a gold digger. It's been humiliating."

And horrible for the baby.

The baby.

"The poor thing, I've been so wrapped up in the drama and media circus that I haven't had time to enjoy the moment properly. Did you even know I didn't know I could get pregnant? Doctors told me I had a slim chance, so the fact that..." My hand is on my stomach. "You stole the happy news from me. I couldn't even tell Mom and Dad first."

I glare at him, wanting him *out* of the apartment.

I'm anxious for Drew to get here and don't want them to see one another.

What a freaking disaster that would be.

"Tess." My brother looks stricken. "Tess, I didn't mean for things to happen like this. I thought putting it out there might force you two to confront the situation."

That is the stupidest logic I've ever heard.

What an idiot.

I shake my head, feeling a surge of frustration and sadness. "Confronting the situation is one thing, Grady. Ruining any chance of a future between us is another."

He rubs his temples, his smirk fading. "I messed up, okay? I see that now. But I don't want us to be…I don't want you to hate me."

Too late.

I glare at him, my patience wearing thin. "And how exactly do you propose we salvage this mess? Huh? You've already threatened to beat the shit out of Drew a few times."

His jaw clenches.

I frown at him. "I can't shake the feeling that everything's changed, that there's no going back."

"You know what Nona used to say. You make your bed; you have to lie in it."

I state, shocked, "Did you not just say you don't want things between us to be horrible? You don't want me to hate you, yet this is a funny way to show it."

"What do you want from me? Huh?"

"Oh my god—get out. All you've done is make this about you. I do not need this right now."

The door to Miranda's apartment is still wide open, and a figure fills the doorway, a duffel bag at his side.

Drew drops it to the ground, eyes going back and forth between Grady and me.

His sudden arrival fills the room with a mix of tension and anticipation. I'm both nervous and excited to see him, hoping we can somehow navigate the mess with my brother. Honestly, he's the least of my worries.

I know things will get better. He just has to get over himself.

But before I can even utter a greeting, Grady's anger and resentment boil over, his fists clenched at his sides. He goes from zero to one hundred in a second.

"What the hell are *you* doing here?" He steps toward Drew.

"Grady, don't," I plead, my voice barely a whisper, but he's already beyond reason, and seeing Drew just made it worse.

But it's too late.

Grady lunges at Drew, his fist connecting with Drew's face before anyone can react. Time seems to slow as Drew stumbles back, a mix of shock and pain contorting his handsome face. My heart races as I rush forward, my hands reaching out instinctively.

"Drew!" I cry out, my voice a mixture of horror and disbelief. "Grady, what the hell is wrong with you?"

Drew raises a hand to his cheek, blood trickling from a cut near his lip. He looks at me, his eyes a mix of pain and confusion, and I'm overwhelmed with guilt.

This mess, this pain, *it's all my fault.*

All I had to do was be honest and tell him.

I told dipshit instead, and now, look at where we are.

Grady's chest heaves as he glares at Drew, his anger unabated. "You think you can just waltz in here and mess with my sister, then walk away like nothing happened?"

"I didn't walk away like nothing happened. I had no idea what was happening until I saw it on the news, asshole. Fuck you."

Drew takes a deep breath, his voice strained. "Do you think I meant for any of this to happen? I care about Tess. Jesus, bro, bring it down a notch."

I watch my brother's reaction, fists clenching at my sides.

"Grady, you have no right to hit him!" Drew could press charges, for crying out loud. "We're all adults here. We can handle this without violence."

Grady's nostrils flare as he glares at Drew, but he finally steps back, his fists slowly unclenching. Drew wipes away the small amount of blood from his lip, his eyes never leaving Grady's face.

"I think it's best if you go," Drew says, his voice tense.

I turn to him. "Drew, I'm so sorry. This isn't how I wanted any of this to happen."

"So I have to leave, and you get to stay? That's fucked up. We're family."

"Well, this whole situation is fucked up, so there. Deal with it."

Grady's anger has left a trail of destruction, a stark reminder of the consequences of our actions. I turn to Grady, my voice trembling with anger and disappointment.

"You had no right, Grady. None at all." I cannot say it enough because he doesn't seem to get it.

He looks at me, his anger slowly giving way to remorse. "Tess, I was just trying to protect you. I didn't want to see you hurt."

"Protect me by taking money."

Hilarious.

My frustration boils over. "You don't get to make decisions for me, Grady. You don't get to play hero and ruin everything in the process."

Tears sting at the corners of my eyes as I storm out of the room.

Drew's pain and Grady's anger intertwine with my own, and I'm left to pick up the pieces. I feel so alone even though two men I love are standing so close.

My hand runs over my belly.

"I'm sorry, peanut."

THERE'S a soft knock on the door.

My eyes crack open, and I realize that Miranda's room is getting dark, and I must have fallen asleep.

"Hey, sleepyhead." Drew's voice is quiet, as if he feels guilty for waking me up. "Can we talk?"

"What time is it?"

"Six-ish?"

Six!?

I sit up.

I nod, heart in my throat. "Yeah, of course. Come in."

I move over on the bed, giving him room to sit without sitting on my legs.

A silence lingers between us like a heavy fog.

"How is your lip?"

He touches a finger to it. "Fine. Honestly, I've had worse. This will heal in a few days."

He's acting like it's no big deal, but that couldn't be further from the truth.

My brother hit him.

"I know what you're thinking, and for the record, this isn't the first time Grady has walloped me."

"It's not?"

"No." He laughs. "He loves a scuffle—should have been a wrestler, not a football player."

"I had no idea he liked to fight."

Drew shrugs. "Eh. You know how guys are."

"Um. That's no excuse for being an asshole and seriously no excuse for hitting people."

He concedes with a terse nod, running a hand through his hair.

"I've been thinking a lot about everything," he starts, his voice tinged with uncertainty. "About us and the baby."

I can't help but notice that he hasn't shaved in days, and his hair is too long. He looks tired, as if he hasn't slept.

I take a deep breath, trying to steady my nerves. "Drew, I need you to know that I didn't want any of this to happen the way it did. I didn't want Grady to go to the press, and I certainly didn't want to keep the truth from you."

He sighs, his gaze dropping to his hands. "I know, Tess, but… I was really blindsided."

"I understand," I say softly. "I should've been upfront with you from the start. But please, don't let Grady's actions define what we do next."

He reaches out, hand brushing against mine, and I feel a spark of chemistry. "We have a lot to figure out. We live so far apart, which sucks, because I don't want you going through this alone."

"Uh, yeah—I don't want to go through this alone, either." I laugh. "It's scaring the shit out of me."

He nods, his grip on my hand tightening ever so slightly. "I know. I'm freaking the fuck out, too."

As we sit there, our hands intertwined, a sense of cautious optimism washes over me.

CHAPTER 41
DREW

DATE SOMEONE YOU THINK YOU MIGHT WANT TO ANNOY FOREVER...

NOW IS NOT *the time to tell her your family wants her to take a paternity test.*

Don't do it.

Not now.

That shit can come later.

Things have been tense since I got here and her brother sucker punched me in the freaking face.

I won't tell Drake—at least, not yet—but my twin already knows something went down.

> Drake: Are you alright?

> Drew: Yeah, why?

> Drake: Don't know, I feel weird.

> Drew: Maybe coz you ARE weird?

We can't fake the connection between us or the spidey senses we have when something is wrong or not right.

He had to have felt it in his face when I got hit in mine.

That's just how this shit works.

Crazy, right?

After I shower and get ready for bed, I lie in it, staring up at the ceiling, the soft glow of the moonlight filtering through the curtains. It's bedtime, but sleep feels like a distant companion tonight—there's no way I'm falling asleep any time soon.

My mind is restless, consumed by thoughts of Tess, as it's been for the past two weeks.

Earlier, as we chatted in the living room, I stole glances at her. I watched her talk—apologizing repeatedly for how her brother has behaved, none of which is her fault. I get that. I know that. I mean, try telling that to my family, but I know in my heart that Grady's issues are his issues and have nothing to do with Tess.

He seems to have lost his damn mind, but that's a him problem.

Tess looks different; she's glowing. I don't necessarily think it's because she's overcome with joy, but maybe it's just the hormones?

How can she possibly be happy with all this drama?

It can't be healthy, yeah?

Dammit.

What a mess.

I visualize her small pregnant belly. It's barely noticeable under her shirt, but it couldn't have been more evident.

I close my eyes for a moment. Her image burned into my mind.

It's not that Tess wasn't attractive to me before. She's always had a magnetic charm that drew me in. But now, this bond between us will never be broken, making her all the more beautiful to me.

It's weird.

She and I barely know each other—we still don't—but somehow, we do?

Or don't.

Only time will tell, but she's stuck with me.

The way she laughed at my jokes and gently touched her belly absentmindedly made me ache with a desire I hadn't expected. It's not just about physical attraction, though that's definitely part of it. It's the way I want to be there for her, support her through this journey, and share in the anticipation and joy.

Drake would be gagging right now if he heard my thoughts.

A faint smile tugs at my lips as I imagine her in the other bedroom. The thought of being close to her, holding her, and feeling her body's warmth against mine ignites a fire within me. I want to kiss away any worries she might have, to make her feel cherished and desired 'cause I've done a shitty job of it so far.

But we can't ignore the complexities of our situation.

Grady's interference and the colossal fuck up created all stands between us. It's a barrier I'm not sure how to overcome.

And then there's the practicality of it all. How will we make this work when we live so far apart?

As I toss and turn, my mind dances between desire and uncertainty.

It's more than just physical attraction. It's a longing to connect on a deeper level, to bridge the gap. I want to be there for Tess, not just as the father of her child, but as someone who cares about her well-being and happiness.

Is that strange?

The moonlight shifts, casting patterns on the walls, and I find myself lost in thought. I know it won't be easy. We're navigating uncharted territory, trying to find a way through the mess. But I'm more determined than ever to see where this path leads.

With a sigh, I close my eyes, the image of Tess's smile still vivid in my mind. The pull between us is undeniable, and as I drift into a fitful sleep, I can't help but hope that somehow, against all odds, we'll find a way to be together. Not just in the other bedroom but in a way that encompasses all the complexities of our feelings and the future we might share.

Do not go into her room.
Let her sleep.
But she wasn't tired when we came to bed—she had that nap.
I can check on her. That's not a crime.

And if she isn't sleeping or tired, we can talk some more. Lord knows we have years' worth of stuff to discuss.

I stand before her bedroom door, heart hammering against my rib cage.

Should I even be doing this? What if she wants her space?

I need to know how she's feeling, if she's okay, and if there's a chance for us to bridge the gap that's formed between us. They don't call me the Sensitive Colter for nothing…

With a quiet exhale, I gently knock on her door. "Tess?"

"Hmm?"

She's awake, and the television flows like a night-light.

I nudge the door open, revealing Tess in a loose-fitting shirt that accentuates her very small baby bump. Her hair is slightly tousled, and her eyes hold a mixture of surprise and curiosity.

"Drew? Is everything okay?" Her voice is soft, tinged with a hint of vulnerability.

"Yeah. Yes. Everything is fine. I just, I couldn't sleep," I admit, my gaze locking onto hers. "And I thought…maybe we could talk? As long as you're not too tired."

The room is bathed by the television light, casting a cozy atmosphere that's a stark contrast to the tension that's been swirling around us.

I wish like hell I had something funny to say.

"No, I had that nap, remember?" Still, she yawns, which is a good sign, considering it's so late.

She pats the mattress. "Don't be shy. Sit."

I sit, sprawling out when she makes room for me.

"On a scale of one to ten, how tired are you?" she asks.

"Why are you asking me? You're the one who's pregnant and going through it. All I have to deal with is trolls and my family. You have…the physical side of it."

"So is that like, a four?" She laughs.

"More like a five, but sure. Or a six. What about you?"

"Twelve." She laughs again, her head resting on the pillow and her hand resting on her stomach.

"Tess," I start, my voice a whisper, "I know this is going to sound weird, but can I...touch your, you know—bump?"

Tess looks up, surprise and uncertainty flickering in her eyes before a warm smile graces her lips.

"Yes, of course. I mean, it's your baby too."

Maybe, but it's not my body, and I'm terrified to touch her.

But her permission is all I need as I settle myself, and my eyes locked onto her stomach. Whoa—a tiny life growing within her, and I reach out, my fingers hovering over her belly for a moment before making contact with her tee shirt.

Awe and wonder course through me.

I feel the warmth of her body beneath my fingertips, the soft curve of her belly beneath my touch. This is wild; a connection unlike anything I've ever experienced, a tangible reminder of the life blossoming inside her.

Her and me.

Crazy.

Unbelievable.

Unexpected.

Scary as fuck.

Tess's breath catches when my hand makes contact, and I glance up to meet her gaze. Her eyes shine with a mix of emotions—vulnerability, gratitude, and something more I can't quite define. It's as if this simple touch has opened a door, allowing us to share in this intimate moment together.

Here I go overthinking things.

One step at a time, bro.

"It's amazing," I murmur, my voice barely above a whisper. "I can't wrap my brain around it, honestly. Can you feel it kick?"

"Uh, no, it's way too soon for that. And I don't know if I'm out of the woods yet. It's pretty early, you know?"

"Not out of the woods? What does that mean?"

She shifts awkwardly.

My hand is still on her stomach.

"You know we're not in the safe zone yet."

"What's the safe zone?"

She giggles. "I thought if I used a football reference, you'd get it."

"I don't get it." I laugh, moving my hand in small circles over her belly, if not for the sake of simply touching her.

"Safe zone is usually twelve weeks."

"What happens at twelve weeks?"

"You have less of a chance for, a. Uh. You know. Miscarriage."

Oh.

"Shit." I don't love the sound of that. "That sounds horrible. So what are you supposed to do? Stay in bed for the next few weeks?"

Tess laughs again. "No. The rest is up to fate."

I don't love the sound of that, but she seems fine with it.

"I'm not worried," she tells me confidently.

Tess's smile grows, a soft chuckle escaping her lips. "Just don't start plannin' playdates."

Playdates.

Dear god. What the fuck is a playdate? I don't think I had those unless you count peewee football as a playdate.

"Well, who knows what the future holds, right?"

My fingers trace gentle circles on her belly, and I'm filled with a sense of protectiveness and affection, especially after she brought up all the "safety in the end zone" stuff.

This isn't just about Tess and me anymore. It's about the life taking shape, the tiny heartbeat that echoes within her.

It's a responsibility and a gift and a connection that goes beyond anything I've ever known.

As I continue to touch her baby bump, Tess's hand covers mine, her touch warm and reassuring. Our eyes meet, and at that moment, it's as if all the complications and uncertainties fade away. There's a sense of unity between us, a shared understanding that we're in this together, no matter what lies ahead.

"Drew…" Tess's voice is soft, her gaze locking onto mine. "Thank you for coming. I needed you here."

"I'm sorry I wasn't here sooner."

We lie in comfortable silence for a while, the weight of the moment hanging in the air. There's so much we still need to figure out, so many challenges to overcome, but for now, in this small, intimate space, none of that matters. All that exists is the life growing that's ours and the hope that we can find a way to figure this out.

Together.

Eventually, I pull my hand away from her belly.

I immediately feel the loss of our connection but don't want to make it weird or put the moves on her even though I'd rather stay.

I give her a smile in the near dark. "I should probably let you get some rest."

Tess nods, her smile softening.

"It's been a long day."

"Long week," I amend.

"Long month!"

I take a step back, my heart heavy with a sense of longing.

"Drew?"

"Hmm."

"Would you stay? You can sleep here. I mean, what's the worst thing that can happen? We have sex and I get pregnant?"

I stare. "Oh, we're making jokes now?"

She nods, grinning. "Too soon?"

I shake my head, settling back down, pulling a pillow to my head and fluffing it. "Nah. This is your story, not mine. You can joke all you want."

She leans forward and presses a kiss to the underside of my

jaw, and I want to touch the spot where her lips warmed my skin.

"Go to sleep."

My fingers caress her hair, and she closes her eyes.

Gently, I stroke her long, silky strands until she's softly snoring, breathing in and out.

CHAPTER 42
TESS

I LOVE HIM. AND THAT WAS THE
START OF EVERYTHING...

I JUST ASSUMED no one knew he was here, but I was wrong.

> Miranda: You're on the news again.

> Tess: WHAT? WHY????

> Miranda: Calm down, it's not bad. Photographers took photos of you and Drew on the swings at the park and holding hands walking to your car.

> Tess: Why didn't you lead with that? Jeez, give me a heart attack.

> Miranda: I'm assuming they've been following you? And now they have dirt, but at least the two of you look cozy, and they can't print anything salacious about you, right???

> Tess: Sure. I guess?

We spent the day together in a spot we thought was quiet and private and out of the way.

A coffee shop.

The lakefront.

A park.

Talking, walking, holding hands, trying to figure out what we were going to do about…

Everything.

At one point on our walk, Drew pulled me into him and kissed me. I wonder if that photo will make it into the news.

Why does anyone even care what Drew does in his personal life? This is crazy to me. He's not even on a professional team. He is literally a college student.

Nuts.

It's invasive and a bit scary, to be honest, not knowing who's watching and where.

I'm a nobody.

I do not need the paparazzi stalking me.

"*Could you be any cuter?*" Drew had asked me while we were swinging at the park, our sneakers hitting the wood chips beneath us as we idly moved back and forth.

"*You think I'm cute?*" I teased, fishing for compliments.

"*Stop it, you know I do.*" He reached for the chain of my swing and pulled it toward him so he could plant a kiss on my mouth.

"*Wow. My being pregnant is making you horny.*"

"*My being horny has literally nothing to do with your being pregnant.*" He paused. "*Dude, that sentence is so freaky. It's, like, not something I thought I'd say until I was like, thirty-five.*"

"*Thirty-five! Did you never imagine yourself as being a dad or what?*"

"*Yeah, of course I always thought I would have kids.*" He'd gone quiet and thoughtful. "*Actually, out of the four of us, I guess it makes the most sense that I would be the one who's a young father.*"

"*How so?*"

"*'Cause you know, I was always the one who wanted a relationship when none of the other three did. Ironically they're the one's with steady girlfriends, and here I was, the one alone every night. Plot twist: gonna be a dad. Still no girlfriend.*"

Still no girlfriend.

Still.

No.

Girlfriend.

Ouch.

Kind of stung a little despite it being the truth.

I am not Drew's girlfriend.

I can't even call myself a one-night stand 'cause look how that turned out for us both.

A cautionary tale of banging without protection.

Ha.

Funny, not at all funny.

Still. There seems to be a magnetic pull between the two of us; and I wondered out loud, *"What do you supposed would have happened between the two of us if we'd done this sooner?"*

"Gotten pregnant sooner?"

"No." I laughed. "Dated. Or…if I'd told you I liked you and you'd done something about it then."

"Maybe we didn't have the chance to date before all of this, but I believe everything happens for a reason."

I tilted my head. "*And what reason do you think brought us here, Drew?"*

"I don't know." He laughed. "*I'm just tryin' to be optimistic. It'll at least give us one helluva story to tell our kid when it's older. The ultimate story of* How I Met Your Mother."

"Except you already knew me."

"I mean, knew you knew you, if you catch my drift."

I swatted at him, reaching across the swing to give his arm a tap, and he uses that opportunity to kiss me again.

This.

This was all I wanted—the chance to kiss him and have him touch me.

Be careful what you wish for, right?

All I wanted was Drew Colter to notice me, and well—he's noticed me all right!!

And now I have to tell him that the media has noticed us, too.

I walk into Miranda's small kitchen, ready to break the news.

"So. We need to talk."

He was about to check his phone but sees me and sets it down. "Again?"

He's grinning, but concern crosses his face when he notices my expression. "Shit. Sorry, what's going on?"

I sit across from him, my fingers nervously tapping against the tabletop. "While we were at the park earlier, we were... photographed."

I whisper the word as if someone is going to jump out of the closet and take more pictures.

He looks confused. "Photographed? By *who*?"

"The paparazzi," I admit, my voice barely above a whisper. "They took pictures of us—Miranda texted."

Drew lifts his phone off the counter and looks at the screen, holding it toward me. He has a million text message notifications on his screen.

Dang.

He's way more popular than I am, ha.

His jaw tightens, his expression shifting from confusion to anger. "They invaded our privacy like that? We're in the middle of Nowhere, Texas. How did they find me?"

Let me count the ways…

"You're kind of hard not to notice, and I'm sure you were spotted at the airport, all six foot something of you. Without a ball cap, Drew? Shame, shame."

He runs a hand through his hair, his agitation palpable. "Dammit. This is exactly what I was afraid of."

"Soo…what do we do?"

Hide?

Flip off the next pap we see?

He lets out a frustrated sigh, his gaze locked onto the table. "We can't just let this slide. I need to do something about it."

"Drew, I get that you're angry," I say, my voice gentle, "but what can we really do? The paparazzi are relentless, and confronting them might just make things worse."

He looks up at me, determination in his eyes. "I can talk to Drake's agent, and have him deal with it. We need to protect our privacy, Tess. Especially now, with everything that's going on."

"I get that, Drew, but going after them might just give them more attention. We're already in the spotlight because of the baby news, and we don't need any more drama."

His grip tightens on his phone, his frustration evident. "Tess, I can't just let them get away with invading our privacy like this. It's not right."

I chew on my lower lip, thoughts racing through my brain as I consider his words. "Okay, I understand your point. Maybe we can find a middle ground. Let's see if we can handle it discreetly without drawing more attention to ourselves. Hang out at the park and invite them to a picnic?"

Seriously, can you imagine?

Drew's gaze softens as he looks at me. "You're right, Tess. I don't want to make things worse. But damn, it's infuriating."

I offer him a reassuring smile, squeezing his arm gently. "We'll just have to lay low."

He nods, his frustration slowly subsiding. "We are not laying low. We're gonna do whatever the hell we want and you're not going to be afraid to go out."

We may not have all the answers, and the road ahead might be bumpy, but thank god we're navigating it side by side.

Drew's phone buzzes, and he glances down at it before looking back at me with a small grin. "It's Drake's agent. Looks like he's on it already."

I watch as he taps out a reply.

I chuckle, relief washing over me. "See? Teamwork."

He reaches across the table to fist bump me.

I stare at his fist.

Shove it back in his direction. "Um, this makes me feel friend zoned."

He lets out a bellowing laugh as he rises from his side of the counter, walking around to my side and planting a wet kiss on my cheek.

"I think it's safe to say you're out of the friend zone."

Our lips meet and it feels as if it's been an age since he's kissed me on the mouth—not since we had sex the morning he left for Illinois, the weekend of the bachelor party.

It's tentative at first; he's gauging to see if I even want to kiss him and I do, turning in my seat, spreading my legs so he can stand between them, my hands sliding around the back of his neck.

His lips brush against mine in a gentle, featherlight touch.

It's a soft, exploratory kiss, a hint of something more to come. I respond in kind, my lips parting slightly as if inviting him closer. And as he accepts the invitation, deepening the kiss with a slow, deliberate movement…

…a shiver runs down my spine as Drew's tongue brushes against my lips.

Without hesitation, I open my mouth, allowing him to deepen the kiss even further. Our tongues dance in a sensual tango, a passionate rhythm that ignites a fire within me.

I can feel his hands on my waist, his touch both tender and firm as he pulls me closer. Can feel him between my legs as his desire goes from sweet kiss to semi-erection that may or may not be pressing into my parted legs.

Delicious.

A rush of heat grows between my thighs.

My fingers slide around the back of Drew's neck, tangling in the soft strands of his hair. I pull him closer, the urgency of our kiss intensifying. His hands move from my waist to my lower back, his touch sending a jolt of electricity through me.

Every sensation is magnified, every touch sending waves of pleasure cascading through my body.

Lord.

These pregnancy hormones are making me horny as hell.

Drew's lips leave mine, trailing a line of heated kisses along my jawline, down my neck. I tilt my head back, giving him better access. A soft moan escapes my lips as his teeth graze the sensitive skin of my neck.

The combination of his kisses and the subtle nip of his teeth sends a delicious ache

Straight.

To.

My.

Vagina.

Yeah, I said it.

His hands move higher, his fingers tangling in my hair as he captures my lips once more, and my boobs are heavy, wanting to be touched.

The kiss is hungry, a mix of longing and desire. I let out a soft whimper because I cannot get enough of him, my body arching into his.

I want more but like, down girl.

Chill.

It's just a kiss…

Our breaths come in ragged gasps as we break the kiss, our foreheads resting against each other. His eyes are dark with desire, his chest rising and falling rapidly.

My own heart pounds in my chest, my body humming with need.

"Drew," I whisper, my voice barely audible in the charged air between us.

He looks at me, his gaze filled with a mix of longing and uncertainty. "Yeah," he says. "I know."

Ah, good.

He wants it, too. No

I give him a small, reassuring smile, my fingers gently tracing the line of his jaw.

Any trace of hesitation evaporates.

Drew's lips crash down on mine once more, and the world

around us fades away, leaving only the two of us and the intoxicating heat of our desire. At this moment, there's no room for doubts or worries—there's only the overwhelming sensation of being wanted, of being desired, and the promise of a connection that's only just beginning to ignite.

Drew reaches down and does what I've been wanting him to do since he put his lips to mine; he slides his hands under my ass and lifts me, setting me on the countertop.

Pulls me forward.

Steps between my legs again.

I wrap them around his waist.

Game.

On.

DEAR DIARY...

It's so weird with all the guys gone. They graduated in June and it's just bizarro being at school without them all here. Quiet somehow. I cried a lot last night cause Grady told me Drew and his brothers finally left for college, which is like, a twenty hour drive. Which means they won't be coming home at all and what are the chances I'll ever bump into him again? All I wanted was for him to ask me to ONE stupid dance and now that will never happen because no one who goes to college ever comes home for a HS dance. Going to cry myself to sleep now, bye.

CHAPTER 43
DREW

YOU WERE BORN TO BE REAL.
NOT TO BE PERFECT.

TESS WRAPS her legs around my waist, and you know she's wearing shorts, so my hands automatically go to her smooth legs. I run my palms over the thighs wrapped around me, back and forth, our kisses becoming more heated.

I'm tall enough that when I press forward, my erection flirts with her pussy, and it's a damn shame her shorts are denim 'cause, damn, I'd love to feel her through thinner fabric.

"I'm so turned on right now," she moans. "You have no idea."

Oh, I have some idea.

"Are you?"

There's been a magnetic pull between us since she picked me up at the airport; a current of excitement that's been impossible to ignore. I take a step closer, my heart pounding as I reach out to tuck a loose strand of hair behind her ear.

She's so fucking pretty.

Her breath hitches when I move my hands, sliding them up her waist and over her rib cage.

Our tongues mingle…

Hot and wet and frantic.

Tess's arms wrap around my shoulders, pulling me closer

still—as if that were even humanly possible—desire coursing through my veins. My lower half.

My cock.

Obviously.

I deepen the kiss, my fingers tangling in her hair as I lose myself in the taste and feel of her. There's an urgency to our make-out session, a desperation that's been building between us since the moment we met.

We're breathless, our foreheads resting against each other's.

I could literally tear her clothes off right now. I want her so bad.

"I want you so bad," I admit, my voice a whisper in the quiet room. "I want to hold you and kiss you and touch you."

Fuck if I don't.

"Say yes."

And then, with a small nod, her lips find mine once more, the kiss turning deeper, more fervent. Our bodies press against each other, a tangible reminder of the connection that's been building between us.

My hands slide down her back, my fingers tracing the contours of her body, and a soft moan escapes her lips. The sound sends a jolt of desire straight to my core, and I deepen the kiss, my lips trailing down her jawline, her neck.

Tess's fingers find their way to the hem of my shirt, her touch igniting a fire within me. With a sense of urgency, I pull away just long enough to rid myself of the fabric that separates us, yanking it over my head and tossing it to the kitchen floor.

Then I remove hers.

Her hands go behind her, and within seconds, her bra joins our shirts on the ground.

Skin on skin, we slowly, almost hesitantly, explore each other's bodies.

I'm overwhelmed by a mix of desire and tenderness.

On one hand, I want to fuck her hard.

On the other—she's pregnant.

I don't want to hurt her.

You can't hurt her. And you can't get her pregnant. She's already pregnant, you idiot.

Still.

The urge to be gentle has me tentatively inching forward, my fingers tracing down her collarbone to her breasts. I trace the curve, drawing a line to her nipples, round and round the areola.

So pretty…

Her breath hitches as she watches me touch her, her back arching.

It's more than just physical intimacy—it's a way for us to bridge this gap that's been wedged between us.

A way for us to reconnect.

Out of all the Colters, I'm the most sentimental, and yeah, it can be a drag, but it can also save a situation.

Tess's fingers dance across my skin, her touch setting every literal nerve in my body on fire.

I'm combustible.

Our kisses turn languid, filled with a mix of longing and since both of us are hurting it makes sense that we're both a bit desperate.

Her hands frantically push down the waistband of my boxer shorts.

Like I said—desperate.

Or maybe it just feels that way.

There isn't much foreplay—we're too interested in getting naked and getting my dick inside her vagina for that. Foreplay can come later, *Tess wants it now…*

God it feels so good having her body pressed against mine, the cold air hitting my ass cheeks as my shorts go down to my ankles.

My dick is so hard…

It seeks her heat because that's what it was born to do.

Tess scoots her ass closer to the edge of the counter, wiggling her hips, still wearing her bottoms—they have to get gone.

She lifts her hips; hooks her fingers into her denim shorts and shimmies them down her hips, frenziedly to get them off.

Now we're both naked with pants around our ankles, like two thirsty teenagers who have to sneak around on their parents to screw—and get it done quickly so no one walks in.

I swear to god I'm already thrusting, and I'm nowhere near inside her yet…

"Do it already," she whines. "Oh god—I'm sorry, I didn't mean to blurt that out."

It's fine. Seriously, it's fine. She's only saying what I'm thinking. That I want to fucking do it already and sink into her…

I slide in bareback, and she's already wet. So wet and hot, but still, I move forward slowly, not wanting to hurt her even though she's telling me to "do it already."

"Thank god I can't get pregnant." She laughs but shivers at the same time, moaning when I pull out…and push back in…

In…

Out…

Arching up slightly so I'm not too short to fuck her standing up, making sure my pelvis and her pussy line up. No need to break my dick for a quick fuck, eh?

Doesn't sound like fun to me, not one bit.

"Faster," Tess demands.

I pump faster, balls already tingling.

Not a good sign—it means I'm gonna come sooner than later and probably before she does, which would be embarrassing as hell.

"Harder," she tells me. "Harder, Drew, oh god…"

Her head is tilted back and her eyes are hooded, lips look as if she's been thoroughly kissed. Plump. Juicy.

I lean forward and press another kiss to them, and her lips part, tongue mingling with mine.

My arms go around her, and I pull her in.

Lifting her off the counter completely, I turn, walking toward the wall, still buried inside her.

Pressing her back against it, I heft her up.

Pump in and out…

In and out…

She moans.

I moan.

She grunts.

I grunt.

"Oh fuck…"

I fuck Tess good and hard against that wall, never letting go of her, never stopping, not until we both cry out, moaning at the same time, coming at the same time. I spill inside her, hips braced as my body convulses from the pleasure.

We hold still, and I breathe into her neck.

So still, body shaking.

Hers too.

"Shit," she says. "Now what?"

"What do you mean?"

"Ugh. As soon as you pull out, all the come will drip down my leg."

My body rumbles with a low laugh. "That's what you're worried about?"

"I mean, it's not like I can get pregnant."

"Touché." I pause, never having this problem before. Literally no girl has ever said she was concerned about come dripping down her leg. "What do you want me to do?"

"Um, nothing, I guess. I'll deal with it."

CHAPTER 44
TESS

HIS HAIR. HIS VOICE. HIS SMILE.
HIS LAUGH.

I SERIOUSLY SAY, *"As soon as you pull out, all the come is going to drip down my leg?"*

"You don't have to say everything that pops into your brain, Tess," I remind myself as I wash up in the bathroom, putting myself back to right so I can return to the bedroom and climb back into bed.

I've never had sex against the wall, and now I can easily give it a four-star review.

I wouldn't say it was the best sex I've ever had—I come easier when I'm on top—but it was the most exciting sex I've had, so far.

Listen.

Don't judge me for having a mediocre sex life. Vanilla, if you will.

Not like I have a ton of opportunity to have wild, crazy sex and even if there was I'm not sure I'd take it.

Vanilla and regular is quite fine with me, thankyouverymuch.

After I'm done washing up I join him back in the bedroom, sliding in under the covers in an oversized tee shirt and clean pair of underwear.

He pulls me closer, both of us facing one another on our sides.

His expressive blue eyes lock onto mine and I can't help but let out a nervous chuckle. "Well, I guess the fact that we keep having sex just makes our story more interesting, doesn't it?"

He grins. "Oh, absolutely. I always knew our story was missing a classic 'surprise pregnancy' trope."

Surprise pregnancy trope? "I mean, it started as a secret baby," I playfully tease, nudging him with my elbow.

"Oh, you think that's funny now, do you?"

He catches my hand and traps it against his chest, over his beating heart.

I can feel it thumping beneath my palm.

"Listen. We've tackled a lot of shit, both separately and together. Midterms, practice, my brothers, your brother, the trolls on social media. We got this."

I twirl a strand of my hair between my fingers, my mind racing with thoughts of what lies ahead.

The reality is, this isn't going away, and we haven't actually discussed the future—which is what he came here for, isn't it?

"Seriously, Drew, what are we going to do? I barely just moved out of the dorm rooms, and now I have a baby on the way."

He leans closer, his fingers tracing absent-minded patterns on the back of my hand. "First things first, we're going to take a deep breath. Then we're going to figure things out—together."

Not exactly a plan of action, but it's a start.

"Okay, I'm breathing." Deep breath, in and out. "Now what?"

"Well, we're going to be pros at diaper-changing and baby-proofing. And I've heard 2 a.m. feedings are a blast!"

"Was that sarcasm, Drew Colter? And how are you going to be around for a two o'clock feeding?" I burst out laughing. Honestly, has he not thought about that?

"I have no idea. We can both still finish college, even if it means adjusting our plans a bit. We have an incredible support system, and we're in this together."

"But my parents don't live anywhere near school, and I have two semesters left."

He has one.

And then there's the draft…

We haven't talked about his future at all, just mine.

"This will be like planning a wedding," he informs me. "Let's get a big binder and fill it with information."

I laugh again, rolling back on the bed. "A binder? Stop it."

He's not entirely wrong, though. I guess the process will require a ton of planning because we're so far apart.

"I'll get a blue binder. You can have a pink one."

"Why does my binder have to be pink? Why can't it be blue?" Or yellow or sequins.

"You can have whatever color you want." Drew's fingers tuck a strand of hair behind my ear, his touch gentle and reassuring. "We'll make sure our baby knows they're loved and cared for every step of the way."

Our baby…

I shiver.

"This whole thing is surreal. And if I'm being honest I don't feel ready for it, at all. I had wanted to…I had wanted…"

"Wanted to what?"

"Date you. Date you and like, have you fall in love with me and then we could live happily ever after. We haven't gone anywhere yet, not to dinner or to the movies, and it makes me sad in a way that the whole thing god sidetracked."

I don't want to say "screwed up" because the thought makes me feel guilty even having it; like I'm somehow talking shit about my unborn child.

"Yeah—in a perfect world, that's how this would have gone. I mean—you falling in love with me and all that."

He winks, our fingers brushing.

I move mine to his face; to brush the bruise on his mouth where my brother hit him.

"Does this still hurt?"

"No."

"Are you telling the truth?"

"Yes." He grins. "Do you know how many times I've been damn near knocked out from taking a hit or gotten concussions from a collision? Dozens. This little gash was a pussy move, and I'll tell Grady I said so."

"God, please don't."

He grins, that familiar twinkle in his eyes. "Well, if it's any consolation, our future just became the plot of a seriously entertaining rom-com."

Is it?

Really?

At least he's optimistic and at least he's here with me now.

"I can't imagine doing this alone." I have Miranda and I have my parents but it's not the same. "Guess we're the stars of our own unique story."

"We aren't even dating, and now we're having a baby," he says, his voice a mix of incredulity and uncertainty. "Seriously, what *are* we going to do?"

My heart flutters like a trapped bird in my chest, fingers tracing the intricate patterns of the bedspread, my mind racing as I search for the right words.

"I have no idea."

The word hangs in the air, heavy with implications.

I shift my gaze to the window, where the world beyond seems to stretch out in a vast unknown. "But what about us? What about our friendship?"

Drew's voice is gentle, a soothing balm to my swirling thoughts.

"Our friendship." He clears his throat. "Are you friend zoning me again?"

I let out a shaky laugh. "Do you not want to be friend zoned by your baby mama?"

"Not really."

"So what do you want? To be my boyfriend?"

Ironically, it feels too soon.

We skipped a million steps in the process, jumping straight to 'lifelong commitment' of the offspring kind and it muddles the waters by a million.

Dating. Babies. School. Football.

Family.

Telling people. Not telling people. Keeping it private. Having our privacy invaded and our faces plastered on the news.

My tiny apartment. My roommates.

Classes.

Morning sickness. Going to the doctor. The fact that we're long-distance.

Yeah. We definitely need binders.

Or five.

My head would spin if it wasn't attached to my head.

"I would be your boyfriend."

I squint at him. "Are you just sayin' that because you knocked me up before our first date?"

He shrugs, which is comical.

How real could we possibly be tonight.

I would be your boyfriend.

His words settle over me like a comforting embrace, reminding me that strength often lies in the willingness to face the unknown—and he's had his fair share of it, being a football player at a Big Ten school.

He smiles. "I won't pretend I have all the answers, Tess and we don't have to figure this shit out tonight. But I do know that I'm here for you, for us. And together, we'll figure things out."

Together we'll figure things out.

When, though?

"Why do you always say the perfect thing?"

Drew chuckles, his fingers lacing through mine. "I don't. In fact, ask Drake—I say plenty of stupid shit and he probably has screenshots of most of it."

As we lay there, side by side, the weight of the situation feels a little lighter.

"Hey. Promise me something," Drew says.

"What is it?"

"Promise me that we'll be honest with each other no matter what happens. That we'll communicate and not keep anything from each other. Finding out from the press was horrible—and not because I felt betrayed but because I thought you did it because you had no other choice. And I know that's not true, but…no more surprises."

"No more surprises." Tears prickle at the corners of my eyes, touched by the depth of his request. "I promise, Drew."

His smile is like a sunrise, warm and full of promise. "Then we've got this. And we've got each other."

DIARY...

Why am I so sad lately? It's my junior year, I should be excited—one more year until HS graduation but I can't get myself out of this funk.

I didn't even care when Grady moved out but I can't stop feeling...empty inside now that the Colter boys aren't in school anymore and I never see them in the hallway. Not the Colter Boys. THE Colter. As in the ONLY Colter for me.

Drew.

I see him on TV now. The news is covering their freshmen year in Wisconsin and acting like they're the second and third coming of Christ but I don't see what the big deal is. Everyone needs to stop treating them like Gods, Drew would HATE that. He is the most down to earth, nice guy and I know the attention must be killing him.

Not Drake—he probably loves is, LOL. But Drew.

I always liked him because he's sensitive and seeing him on TV makes me want to...reach out and hug him, you know? I can tell he's not happy, don't ask me how I know. He's never said ten sentences to me but I just...

...know.

Wish I was brave enough—and smart enough—to apply and get accepted to Madison but we all know I'm not getting anything above a 3.0 this semester.

Gonna go torture myself some more by looking at social media for tagged posts of the boys.

Hearts, T

CHAPTER 45
DREW

HER EYES. HER HAIR. HER FRECKLES. HER VOICE.

I FEEL a soft hand beneath the hem of my shirt, slowly moving up my stomach to my chest.

I stir, yawning.

It's pitch black in Tess's bedroom, and I can barely see a thing when my eyes crack open.

I can't see a thing, but I can feel.

Gotta love those five senses heightened by darkness…

"What are you doing?" I croak, voice raspy from sleep.

I yawn again.

Tess inches closer, pressing up against me, hand over my pec, fingers going round and round my nipple.

"Well, first, I was thinking of doing this."

A kiss is pressed to the underside of my chin.

Her fingers dance along my skin, causing a shiver that I can't help.

"Is that so?"

I can feel her over me, capturing my lips in a lingering kiss.

"Mm-hmm. And then maybe a little of this."

Her fingers continue their exploration, tracing a tantalizing pattern along my collarbone.

"Remind me again why you wore a tee shirt to bed," she

whispers. "I can barely get my hand underneath with the weight of these stupid blankets."

My chuckle is soft. "You know, this is how we got in trouble in the first place."

"True, which means there are no more consequences to our actions."

"I wouldn't exactly say that. I have a feeling it's going to be a shitstorm when I return to school."

Tess groans. "Can we not talk about that in the middle of the night? It's like, one o'clock."

I laugh again. "You're the one accosting me. I was just lying here minding my own business." Not that I'm pushing her out of bed for wanting to have sex again. I'm just pointing out the obvious.

"I'm lonely and don't want to be ignored," she whispers in my ear. "Play with me."

I pull her, hands around her hips, lifting her onto me.

Tess straddles my hips. "This is more like it."

She wiggles her hips. "And I don't even have to take my panties off this time."

My hands move south to discover she's not wearing any. The only thing separating us is my dumb briefs, which she's right about—I never should have put them on.

I don't know if it's normal for a pregnant woman to want sex this early in her pregnancy or if Tess normally has a high sex drive, but I'm game for it regardless.

She moves over me, positioning her pussy over my hard cock, rubbing back and forth, back and forth, mimicking sex and dry fucking me.

It's not the same, but it's just as exciting, my cock aching to be inside her and begging to fuck.

Poor little dude has to wait. Tess wants to play and tease. She can tease all she wants but…

"Babe, careful—I don't want my balls to chafe."

Underwear and dry fucking do not a great combo make.

"Aw, you called me babe." She pauses. "That's so hot."

"Is it?"

"Mm-hmm. I don't think anyone has ever called me that before."

"*They haven't?*" *How is that possible*, Tess is like—the fucking coolest and if we went to the same school I would have claimed her years ago. "I'll babe the shit out of you if you want me to."

It's the least I can do for getting her knocked up.

"You would do that?" she mewls, gently rocking back and forth over me.

Her fingers fiddle with the front of my briefs; pulling the fabric aside and then lowering herself down over me.

"Are we seriously going to fuck with me in my underwear?"

Tess laughs. "It feels too good to stop…"

Yeah, I don't exactly hate it.

She can fuck me while I'm fully dressed for all I care. Her insatiable spirit isn't something I'm going to complain about—not tonight, not tomorrow, and probably not ever.

CHAPTER
FORTY-SIX

Tess: What are you up to? Anything exciting...?

Drew: Sitting in class—not exciting at all.

Tess: Which one?

Drew: Mass Comm—confession: this is the second time I'm having to take it.

Tess: What?! Why?

Drew: 'Cause I bailed on it so often last semester and had Drake go for me, ended up getting a D

Tess: Oh shit—that sucks...

Drew: Yeah, it does, because this professor is a dickhead and loves listening to himself talk.

Tess: Don't they all?

Drew: This one wrote the textbook and wants everyone to know it.

Tess: Ooooh one of thoseeeee

Drew: Yeah—one of those.

Drew: What about you, what are you doing?

Tess: Same. Sitting in class. It's an easy one, though, English Lit. I'm practically napping and need some distraction.

Drew: Ahh, so that's why you slid into my messages, LOL. Lucky for you, I'm an expert in the art of distraction.

Tess: Oh, please. I've seen your attempts at distraction.

Drew: Ouch. I see how it is. How about some captivating conversation?

Tess: Captivating conversation? What are you, a thesaurus? *yawns* I suppose I could be persuaded.

Drew: So have you ever wondered if aliens are secretly among us, posing as normal humans?

Tess: LOL oh god—classic alien conspiracy theory. I'm pretty sure I've met a few aliens on campus.

Drew: Same. This professor might actually be one. They're probably here to gather advanced equations to take back to their home planet.

Tess: Makes sense. That's the only logical explanation for their presence.

Drew: And you, my dear, are clearly their leader, gathering intel on quadratic functions.

Tess: Shhh, don't blow my cover. I'm deep undercover.

Drew: I'll keep your secret safe. But only if you promise that next time I see you, I get to see those amazing boobs again

Tess: I'm flattered you're still thinking about those...

Drew: Uh, have been since that first weekend.

Tess: Awww... you say the sweetest things.

Drew: And they say my brother has all the best moves. Ha.

Tess: Speaking of the best moves, I'm seriously on the edge of falling asleep... if it happens, I'm blaming the baby.

Drew: No worries, I'm here to rescue you from the clutches of boredom. How about we play a game?

Tess: A game, you say? I'm listening....

Drew: Game of questions. I just googled "Best questions to ask on a first date."

Tess: Is this our actual first date?

Drew: God, I hope not.

Drew: Shit. I should have taken you out on one when I was there. I'm such a fucking dick. Dammit, Tess, I'm so sorry.

Tess: Listen, my brother gave you a bloody lip. I'd say we're even?

Tess: Let's just play the game, LOL. I need the distraction.

Drew: K. First question—If you were stranded on a desert island, what three items would you bring?

HOW TO SCORE OFF FIELD

Tess: Dang, I don't know. You answer first.

Drew: That's easy. A hammock, a never-ending supply of sunscreen, and a survival guide titled "How to Escape from Desert Islands for Dummies."

Tess: Ambitious choices. Okay, next question: If you could travel anywhere in the world, where would you go?

Drew: New Zealand. It's like a fantasy world filled with stunning landscapes and hobbits.

Tess: Hobbits? LOL. Lord. A true adventurer's dream **eye roll** I'll start saving for our New Zealand escapade.

Drew: Sounds like a plan. Alright, last question: What's your go-to karaoke song?

Tess: Oh, you're really digging deep now. I'd have to say "Livin' on a Prayer" by Bon Jovi. I like to pretend I'm a rock star from the '90s.

Drew: A rock star, huh? I'm definitely requesting an encore at the next karaoke night.

Tess: You better believe it. Alright, your turn to ask.

Drew: Hmm, let me think. If you could time travel, would you go to the past or the future?

Tess: Ah, the eternal time travel dilemma. I'd go to the past—there's so much history to explore and learn from. And maybe I'd have you wear a condom?

Drew: Oh. My. GOD, Tess, SICK BURN. Shit. Ouch.

Tess: I'm kidding but also, not kidding. Bwahahaha. Sorry, I didn't mean to ruin the moment. Next question and go.

Drew: Alright, last question from me: What's your favorite way to spend a lazy Sunday?

Tess: Lounging around in comfy pajamas, a movie marathon (reality TV, obvi), and consuming ridiculous amounts of popcorn.

Drew: A true Sunday champion. Alright, I think we've successfully navigated the first date questions. I have to say, I'd give you a second date based on your answers.

Tess: There you go, charming me out of my panties…but you know. I could probably come up with a better list of questions than those.

Drew: What do you mean, better?

Tess: You know…spicier.

Drew: **sweating laughing emoji** Do your worst.

Tess: Okay. Here I go. I'll start with a tame one…

Tess: Do you prefer making out or cuddling?

Drew: I prefer cuddling while I make out. Does that count? LOL

Tess: Yes?

Drew: What about you?

Tess: I don't mind a cuddle, especially when it's on the couch, watching one of my shows while elbow-deep in popcorn. Literally the perfect evening. Ready for the next question?

HOW TO SCORE OFF FIELD

Tess: When is the first time you pictured me naked?

Drew: Probably when we were playing miniature golf.

Tess: WHAT? **sputters** You seemed so...like, were you even checking me out? I didn't notice.

Drew: As if I was going to let you notice me checking you out? We already established that at the time, I still had you in the "Grady's sister" box, and I'd set it on the shelf.

Tess: Fair enough. But damn, I'm shocked.

Drew: What about you? When did you first picture me naked?

Tess: Uh, like—tenth grade? LOL. You already know I had a massive crush on you, so this should be no surprise. Ready for the next ???

Drew: Yup.

Tess: What's your least favorite position?

Drew: Shit, you weren't fucking around when you said you could come up with spicier questions. Mine were so freaking lame compared to these.

Tess: Uh, YEAH, they were... So. What's your answer? Stop stalling.

Drew: Er. I don't know. Is there such a thing as a least favorite position? I'd have to go with.... anal.

Tess: ANAL??! When have you had anal????

Drew: Never. That's why it's my least favorite, because all of them are pretty okay

Tess: OMG lol Fair enough, I guess. Mine is… probably missionary LOL

Drew: Oh boy…

Tess: Here's one. Where do you like to be touched?

Drew: Besides my junk?

Tess: No, I think "junk" counts as an answer.

Drew: My junk. My leg. My…butt? You?

Tess: Boobs. Butt. And my business…

Drew: We get along so well.

Tess: Yeah, and I have the growing bump to prove it.

CHAPTER 47
TESS

MY HEART WAS FULL AND THEN IT BROKE.

OH NO...

Is this what I think it is?

I inhale a sharp breath not sure what I'm looking at, googling on my phone to be sure, staring down between my legs.

And here I thought this was going to be a regular visit to the bathroom.

No signs that this was going to happen, if you don't count... *This.*

I sit here, debating and debating and debating, not sure what to do first.

What do I do?

How do I react?

I wasn't ready to be pregnant but I'm not ready for this, *either.*

Do I call my mom?

My roommates?

Do I call Drew?

Wipe.

Flush.

Text?

Cry?

Yes, I'm definitely going to cry....

CHAPTER 48
DREW

I GUESS MISSING HER THIS MUCH IS THE UNIVERSE REMINDING ME THAT I'M FALLING FOR HER.

IT'S LATE.

Like—too late for a friendly call.

So when the phone rings, I scramble to answer it, heart racing with a mix of excitement and apprehension when I see Tess's name flashing on the small screen. I smile though I'm tired as I accept the call and press my phone to my ear, yawning.

"Hey," I greet her, trying to keep my voice steady despite the fluttering in my chest. "Is everything okay?"

The question everyone asks when they get a random call past a certain hour in the day, yeah?

"Hey," her voice responds, but there's an edge to it, a hint of something I can't quite place. "No, I don't think…everything is okay."

I lean over, flip my bedside light on, and lean back against the pillows propped against the headboard.

"What's goin' on?"

There's a pause on the other end, a weighty silence that stretches out for a moment too long. My mind races, my imagination conjuring up a thousand possibilities—some mundane, some heart-stoppingly serious. Or maybe I'm just too fucking tired.

We had our first practice today.

A meeting, too, and I crashed when I went to bed after texting with Tess—everything seemed okay at the time. What could have gone wrong in the few hours I've been in bed?

"Did your brother do something?" I ask, immediately suspecting Grady of another verbal lashing.

"I... I don't know how to even say this," Tess begins, voice trembling. "I was on the toilet, you know, and something wasn't right."

I was on the toilet...

Something wasn't right...

"Okay?"

I'm not exactly sure what her words mean.

But my heart skips a beat anyway, a cold chill running down my spine.

I was on the toilet...

Something wasn't right...

Her words hang in the air, charged with meaning. A thousand thoughts rush through my mind, and I try to make sense of what she's telling me.

"Something wasn't right?" I repeat, my voice barely above a whisper.

"Yeah," she replies, her voice a mix of vulnerability and uncertainty. "I'm sorry, Drew..."

"Sorry for what?"

"Maybe I just wasn't far enough along..."

Wasn't far enough along?

The unfinished sentence hangs there. It's a heavy, heavy silence, filled with words she can't get out of her throat, and I close my eyes as if that will help my mind race to piece together the puzzle.

It's too soon to jump to conclusions, too soon to let fear and worry take over, but her words are hanging in the air like a damn storm cloud threatening to burst.

I take a deep breath, my voice steady despite the turmoil within me.

"Are you saying what I think you're saying?" More whispered words.

"I think so."

Does that mean she's not pregnant anymore?

I clear my throat around the lump forming there, needing to actually ask what's only in my head. "Does that mean you're not pregnant anymore?"

She pauses, and I swear I hear her nodding. "I think so."

I think so.

She's not pregnant anymore.

It's on the tip of my tongue to ask, "How?" Or "Why," but that would only make me sound stupid and possibly insensitive, so the next thing out of my mouth is, "I'm so sorry."

Although…

My shoulders sag.

With relief?

With grief?

I have no idea.

All I know is that I'm starting to feel sick in my stomach.

I wish I could reach through the phone and wrap my arms around her to offer the comfort and reassurance that I know she needs.

"I'm so sorry," I say again on account of *I literally have no idea what else to say.*

I might be the Sensitive Colter, but I've never claimed to have a way with words.

"Honestly, I still hadn't been to the doctor, figuring that a dozen tests would suffice," Tess says with a strangled laugh. "And I was you know, researching after I went to the bathroom because I wasn't really sure—and then I called my mom because—moms know stuff. And yeah, that's what this was."

She's talking in circles, words and thoughts not making sense to me, but I don't interrupt to ask questions, keeping my mouth shut and letting her speak.

"I'm glad you called your mom. What did she say?"

"She said what the internet said; that I can take a test in a few days so I'm sure I'm not pregnant anymore but not for a few days because my body is still full of hormones."

That makes sense.

"What do you need from me, Tess? Do you need me to fly out there?"

"No. No, no, I'll be fine. It'll be fine." She pauses, breathing in a long breath. "Can I be honest with you?"

"Yeah, of course."

"I'm confused."

"You are?"

"Yes. I know we weren't ready, and we barely know each other—even though I've known you half my life, and now I'm just freaking out because I don't want to lose you because I feel like I need you. That's what went through my mind first, you know? Is that bad?"

I hear sniffling on the other end of the line.

She's crying.

"No, it's not bad." I reassure her, softly. "You're allowed to feel however you feel."

"So are you. I wouldn't blame you for being pissed."

"Tess. Not to sound cheesy, but…everything happens for a reason. You got pregnant for a reason, and you got…unpregnant for a reason." I have no idea how else to say it. "That's how the world works, and not to bring God into it but he has a plan, you know?"

I will not cry. I will not cry.

I hope she doesn't think I'm preaching, but I honestly believe that the things that happen to us, the people who come in and out of our lives, are all supposed to, regardless of the circumstances.

I feel fucking horrible, mostly for her.

I had it easy, if you consider being hounded by the media, getting my ass chewed out by your coaches, brothers, mother, and everyone else with anything to do with my football career—

easy. There's going to need to be damage control for this, too, but it'll pass the way things always do. For me, but maybe not for her.

All I had to do sit and take it. Listen to my coaches and brothers insert themselves into my personal life.

All I had to do was suck it up and keep my thoughts and opinions to myself in the face of so many people bitching at me, lecturing me, telling me I may have ruined my career.

Tess? Had most of the emotional and all of the physical burden.

"You get that none of this is your fault, right?" I say, my words steady and sincere. "I don't want you to carry any guilt or feel bad about what's happened. Life is unpredictable, and what we're going through isn't something you should blame yourself for."

Don't I sound so altruistic?

Cause I am.

And none of this was her fault.

I don't know jackshit about pregnant people, but I know that things can change in the blink of an eye, and they did.

"I appreciate you saying that. But it's hard not to feel responsible, you know?"

"I know," I reply gently. "You know I'm not mad, and I don't want you to feel guilty. We're in this together, and we'll face whatever comes our way as a team."

"A team," she repeats.

"Are you smilin'?"

She scoffs. "If I was, how would you be able to tell?"

"I just can."

There's a soft sigh on the other end, and I can imagine her nodding in understanding.

"Can I just say…I'm really glad that if anyone was going to knock me up, I'm glad it was you."

"I'm really flattered." I laugh.

"No, for real. If I was going to go through this shit with

anyone, thank god it was you because I can't imagine some asshole ghosting me. or blaming me, or telling me that it wasn't his. You could have done all those things." She sniffs again. "Even though you were probably planning on makin' me get that paternity test."

I let out a laugh. "I mean—not me, my mama." And a few dozen other people.

Ha!

"Where do we go from here?" Tess's words hang softly in the air, carrying a weight of uncertainty. I can hear the vulnerability in her voice, the unspoken question that lingers between us as she switches gears.

I pause for a moment, my thoughts racing as I search for the right words. "Tess," I reply gently. "Just because we're physically far apart doesn't mean there's no reason for us not to talk every day. If anything, our connection is more…" I search for the right word. "Important now than ever. We're friends."

"Friends."

"That's not what I meant. Not in that way, it wasn't a slight. I meant—we're freakin' bonded now. You're not getting rid of me just cause you're no longer stuck with me for the next eighteen years."

"I hope I'm not getting rid of ya."

I worry my bottom lip as my brain goes off in ten different directions. "So what are you gonna tell your brother?"

"I'm not. I'm gonna have my mom tell him. Grady and I haven't spoken, and I don't think I'll be ready to speak to him until *he* comes to apologize."

I rub the spot on my face where my best friend hit me. "Yeah, I wouldn't mind an apology either, though I doubt he's gonna give me one."

"He will. You wait and see. He's going to feel like total shit when he hears the news, you know? Deep down inside, they were all excited about having…a grandkid. A niece or nephew."

She sounds so sad.

I pause, not sure if what I'm about to say is going to make things conversation worse or not, but it has to be said.

"Now you know you can get preggo. Who's to say you can't get pregnant again someday when the timing is right?"

"Or maybe you had super sperm."

Super sperm. "I love the sound of that. Can I put that on a tee shirt?"

Tess can't help but laughs. "Please don't."

Or maybe I will. "It'll be one of those shirts with two thumbs on it, pointing inward, and it'll say 'Know who has super sperm? This guy.'"

"I would kill you." She's laughing when she says it.

"Come say that to my face." I make a pffft sound. "Don't make promises you ain't gonna keep."

"Just don't ever say super sperm again."

"I'm sayin' it over and over, starting tomorrow."

We keep laughing, the mood lightening.

I take a deep breath.

"We should make a pact, eh?"

"What kind of pact? Like the pinky promise kind?"

"Sort of." I laugh. "No matter where life takes us, we'll continue to be a part of each other's journey. We'll share successes, our challenges—everything in between. Distance doesn't have to define our connection."

I mean, she's basically part of me now.

There's a brief silence, and then I hear Tess's voice, soft yet determined. "You're right. I don't want to lose what we have just because circumstances have changed."

"We won't lose it," I reassure her. "So let's keep talking, keep sharing, and keep supporting each other, no matter the miles between us." I hesitate. "You know, if Drake were here, he'd be making barfing sounds in the background."

"Whatever, he's an idiot. This is nice, and now I won't feel alone."

I know she's not actually alone, but I get what she's saying.

Miranda and her parents and her other friends won't ever know what we went through.

Only I do.

"You know what you need to do?" I say, feeling daring. "You need to come and see me. Are you up for it?"

There's a moment of anticipation as I wait for her response, the excitement in my chest threatening to burst free. The seconds stretch as she considers it.

"It might be exactly what we both need."

My breath exhales.

I'm glad she agrees because I'd feel like an ass having suggested it.

"I'll take you on a date," I announce. "Like a real one."

"A real one? We haven't been on a date, period." She sniffs, affronted. "The least you can do is take me somewhere with desserts." A pause. "I'll probably get two."

"You can have as many desserts as you want."

"Okay. Yes. I'll come and see you."

CHAPTER 49
TESS

DAMN. I REALLY MISSED HIM.

I CAN'T BELIEVE I'm here.

In Illinois, I mean.

My parents offered to pay because they thought it would be good for me to visit Drew, too, but he's the one who bought my ticket.

First class.

"You realize our families might have something to say about it, right?"

He had hesitated. "True, they might have their reservations. But what's life without a little bit of rebellion?"

I've never been a rebel a day in my life and neither has Drew.

Except for this one thing apparently where I did what no one in my family ever thought I would do; get pregnant from a one-night stand, and the father was my brother's best friend.

Was.

Past tense.

They obviously haven't spoken, but mostly because my brother has been acting like a dick.

Color me surprised that he treated me with respect on our call last night—the last call I was expecting.

"*Hey, sis,*" Grady's voice came through, casual and familiar—

yet unfamiliar at the same time. In the past few weeks, I feel like I don't know him at all.

"*Hey,*" I replied, my heart racing a little. "*What's up?*"

"*Nothing much,*" he said. "*Just wanted to talk to you about something.*"

My mind raced through the possibilities of what this conversation could be about. "*Sure, go ahead.*"

I stood at the kitchen counter in my apartment, arms and ankles crossed as if he were standing in the room, talking to me face-to-face and I had to be in defense mode.

There was a brief pause before Grady spoke again. "*Mom and Dad told me about your plans to visit Drew.*"

My brows shot up. "*Yeah, that's true.*"

"*I gotta admit, I was surprised,*" Grady said, his tone light. "*I mean, you're hopping on a plane to see the guy who got you pregnant. Illinois isn't exactly your typical vacation destination.*"

Vacation destination?

What an idiot.

I couldn't help but chuckle. "*Yeah, I guess it's not your usual vacation spot. Lots of farm fields and cattle, I would imagine.*"

Same as here.

"*But seriously, Tess,*" Grady continued. "*Are you sure about this? I know you're a grown-up and all, but I can't help but worry.*"

"*Worry about what?*"

Nothing more could happen to me. The month has been one of the shittiest on record for me in the history of shitty things happening to me. Not getting a bid from my top sorority choice my freshman year used to be at the top of the list.

Ha.

And I thought that was rough...

What a fool I'd been.

"*Mom and Dad told me about...you know. Everything. The baby and stuff.*"

The baby and stuff...

I picked at a piece of lint on my hoodie. "*I appreciate your* concern, Grady, but…you know Drew better than anyone, and I want to see him. He wants to see me. We need…time together to..."

Shoot, how do I put this?

"Heal."

The word feels so foreign to me; a word I never thought I would assign to myself or my feelings or my state of well-being, but here I am, needing to heal and not wanting to do it alone.

"Look," he said, his tone softening. "I might have given you a hard time"—he cleared his throat—"about your choices, but, uh. I love you, you know? And I, uh, I support you."

I let the silence take up space in the universe so he can choose his next sentence.

"Just promise me you'll be careful, okay? I know you, Tess – you jump in headfirst, and I don't want to see you get hurt."

"Jump in headfirst?" I laughed. "What are you even talking about? I don't know if I ever told you this because it was none of your business but I've been in love with Drew Colter since I was in middle school—there was nothing 'headfirst' about it."

I smiled despite the seriousness of the conversation.

I lowered my voice, getting serious. "Listen. I promise I'll be careful. I want you to consider contacting Drew and apologizing—I don't think you and I will be 'good' until you do."

If you could hear a nod through a cell phone, I could hear his.

"Okay."

"Good."

"Good," he repeated. "And you better bring me back a souvenir or something. I haven't been to the Midwest in years."

I laughed. "I'll see what I can do. Maybe a keychain or a postcard from the airport?"

"Now you're talking," he said. "Tess?"

"Hm?"

"I'm really fucking sorry. About everything."

"I know."

And I do. My brother might have been acting out the past few weeks but he's had my back my entire life. This was the first time in our lives we'd been at odds, and it was one of the loneliest, not having him supporting me because he was butt hurt about Drew.

Would it have made a difference if some other guy had gotten me, you know—preggo?

Maybe.

Maybe not.

"DAMN, Tess, I haven't seen you in years. Drew wasn't kidding when he said you were all grown up."

Drake Colter, looking so much like his twin, but at the same time so unlike his twin, wraps me in a hug, his massive body swallowing me hole.

I wasn't sure how he'd be.

Drake isn't warm and fuzzy like Drew is and with all the drama and excitement that's been going on, I wasn't sure how he'd receive me.

My worries fade as I'm ushered through their door.

Upstairs to his room.

The first thing I notice is the balloon bouquet floating in a mass above the desk. I quickly count them and come up with six, one of them loose and bouncing against the ceiling when we move through the room.

The balloons don't say anything. They're just hearts.

Silver and purple hearts.

And there are flowers.

Lavender roses in a glass vase.

"I didn't know what your favorite color was, so I just picked purple," he says from behind me, setting my suitcase near the closet.

I don't even know what to say.

I turn to face him. "No one has ever gotten me flowers before."

"There is no way that's even possible."

"Way." I laugh, folding my hands in front of me, not knowing what to do with them. I want to… hug him. Kiss him.

Kiss his face.

So I close the gap and lift onto my tiptoes, pressing my lips to the underside of his jaw, his stubble scratching my mouth.

"Thank you."

"You're welcome." His voice is low and gravelly, a mix of embarrassment and happiness.

He kisses me like he means it, his lips meeting mine with an intensity that sends shivers down my spine.

This kiss isn't like the horny, semi-alcohol-induced kisses we shared that night we had sex at Miranda's place. This isn't like the kisses we shared after I found out I was pregnant.

This isn't a fleeting touch. His hands cradle my face gently, as if I'm something precious, something he's been waiting for since before I arrived here.

I can feel the weight of our emotions in that kiss – it's heavy, if that makes any sense at all.

Our longing, the passion, the unspoken words hanging between us that I'm sure we'll share later, tonight, at dinner.

It's as if he's trying to convey everything we feel in this kiss; every thought running through his mind. And at that moment, I understand.

His lips move against mine.

My fingers find their way to his hair—which he's trimmed, by the way—my heart racing in sync with the rhythm of our breaths. It's a kiss that speaks volumes, that bridges the gap between us, erasing any doubts that I shouldn't have come to Illinois to see him and work things out.

As the kiss deepens, I feel his heartbeat against my chest, a steady rhythm that matches my own. *Or maybe I'm imagining it because* of our connection and this raw emotion.

When we finally pull away, it's slowly.

I look into his eyes.

There's a new understanding there, a shared knowledge that goes beyond words. In that kiss, we've said more than we ever could have spoken aloud. And as I stand there, feeling the warmth of his touch still lingering on my lips, I'm excited about…

Everything.

It's like I went back in time and we're starting over—if that's even possible.

Anything is possible, a small voice in the back of my head whispers.

There's a pounding on the wall, coming from the hall.

A fist.

"Hey, no foolin' around!" Drake shouts from the hallway with laughter in his voice.

The door flies open, and his eyes scan the room, seemingly disappointed at finding us standing in the middle of it and not on the bed.

"I've always wanted to bust in on him and catch him foolin' around," Drake jokes, leaning against the doorframe.

"Reallly?" Drew asks sarcastically. "This is what you've always wanted?"

"Forever in my whole entire life." His eyes close as he holds a hand over his heart like a Scout.

Drew snorts. "Bro, you need to raise your standards."

"Oh my standards are the right high, thank you very much." He crosses his arms. "What are y'all gonna do later? Wanna do something?"

"We have plans," Drew tells his twin. "We're doin' a date."

"Doin' a date?"

"Shut up, dickhead, you know what I mean."

This is the Drew and Drake I remember from our youth—the teasing, the snark, the sarcastic back and forth that's a borderline pissing contest.

My gaze volleys back and forth as they argue until finally,

Drew shoves his brother back into the hallway and shuts the door in his face.

Locks it too.

"Alone at last," I joke, walking to the desk and poking one of my balloons with the tip of my fingernail.

"Don't get used to it. He's a huge pain in the ass, and he's not happy unless he's all up in my business."

Yeah, Grady is the same way for the most part. I don't want to bring his name up though because I don't know how Drew is feeling about it, and my attention turns to the bruise next to his lip, a reminder about everything that went down last time they were in the same room together.

It's healing, though.

I glance out the bedroom window and out into the back, his view overlooking the backyard for the house next door.

Four girls lounge around sunning themselves, despite the temperature outside not being all that conducive to sunbathing.

I let the curtain fall back into place.

"Who are they?"

"The irritating girls next door."

"Irritating?"

"Trouble." He walks to his desk and sniffs the roses. "You don't even wanna know."

"Oh yes, I do. I totally do. Spill."

Now I'm lying across the bed, taking up most of the space, bracing my chin in my hand, watching him intently as he fusses around the room.

"So basically, in a nutshell, two of the girls tried trapping my brothers into relationships. It was pure evil."

"How!" I feel my eyes get wide.

"Erm. Shannon—there's a girl named Shannon—sent a picture to the media that made it look like she and Drake were making out on our front porch, and it caused a huge fight between he and Daisy. Total mess."

"The media?"

"Yeah. Sent it to the tabloids and *SportsCenter* picked it up. She was basically framing him for something he didn't do so his girlfriend would break up with him and she could swoop in."

"That's...that's..." A knot of guilt has my stomach clenching.

That's not what I did to him, is it?

I didn't go to the media, but Grady did and almost ruined everything.

Thank god it was short-lived. I don't know how we would have survived if Drew was a different kind of person than he is. Understanding, kind, and totally cool.

He looks at me now that I've gone quiet. "Tess."

My head gives a little shake. "What?"

"Don't compare yourself to the trolls next door. They're not even supposed to be here. They should have graduated by now. Like, move, dude—you don't go here anymore."

I laugh, despite the thoughts running through my brain.

It's been a lot.

I let my head hit his comforter.

CHAPTER 50
DREW

WE GET SECOND CHANCES WHEN WE'RE NOT READY THE FIRST TIME.

"WAKEY, WAKEY..."

Her eyelids flutter, but she doesn't open them.

"Hey. Sleeping Beauty, we have to get ready for dinner. We have that date, remember? The one where you order nine desserts, and I don't complain?"

That gets her attention.

She stirs.

I lean in and press a gentle kiss to her cheek.

Temple.

Lips.

"Wake up, sleepyhead," I whisper, my voice a soft murmur.

She lets out another contented moan but doesn't fully open her eyes, only lays there as if in a dreamland.

I don't feel guilty for trying to rouse her. Continuing my gentle assault, I brush my lips over her skin in a series of featherlight kisses. She's wearing a crewneck sweatshirt cut at the neck and hanging off her shoulder, bare skin begging to be peppered with kisses.

"Mmm," she murmurs again, a slow smile tugging at her lips.

"Rise and shine, gorgeous," I whisper. "Time to wake up."

Tess finally stirs, her eyes fluttering open.

She blinks up at the ceiling a few seconds before turning her head to look at me.

"Hey." Her voice is sleepy. "What time is it?"

"Four."

"Hmm." She reaches for me, pulling me toward her—on top of her, arms wrapping around me, hands lacing behind my neck. "You're so warm."

So is she.

"I feel so lazy." Tess yawns.

"Do you want to stay here tonight? We can order pizza or pasta or something else?" Whatever she wants.

"No. No, I want to go out. If we stay in we'll just spend all our time being lazy, and that's not why I'm here."

When she sits up on the bed, I kiss her exposed shoulder again, letting my lips linger there.

"All I need is a shower, and we'll be good to go."

CHAPTER 51
TESS

I'M ABOUT TO TAKE A HOT SHOWER. THAT'S LIKE A REGULAR SHOWER, BUT WITH ME IN IT.

WARM WATER CASCADES OVER ME, the day's travel stress washed down the drain with the suds, every drop of water that hits my skin warming me like a blanket.

Closing my eyes against the spray, I revel in the simple pleasure of this moment of solitude.

I hug myself.

Sputter when the water hits my face, hand reaching for the shower gel on the shelf.

A smile tugs at my lips when I take the brown, wood-grained bottle and pop it open, giving it a sniff. It reminds me of Drew, a mix of earthy and fresh that I've come to associate with him. Granted, it would also smell like Drake, but that's not where my head is at the moment.

Ha!

I put it back on the shelf and grab the feminine shower gel—Ryann's, no doubt—and give that a whiff, too.

"Much better."

I lather up with a loofah, not wanting to use anyone else's, not knowing who they belong to—obviously. A bit like borrowing someone's toothbrush? I hadn't thought to pack anything for the shower, and no washcloths are to be found…

I'm lost in my own thoughts until the soft sound of the bathroom door opens catches my attention.

I go still.

Rub my hand on the glass to clear the steam off, my view no longer obstructed.

My heart literally skips a beat at the sight of Drew.

Stripping down, removing his tee shirt, then his shorts, he stands in his underwear at the sink, regarding me.

"Mind if I join you?" he asks, his voice a low rumble that sends shivers down my spine.

I've never showered with anyone before.

"Uh. Sure." I shake my head—I don't mind at all—lips curving into a grin. "Not at all. It's already a bit crowded in here with all these loofahs, but I think we can make it work."

He chuckles, the sound filling the space between us as he slides open the door and steps under the spray of water. I watch, captivated, as he reaches for his own shower gel, the muscles in his arms flexing as he lathers it up.

I look down.

Check out his belly, his belly button, his hips, thighs…

As if on instinct, I move closer to him, our bodies just barely brushing against each other.

The steam rises around us, creating an almost dreamlike atmosphere. His eyes never leave mine as he lifts his hand, his fingers tracing a slow, sudsy path down my arm.

I shiver.

Without a word, he reaches for the gray sponge, applying just enough pressure to create a gentle friction as he drags it against my skin.

Up my arm.

Down my arm.

Over my collarbone.

His touch is tender. "Want me to wash your back?"

"Sure."

No one has ever washed my back before.

Obviously.

My head dips forward when he slowly spins me around so my back is facing him, and the sponge touches my skin, dragging up the center of my back. He moves it around in circles, over my shoulders, spine, down to the curve above my ass.

I tilt my head forward, allowing him better access as he works his way down my back, his movements deliberate and soothing.

It's an intimacy that goes beyond words, a connection that's as physical as it is emotional.

Finally, I turn to face him, our bodies now pressed against each other.

His arms come around me and mine go around him and we stand, studsy, beneath the spray of the water embracing. When my forehead presses against his chest, I can almost hear his heart beating.

Tears fall but are quickly washed away by the water.

His arms tighten.

His lips kiss the top of my head.

I just want to be close to him.

DEAR DIARY...

    School sucked today. Why are girls so mean to each other?
    Tosha and Charity are arguing over a pair of jeans that are MIA and the whole fight is so over-the-top I want nothing to do with it. I can't wait to go to college and get out of this town. I mean, I love my friends and stuff but we need a break from each other. Does anyone in this town leave besides the football players??? I'm not a senior so it's not like I can have senioritis, but damn.
    Get me out of here.
    Grady is working and turned down a partial scholarship to Texas State. Says he's not big enough—like, size wise?—and doesn't want to sit on the bench his entire football career which pisses mom and dad off cause its FREE money for school and they want him to get an education. I get his point. If he wants to work on cars and own a shop, and he's working with his hands what difference does it make if he goes and plays football at a ? On the other hand—like, it's college? I

don't know, there's just a lot of yelling and it's giving me major anxiety and I hate it.
   Xx
   T

CHAPTER 52
DREW

I SHOWER NAKED.

THE WATER from the shower has done its job, leaving Tess's skin glistening and her hair damp.

We step out of the shower, and I grab a fluffy towel, opening it wide, ready to envelop her inside it.

"Time for the drying-off ceremony," I announce, waggling my eyebrows playfully. "This is a full service rinse off for you."

I kiss her on the top of her head.

Tess smiles, eyes lighting up. "Oh really? And what does this ceremony entail?" She uses air quotes around the word ceremony.

I'm still holding the towel open, waiting for her to step in it.

"Well, we start with the classic pat dry." I demonstrate on myself with exaggerated movements, then pat her damp arm like I'm trying to put out a tiny fire.

She nods, watching intently. "Ahh, I see."

"Next, we move on to the gentle swipe technique." I trail the towel down her arm, making sure to be overly dramatic in my motions.

"It's a really good thing I don't have a spray tan," she says. "Otherwise, you would wipe it off with this technique."

"Would I?" I'm being uber gentle.

"Uh-huh. Probably." She watches me with amusement as I

slowly move the towel over her skin to dry her off. "You're really committed to this, aren't you?"

I'm on my knees, kneeling so I can do the front—and back—of her legs.

Her ass.

"Turn for me, please."

Tess turns, holding her arms out to her sides, slowly going in a circle so I can pat her backside down.

"Nice. I like what I see."

"Don't stare at my butt," she says.

"Too late." I dry her, confident I've gotten her whole rear end sufficiently taken care of. "Turn, please."

She smells good, like soap and shampoo.

Clean.

I stare at her body, run my hands down her belly.

Lean forward and kiss it, just above the belly button.

Press my forehead there, gently resting it on her abdomen.

Tess rests her hands on my head, funning her fingers gently through my hair.

We don't say much of anything for a few moments.

Then,

I rise from my knees and finish toweling her off.

CHAPTER 53
TESS

DON'T GIVE UP ON SOMETHING
YOU CAN'T GO A DAY WITHOUT
THINKING ABOUT. OR SOME ONE.

I'VE ALWAYS WANTED to come to a place like this but have never had the opportunity—and by opportunity, I mean: I've never dated a guy who:

1. Could afford it
2. Made this kind of effort

Not that I know Drew could afford it, but I'm assuming, especially since he's the one who paid for my airline ticket and hasn't asked for reimbursement.

This place is cool in a way that I am not.

Dim.

Classy.

But hip in a way that most old establishments are.

"My brother always wants to come here when he's in town."

"Which brother?" I mean, he has three.

"Duke."

Ahh.

The restaurant's soft lighting casts a warm glow over everything, from the polished silverware to the pristine white tablecloths, and I am here for it.

I fidget with my napkin. I had almost forgotten to put it on my lap when I sat down—the fabric smooth beneath my fingertips.

This is it—our first real date.

I'm excited, nervous, and feeling a mixed bag of emotions all at the same time.

Ugh!

Nerves, go away…

Drew looks incredibly handsome in a well-fitted suit. I was shocked when he walked into the living room sporting it and feel underdressed, too.

I'm in jeans and a dressy blouse, but he's in a suit—dressed to impress, and damn, he looks good enough to make my mouth water.

"Have I mentioned how you clean up nice?"

"Don't you remember us dressing up for away games in high school?"

He mimics my movements, unwrapping his silverware and draping his napkin across his lap.

"Actually, I don't."

"Well, you look great, too." He sounds nervous. "Gorgeous."

I feel pretty tonight, too. After the hell I've gone through and the roller coaster of emotions, it feels good to feel human. And pretty. And put together.

I feel young again—not like a young woman who got pregnant after a one-night stand and had the entire world know about it.

A deep blush creeps up my cheeks, and I lower my gaze to the menu. "Thanks. I'm just... really glad we're doing this."

"Me too," he says, his tone softening. "And you know what? Let's make a deal—no pressure, just two people enjoying a nice meal together."

His words ease my nerves, and I meet his gaze with a grateful smile.

"Deal."

As we wait for our food, our conversation flows naturally in a mixture of laughter and easy banter. It's a reminder of how well we click and how effortlessly we can talk about anything and everything. We share stories from our past, discuss our favorite movies, and even delve into a spirited debate about the merits of pineapple on pizza.

And then, with a sly grin, Drew leans in a little closer. "You know, this restaurant reminds me of a story…"

"Oh, do tell," I say, my curiosity piqued.

Drew leans back in his chair. "A few years ago, my brother and his girlfriend thought it would be a good idea to, uh, have sex in the restaurant bathroom when they were on a date."

I raise an eyebrow, my mouth dropping open in surprise. "Seriously?"

Drew nods, a grin tugging at his lips. "Well. I think what actually happened was he went down on her in the bathroom, and they almost got caught."

"How?"

I select a piece of bread from the basket placed in the center of the table, butter it, and wait for more details.

"They thought they were being all sneaky and discreet, but they were making more noise than they realized, and clearly, my brother isn't small. He literally cannot do anything graceful."

I cover my mouth with my hand. "Oh god. I can't imagine."

Drew leans back, clearly enjoying my reaction. "So they're in the stall, and he's down on his knees trying to go down on her, and the door opens, and someone walks in."

"Did they just stand there and wait?"

"No. I think he kept at it."

"NO!" I breathe. "I would have died."

"Yeah, I'm pretty sure my boner would have shriveled up inside my body, so if you have any ideas about banging in the bathrooms over there, you should probably think again."

"Um, no worries. I think I'm good."

But now that he's mentioning it, my eyes dart across the restaurant to the hallway where the bathrooms are located.

"Do you think it was *this* restaurant?"

"Probably. He's the one who gave me the name of this place."

I make a mental note to check out the bathrooms—not that I want him going down on me in them later, but I am curious. What self-respecting girl wouldn't be?

"I can't say it's on my bucket list of activities to try, but then again—what do I know?" I shake my head in amazement, still chuckling. "Well, I guess that's one way to make a memorable dining experience."

We're both laughing when a voice interrupts.

"Hey, uh—are you Drew Colter?"

A man stands beside our table, his eyes wide with recognition—and excitement, which is wild, considering he's my dad's age and not a young fan.

Drew glances up, a warm smile lighting up his face. He sets down the butter knife and leans back in his chair.

"Yeah, that's me."

"Dang, I couldn't tell if it was you or your brother." The man grins, clearly thrilled. "Man, I'm a huge fan of yours! Huge. I've been following your career since forever. It's crazy that all you play football."

"I know it blows people's minds that all four of us play football. Like the Manning brothers or the Kelce brothers, but times two." He smiles politely.

He doesn't seem to mind the interruption, and it's almost as if it happens to him often enough.

"I'm Mark," the man says, extending a hand to Drew, who shakes it with a friendly smile. "My son Kyle is also a huge fan. He's eight."

"Oh, well, tell Kyle I said hey. Does he play football?"

Mark nods enthusiastically, his eyes darting around. "Look, I'm not supposed to be over here. I'm on my way to the bathroom, and my wife says I'm not supposed to interrupt your date."

He's babbling, but Drew doesn't seem to mind.

"It's okay."

"Can I get you to sign something?" He's patting his pockets

as if a pen will magically appear in one. "Shit, I don't have a pen. Or paper."

A server lingers nearby and overhears him. Digging into her apron, she produces not only a pen but also a ticket pad. She rips off a sheet of paper from it and hands it to Mark.

Who hands it to Drew.

"I'll sign this to Kyle." He scribbles quickly. His autograph is all sharp angles and one long flourish.

It's a masculine signature, and I stare at his hands the whole time he's jotting a note to Kyle. Those rough hands have been on my body. Big. Strong.

Capable.

And listen to me, sexualizing his hands when all he's doing is writing his name.

Wow. It's like I haven't had sex in months, the way I'm objectifying him.

Drew hands the sheet of paper to Mark. "Well, it's been good to meet you, Mark. This is my childhood friend, Tess," Drew tells him.

I do a double take.

His childhood friend?

My heart sinks, damned if it doesn't, and I stop listening to whatever they say.

Childhood friend.

Huh.

Not almost the mother of my child? Not potential future girlfriend?

He could have simply said, "This is my friend, Tess."

But he didn't.

Mark launches into a passionate monologue about his favorite football team that has Drew nodding along in support. He talks about other players on Wisconsin's teams, their best game last year, and the unforgettable moments that have made him a die-hard fan.

I'm annoyed.

Childhood friend.

I mean—yes, that's what I am, but here, I thought I was more. Are we not on a date? Was this not supposed to be romantic?

Drew listens to Mark intently, asking questions and engaging in the conversation with genuine interest, dragging the encounter out even longer. And fine. So what if I can't help but admire his ability to connect with people on a personal level, even when he's the one being recognized?

As Mark finishes his enthusiastic monologue—which almost puts me to sleep, ha ha—he finally backs away from us.

"Shit, I better go back to my table. My wife is going to kill me." He sticks out his hand again for another shake. "It's been such a pleasure meeting you both. Can I get a picture?"

Drew nods, and Mark fumbles with his phone, snapping a quick selfie with Drew and then with both of us. He thanks us profusely, his excitement still evident in every word.

Lordy.

Mark eventually walks off, leaving us alone again until the server drops by with our entrées.

I push the asparagus around on my plate with a fork tine, debating how to begin the conversation or if I should let it go.

It's not a big deal.

It's not.

So why do I feel like it is?

If Drew notices my silence, he hasn't let on. He cuts his steak with a knife and happily pops a piece in his mouth, chewing thoughtfully as he smiles across the table at me.

Clueless.

Like a typical male…

But this is our first date, and I don't want to ruin it by being salty.

Then again, I'm a raging hormone. After all, I was pregnant last week. I literally cannot help this wave of emotion I'm feeling, regardless of how trivial it may or may not be.

Drew fidgets when I frown over at him, and I'm taken back

to high school—to the night I watched him from the corner of our basement, during a party, try to hit on one of the popular girls in their grade and she shut him down.

He stammers, "How's your dinner?"

He talks, but my brain is mush.

This is my childhood friend…

Drew is the boy of my dreams, and now he's telling people I'm his childhood friend, which basically equates to "this is my friend's little sister."

God, I'm a mess.

An emotional mess.

Why couldn't he have said, "This is my date, Tess?"

Would that have made me happy?

Yes.

One hundred percent yes…

DEAR DIARY...

    I thought Drew was coming home for the weekend. I mean—it's Christmas, why wouldn't he? So like an idiot, I made an emergency appointment to get my hair done (my roots look terrible) and got a trim, and bought a new outfit at the mall thinking that MAYBE I would see him? The night before Christmas everyone who's home from college always gets together at the Grain Feedery for dancing and drinks and I'm the idiot because I thought Drew would be there. EVERYONE goes and who doesn't come home for the holiday??? It's Christmas for crying out loud. But no. The Colters have that Bowl game they're playing in so we have to watch them on TV along with the rest of the Nation which isn't fair, is it?

    How dumb did I feel standing around in that new dress, waiting on a boy who wasn't gonna show up. Dumb.

    I give up...
    x Tess

CHAPTER 54
DREW

WATCH ME SCREW UP EVERYTHING. SHOW TIMES RUN STARTING AT 7 AM, DAILY.

AS I STAND HERE, lacing up my cleats and feeling the weight of anticipation in the air, I can't help but wonder why Tess has become so distant since our last date. She was one way when we sat down and another by the time we left. Her laughter and the easy flow of conversation still lingers.

Was it something I said?

I rack my brain, lacing my other shoe.

Something has shifted.

It's as if a cloud has settled over the connection we were beginning to build.

Shit.

We're preparing for our first scrimmage of the season, but all I can think about is Tess. I find myself lost in thoughts of what might have changed.

Was it something I said or did?

Did I miss a cue that could have led us astray? The rhythmic thud of my heartbeat seems to mimic the cadence of my racing mind, both trying to make sense of this sudden change.

Adrenaline should be pumping, but for a different reason. I have to get my head in the game, or I could end up fucking myself.

Literally.

The camaraderie of my teammates surrounds me, their laughter and banter and shared excitement a stark contrast to the unease I feel. Our team captain tries to pump everyone up, prepping us for Coach to come in and give his spiel before we run out onto the field. The campus pastor is also here to lead a prayer.

Before I'd left the house and left her with Ryann and Daisy, she'd been chatting with them both, wearing borrowed team apparel—one of my hoodies that's three sizes too big on her.

Her smile was there, but it was different—*guarded*, maybe forced? I wanted to pull her aside to ask if everything's alright, but it wasn't the place, and I didn't have the time. Now I won't get to see her again for the next four hours at the very least.

Whatever's gnawing at her, I hope she talks it through with one of the girls.

They know what this life is like. Who better than brothers' girlfriends?

What if I'm overthinking?

What if it has nothing to do with me at all?

I mean, it probably doesn't.

I hadn't done anything wrong.

But she was so cold last night—I thought she'd at least cuddle in bed? Spoon me or let me spoon her at the very least.

I like to spoon, what of it?

Stop thinking about it.

I shake the dust out of my brain.

Coach's deep, steady timbre breaks through my reverie. It's time to focus and get my head in the game.

I direct my attention to him. He speaks words about courage and determination and giving it our all.

"Today marks the start of our journey, the first step toward our goals. We've trained hard, honed our skills, and now it's time to show the world what we're made of. Remember, the real victory lies in our unity and our unwavering determination. Leave everything on that field—sweat, heart, soul. Play for each other, for the jersey on your back. Trust in the countless hours you've put in. Play smart, play fierce, and most importantly, play as one. Now, let's go out there and make our presence known." When Coach pauses, you can hear a pin drop. "NOW GO GIVE 'EM HELL!"

The locker room erupts with cheers.

My teammates—and myself—bang on our chest plates, getting ourselves even more amped up.

I jog onto the field, helmet clutched in my hand, and remind myself that I can't let whatever's going on with Tess hinder my performance.

This scrimmage demands my full attention, and I'm determined to give it my all—regardless of the unanswered questions lingering in my mind.

"Dude, what's going on?" Suddenly, my brother is there, clamping a hand on my shoulder like we're the only two people in this stadium crowded with thousands upon thousands of people.

"Nothin'."

He smacks me on my shoulder pads. "We don't have time to fuck around. Just tell me what's going on."

The fans are so loud it's almost deafening.

"I have no idea what's going on," I say honestly because I literally don't.

Drake laughs. "Welcome to the wonderful world of relationships. Congrats, bro. Welcome to the club."

"What the hell is that supposed to mean?" Should I be amused? 'Cause all I am is confused.

"It means that women are a mystery. Don't try to figure them out. When she's ready to tell you what the problem is, she'll tell you." He pulls his helmet down over his head, snapping the chin strap. "Get your head in the game, man. Do you want to end up hurt?"

"No."

"Then shut off the noise and get your head in the game." He smacks me again on the shoulder pads. "It's time to give 'em hell."

CHAPTER 55
TESS

I WON'T LIE, HIS BROTHER IS PRETTY FREAKING AWESOME, TOO.

OF ALL THE *people I thought would come lecture me about communicating my feelings, never in a million years would I have thought it would be Drake Colter.*

Drake.

Of all people.

The Drake Colter I remember from our youth was a cocky, arrogant asshole who never had time for anything other than football.

Granted, Drew didn't really either, but at least he wasn't a dick about it.

But as I lounge around Drew's bedroom, awkwardly waiting for him to finish his shower, the door creaks open, and there stands Drake, his brother, giving me that enigmatic smirk that has "I'm here to stick my nose in your business" written all over it.

"Having fun?" he drawls, leaning casually against the doorframe, bulky arms crossed.

I notice he has tattoos, something I hadn't noticed before.

The gap between his teeth winks at me.

"Am I having fun?" I wouldn't call sitting around a bedroom waiting for a guy to get out of the shower my idea of fun, but whatever. At least I'm here.

I try not to let Drake's sudden appearance in the doorway rattle me, but the truth is he's always intimidated me. Probably because of his Zero Fucks Given attitude that I've never mastered.

"Oh, just soaking in the ambience of your brother's room."

He chuckles, strolling into the room as if he owns the place.

Which technically, I guess he kind of does.

Drew told me that his older brother Duke owns the house, and they're allowed to live in it rent free as long as they're on the team and in school.

Drake is by the desk now, leaning over to sniff the roses still placed in the center of Drew's desk.

My flowers.

"You know, I've always thought the true essence of a person is revealed by their bedroom," he begins. "A lot can be deciphered from the books they read, the clothes they wear, and the questionable decor choices they make."

He pokes at the Star Wars Lego creation of the Millennium Falcon.

Wanders from the desk to the bookshelf.

I raise an eyebrow, unimpressed. "So what's your brother's essence, according to his room?"

He looks around with seriousness. "Well, I'd say Drew is 'post-modern minimalist meets chaotic laundry pile' aesthetic."

I can't help but laugh when he says, "He should go into interior decorating. His room is way better than mine."

Way better than mine…

He leans against the dresser, his expression softening. "What's going on with you and my brother?"

"I…" *Don't know.* "Nothing."

Now he's the one arching his eyebrow. "Funny, that's what he said this morning when I asked him the same thing."

My mouth opens.

Closes.

"You asked him what was going on?" I pause. "What did he say?"

"He said nothin'. Same as you."

I let out a sigh, my gaze wandering to the floor. Bookshelf. Closet door. "It's... complicated."

Drake arches an eyebrow, crossing his arms over his chest. "Complicated, huh? That's a word I've heard quite often lately."

I glance up at him, my curiosity piqued. "What do you mean?"

He tilts his head, studying me for a moment. "I know that you've had a lot going on, what with the baby and then not having a baby, but you're not the only one affected. Drew's been actin' different since your date last night."

I frown. I thought it was just me.

"Different how?"

He sighs. "Look, obviously, I don't know any details, but I know something happened between you two."

He's not wrong.

"I can feel it in my gut." His massive shoulders shrug. "It's a twin thing."

I shift uncomfortably, suddenly feeling exposed. "I'd be lying if I said you were wrong, but I've been trying to figure things out."

Drake regards me for a few moments. Crosses and uncrosses his arms. "Out of the two of us, he's always been the sensitive one. I'm not sayin' you can't count on me, but if you ask anyone who's the most reliable, they will almost always say Drew."

Silently, I nod.

He's not telling me anything I don't already know.

"And before I met Daisy—before we started datin' and getting to know each other—I knew Drew was going through a tough time. He never said it directly, but I think he was thinkin' of quittin' the team."

My eyes widen. "He was?"

He mentioned something about being unhappy but hadn't said anything about quitting the team.

"Like I said, he didn't actually tell me. It's just a feelin' I had, and I wanted him to be happy. And so I downloaded the datin' app and started talkin' to girls for him, and that's how I met Daisy."

This I knew.

"And I got the feelin' that although he was happy for me, he was a bit crushed that now he's the only Colter who doesn't have someone to love—who loves him back."

I am intently hanging on his every word.

"Look, I know it's not any of my business, but when Drew came back from Logan's bachelor weekend—which I would have liked an invitation to, by the way, not that I'm complainin'. But I would have."

Is this the point he's trying to make?

I doubt it.

"When he came back from that weekend, he was excited. I could tell. So I don't know what's going on or if it has anything to do with the baby? But he doesn't seem to know what's going on either, and I know it's not my business—but it kind of is— you should, you know. Tell him."

My lips part. "Last night when we were at dinner, he introduced me to a fan as his—"

"Girlfriend?" Drake cuts me off.

"No. As his childhood friend."

He waits as if there were more to tell. "And that upset you."

"Sort of."

"And now you're letting it fester instead of talkin' to him about it."

I know my feelings aren't trivial, but the reason I haven't brought them up are because I'm not sure I have a right to claim to be more to him. I know he considers me a friend, and we've obviously had a bunch of sex. What if this is a friends-with-benefits situation?

That is not what I want.

"I don't want to overthink things. So I'm trying to process it before I bring it up."

"Well, that ain't gonna make matters better. Whatever scenario he dreams up in his imagination is gonna be far worse than the truth, as we guys so often do." He chuckles. "You know, for what it's worth, Drew's not great with words. He probably didn't even realize that introducing you as a childhood friend would upset you. He probably thought it was bein' polite."

I smile despite the knots in my stomach. "I know."

Drake's expression softens, and he takes a step closer. "You know, I didn't come in here to poke fun at y'all. If you care about my brother, and I can tell you do, maybe you should take the initiative to start the conversation." He sighs dramatically. "I feel like a damn relationship therapist."

I meet his gaze, surprised by the genuine concern in his eyes. "I want to, but I don't know how to bring it up. It sounds so stupid when I say it out loud. Drew, I hated when you called me your childhood friend. It made me feel like your sister."

I pull a face.

Ugh.

He smirks again, that trademark expression of his. "Well, you could always take a page out of Drake Colter's book and just blurt out, 'Hey, let's talk about our feelins like adults.'"

"Oh my god, you do *not* want to talk about your feelins."

"Well no, I don't. But sometimes I don't have a choice. Daisy doesn't let me stew about shit." He rolls his eyes. "Bless her heart."

He sounds so much like his brother it's bonkers, and all the similarities mess with my brain. The way they start sentences with "well" and the way he sighs and rolls his eyes.

Same eyes.

Same nose.

Same beard stubble on his face.

From the next room, the sound of the shower being turned off has Drake and I glancing at one another.

"I should go before he walks in here. He'll want to know what ideas I've been tryin to fill your head with." He laughs good-naturedly.

"True."

"Anyway. Think about what I said. I don't think it's a big deal that he called you a childhood friend 'cause that's what you are, eh?"

"Right."

But what I am and what I want to be are two different things.

Don't I wish I were the kind of girl who could just blurt out everything she felt, whenever she felt it?

But, of course, my brain has to go into overdrive, analyzing every possible outcome, replaying every conversation he and I have had, and it's driving me nuts in the process.

It's like a mental loop that won't stop, and I'm stuck in this cycle of doubt and frustration.

Childhood friend.

Ugh. Why can't I let this go?

I realize it's stupid and small.

Drew probably has no idea that he said a single thing to hurt me or make me feel insignificant, as if we haven't been wrung through the wringer lately!

No clue that I'm over here caught up in a tornado of emotions, trying to keep my cool on the outside. I mean, I've been acting like I have my shit together—everything is fine. I'm fine. We're good.

But deep down, it's a different story.

Guess I'm more insecure than I thought I was, and it's not fair to him that I'm not sharing.

But do guys want to hear our thoughts? Don't the words "What are you thinking, what's on your mind," make their dick shrivel up?

Ha.

Now the more I try to turn my brain off, the more things are creeping back in, mocking me for being so damn… well, childish.

Petty.

Like seriously? Is this what adulting feels like? Because if it is, I want a refund.

So what if he called me a childhood friend. That's what I am.

Sort of.

Okay fine, not really, we were never friends. He was friends with my brother, but maybe in his brain, it's the same thing.

I catch myself stealing glances when he's not looking, then today, watching him play in the football game…was nothing short of surreal.

Confession: it was my first time in a college football stadium. How horrible is that? A Texas girl who grew up on *Friday Night Lights* has never been to a college game? When most of her brother's childhood friends ate, drank, and dreamed the game? Including my brother?

Including Drew.

His brothers.

A first for me.

The way Drew moved on that field; the confidence radiating from him was like witnessing a whole different side of him because with me he gives me room to make the decisions, let me seduce him, let me…boss him around a bit.

This was different.

It turned me on.

The Colter Boys were in their element, and suddenly, I got what all the fuss was about. The way he effortlessly caught the ball, calling plays, light on his feet.

The crowd's cheers.

The adrenaline in the air.

The electric atmosphere.

Every time Drew made a play—or he made one with his brother—excitement rippled through the stadium, and I found myself on my feet screaming with everyone else.

And all this time, he isn't sure he wants to keep playing the game when it's clear he was born for this.

They both were.

It made me realize how much passion he pours into everything he does and how he embraces challenges with his whole heart, whether it's his choice or not.

So, here I am, stuck in this limbo of wanting to tell him how I feel and wanting to pretend things are good. Fine.

It's like I'm standing on the edge of a cliff, teetering between taking that leap of faith and retreating to safer ground.

But hey, at least I have my pride, right?

Yeah, like that's comforting when all I want to do is throw it out the window and let my emotions run wild, which could just be the hormones.

Childhood friend?

Far from it.

Why isn't there a playbook for this stuff? A step-by-step guide to navigating these feelings without feeling like I'm stumbling through a minefield and fucking everything up in the process.

CHAPTER 56
DREW

THE BEST RELATIONSHIP IS THE ONE YOU NEVER EXPECTED TO BE IN.

I'M SO FUCKING TIRED.

1. Because we were out kind of late last night, considering I had a game today.

2. I'm tired from the game, having taken a few hits I wasn't counting on.

I know Tess wants to talk to me, but I don't have the mental bandwidth—not that she's brought anything up, but we went to sleep tonight not talking after spending a quiet evening in bed, watching TV like a couple of old people who don't have a life.

Not like two people who are crazy about one another and have just started dating.

Why is this so fucking hard?

Because you got her pregnant before you took her on a proper date, you fucking moron.

She's entitled to be moody.

Moody.

Is that all this is?

My eyelids are heavy, and the last thing I hear is Lana, the talking, judgey cone from *Too Hot to Handle*—a show about singles living on an isolated island for two weeks. They aren't allowed to have sex, kiss, make out, or get sexually physical in any way, shape, or form—and if they do, they lose exorbitant amounts of money each time.

Cameras follow their every movement.

Every touch.

The hostess announces that two contestants kissed, costing the group two thousand dollars. The other contestants argue about being betrayed.

Next to me, Tess is already sleeping.

My lids slide closed.

So tired.

But maybe I should have asked her again what's wrong.

'Cause I know it's something.

Behind my sleepy eyes, I see her smiling at me. Her ass in those jean shorts at the miniature golf course, her boobs in that dress she had on at the honky-tonk…

She has me on the dance floor, our feet moving, bodies pressed together. Laughing. Steps into me, wearing only that skimpy silk top and that thong, ass on display, an invitation for my palms…

Tess has her hands on my shoulders. Those move, too, until they're behind my head, nails lightly scratching the back of my neck as she kisses me.

I pull her closer, still.

Fingers flirting with the hem of her thin camisole or tank top or whatever this excuse for a shirt is, the fabric as silky as her skin, and I run my hands beneath it—tentatively at first.

It doesn't take long for the tips of my fingers to brush the underside of her tits. Trail along her smooth flesh. Thumbs grazing.

Then.

My hands are covering her tits.

They fill my palms perfectly, just as I'd imagined those few times I'd imagined what they look like, feel like, taste like. Damn, it's been an age since I've felt boobs—and all the reasons I had tried to date with intention last year rush back, sex being one of them.

Sex.

Affection.

Physical touch.

All the same thing, basically, marketed differently.

I groan when her nails scratch my scalp. Fuck that feels good…

She groans when I pinch her nipple, and now I want to see what her boobs look like, reaching to lift the hem of her barely-there shirt over her head.

Damn.

The view does not disappoint, and neither does the weight of her breasts in my hands.

For real.

Best tits ever.

"My least favorite position is missionary…" she whispers, pushing her hands into my chest as she rides me, loving it on top. "You better be careful, or you'll get me pregnant."

Get me pregnant.

That I can do.

My fingers trace gentle circles on her belly, and I'm filled with a sense of protectiveness and affection, especially after she brought up all the "safety in the end zone" stuff.

This isn't just about Tess and me anymore – it's about the life that's taking shape, the tiny heartbeat that echoes within her.

It's a responsibility and a gift and a connection that goes beyond anything I've ever known.

As I continue to touch her baby bump, Tess's hand covers mine, her touch warm and reassuring. Our eyes meet, and at that moment, it's as if all the complications and uncertainties fade away.

There's a sense of unity between us, a shared understanding that we're in this together, no matter what lies ahead.

Drake's laughter rings in the background because he hates it when I talk like that. He thinks it stupid and corny, and it makes him uncomfortable.

"What's wrong?"

"Nothing."

"Tess lost the baby."

"Lost it?" He sounds confused.

"I didn't even know I wanted to be a father until she told me. I didn't know," I repeat. "I didn't know, Drake."

I swear to god, tears come from my eyes. I haven't cried in years. Years. Actual years.

When was the last time I cried? When was it?

I hurt myself, breaking my leg in several places, and my dad had been so fucking pissed as if it were my fault and not something out of my control. I couldn't help it that the linebacker had smashed into me. It wasn't my fault. I didn't see him coming.

The tears run down my cheeks.

I toss.

I turn.

Reach for Tess but she's not there.

"This is my childhood friend…"

Child.

Our child that's no longer there. Why am I just thinking about this now? What took me so long?

Because you were only thinking of yourself and not her, and now she's being distant. You fucked it up. Grady was right, you don't deserve her, and you shouldn't have touched her.

I should have left her alone.

"That kiss is going to cost you two thousand dollars."

If she wanted you, she would have told you.

"Thanks to you, we have no more money left. You should have kept your dick in your pants, asshole! That was twenty-five thousand dollars."

Jerk.

Fool.

"I'm sorry…"

I'm sorry.

"I'm sorry."

"Drew, wake up. Babe, wake up."

My shoulders are being shaken, and I hear Tess's voice. She

sounds tired and confused—but mostly, she sounds awake. Concerned.

"Hmm?"

"You were having a dream."

I turn to face her, blinking myself awake.

"Did you call me babe?"

Tess pulls away from me so she's not up in my face, laughing in the dark. "You're dead ass asleep, and you hear me call you babe?"

"I hear what I hear."

"It just slipped out," she murmurs. "Sorry."

I roll closer, putting my hand on her waist. "Don't apologize. I liked it."

Babe.

I've always been jealous of my dumb brothers and their stupid endearments, having to listen to them call their girlfriends sweetie and babe and bae—and now I have her calling me by a pet name?

Literally what I've always wanted.

"Should I call you babe, too?" I tease in all seriousness, letting my eyes adjust to the dark.

Tess is quiet, and for a moment, I wonder if I'm still dreaming or if she's actually awake.

"Tess? I was kiddin."

"Oh. Were you?"

No.

"I mean, I was kiddin only if you don't want me to call you babe," I try again, not making much sense. But it's late, and we're both half asleep—at least I was. Don't know about her or if she's been lying here listening to me breathe the entire time.

I passed out as soon as my head hit the pillow.

"So you're kiddin', but you're not kiddin'."

Her voice has an edge to it that has me seeking her face out in the dark. It's late so I don't want to turn the lights on.

"Is…something wrong?"

I know she's been acting weird, but so far, she hasn't admitted it. I don't want to push and push and push, but she's leaving soon, and we don't have a ton of time. I don't want that time wasted or spent arguing, or filled with tension.

She moves on the bed, rolling to her back. Not away from me but not closer to me, either.

"Remember the other night when we were at dinner?"

Dinner—not "when we were on our date."

"Yes." Of course I do. I thought we had a good time.

"When that fan was getting his autograph and telling you about his son, you introduced me as your childhood friend."

I blink.

Blink again, trying to think back to that conversation. "I did?"

Had I?

Is that a bad thing? *I'm scared to ask out loud.*

"I felt insulted."

Insulted. "Why?"

She moves, rolling toward me this time, propping herself on her elbow as if she can actually see me and wants to talk face-to-face despite it being pitch black in his room.

"Because. I thought I was more to you than that."

"You are."

Those two words don't feel like enough, and her silence proves it, but for some reason, my brain isn't coming up with anything more sufficient to say.

Fuck, fuck, FUCK.

Think, think, THINK.

"That's not at all how I meant it." I reach for her, feeling around for her hand. "That's not how I meant it at all."

Same words, rephrased.

"You're not just a childhood friend."

Her laughter is quiet. "I didn't think we were friends at all when we were kids, if I'm being honest."

"You didn't?"

"No. I was your friend by proxy, but we weren't friends. When did we ever spend a single second together, alone, up until the past few months?"

"Never."

"When did we hang out laughin' and havin' fun in a group when we were younger?"

"Uh. Never."

She hmphs.

"Okay, point taken." I'm still not sure if it's safe to make a joke, not that I'm like ha-ha funny. Not like my brothers. They're hilarious, and I'm…

The quiet one.

"Tess, do you actually feel like I don't care about you?"

She scoffs. "Of course I think you care about me. You're a nice guy. You care about everyone."

I pause. "Are you…rollin' your eyes?"

I catch her snickering. "How can you tell?"

"I can hear it."

This time, she laughs. "Yes, I was rollin' my eyes."

"Is it a bad thing that I'm a nice guy?" Does she not realize how bad it sucks sometimes being the quiet, kind brother? The one people overlook because he's not the loud one? The attention whore? The famous one?

His mom's favorite, but only because he texts her out of guilt the most often?

The brother who catches shit because they consider him a kiss-ass?

The one who lost his virginity last because he was always too scared to make a move and didn't have any game?

I'm that guy.

And being the nice one has gotten old.

"Of course it's not a bad thing. Why would you think that?"

For all the reasons I just listed off in my head and didn't say out loud.

"Why would I think that?" I tuck a hand beneath my chin

and consider her question. "Actually, never mind. Let's get back to the actual subject."

"Which is?"

"Why it bothered you that I introduced you as a childhood friend."

"Because...I don't feel like I'm just your friend."

"Obviously, we're not just friends." Let's see, how do I put this? "The truth is, the words flew out of my mouth before I could think about 'em. I wasn't exactly gonna start callin' you my girlfriend for the first time in front of some stranger, and I didn't need Mark takin' our picture and sellin' it to the tabloids the way Grady did, based on the way I introduced you."

Fucking Grady Donahue still hasn't contacted me to apologize, that prick.

Have I mentioned that?

'Cause I'm getting pissed about it.

"I hadn't thought of it that way," she allows.

"We haven't had a talk about where our heads are at. Don't people do that? Have a talk?"

"You mean about the status of our relationship? Yeah, I think some people do. Some don't." She yawns.

"It was our first date, so I wasn't gonna..." You know. "I wasn't gonna make things awkward. That guy was a stranger. He doesn't need to know our business."

I'm also pretty confident that unless Mark has been living under a rock, he put two and two together in his brain and realized that maybe Tess was the girl in the *SportsCenter* story that had been splashed all over the goddamn internet and social media.

We're just gonna have to brace ourselves in the event that Mark is a sellout...

"Alright. Pretend we were going to do it all over again, and we're at dinner and Mark comes up, and you introduce me. What do you say?"

Oh shit, she's testing me.

"Uh." I'm an idiot and have to stop and think. "I would be like, 'This is my date, Tess.'"

"Really?"

"Yeah, 'cause you're my date, and your name is Tess."

That makes her laugh—thank god—and suddenly, the tension is gone, and she's caressing the top of my hand with the tips of her fingers.

"That would have been nice."

It would have, but I'm dumb, so…that's not what happened.

"Next time," I say as she scoots toward me, pressing her boobs and body into mine.

CHAPTER 57
TESS

I DON'T ALWAYS FIND MYSELF FALLING IN LOVE, BUT WHEN I DO, IT'S WITH MY BROTHER'S BEST FRIEND.

"NEXT TIME," I repeat, pressing into him.

His arms wrap around me, pulling me forward, his lips pressing a kiss against my forehead.

He smells good—like the shower he had earlier. Aftershave lotion and fabric detergent.

He smells comfortable and warm, like I've been missing him the past twenty-four hours even though we've been mostly together.

His fingers trace a pattern along my back, up and down my spine, igniting a cascade of shivers.

"Mmm." That feels good.

I nuzzle closer. He feels secure.

"Are we good?" he asks, the low timbre of his voice vibrating in his chest, causing me to shiver again.

Love the sound of his voice.

Always have.

It's deep and sexy and...

Mine.

I nod against his chest. "We're good. I'm sorry I was being difficult. I just got into my own head."

How can I possibly explain all the emotions inside my brain

when half of them are still baby hormones? How can I put into words what I feel without sounding needy or like a clinger or like I want to move too fast toward the finish line?

His fingers gently tilt my chin as if he's searching for my gaze in the dark, and all I can do is picture them, beautiful blue eyes that I've been in love with since I was a teenager.

And then, almost as if he's reading my mind, his lips brush against mine in a gentle, tentative kiss.

Soft and sweet and apologetic.

Too soft.

Too sweet.

I pull back, our foreheads still touching as I catch my breath.

"More," I whisper, my voice barely audible, but I know he hears it. "I want more."

I can feel him smile. *"More?"*

I nod, my heart racing. "Yes."

Harder.

Faster.

Don't stop…

I want to make up for lost time. Make up for what we've lost.

Make up.

Make out.

His arms tighten around me as if he's trying to anchor himself at this moment.

And then his lips find mine again, and this time they're hungry.

Our lips move against each other in a dance of urgency, clearly fueled by longing and lust and hormones.

The softness of our first kiss has given way to something primal and more insistent because now Drew knows that's how I like it.

I whimper, needing…

Something.

"We're not rushing." he whispers in my ear.

I nod, realizing to some degree that I was about to use sex as a Band-Aid to heal my hurt, desperate for closeness because my heart and body still have to heal. I know that could be wrong, but at the same time...I long for him.

"Explain to me why it took me so long to realize how fucking sexy you are." His voice croons into my ear and down my cerebellum.

"'Cause Grady and his friends are all idiots?" I let out a soft laugh, my fingers tracing a path along his jawline.

"Whoa. Hey now, not all of us are, just *most* of us." I can almost see his eyes twinkling with mischief as he pulls me closer, his breath warm against my ear. "Lucky me, I'm the only smart one who figured it out in time."

"Pfft. Only like, a million years later."

He hesitates with his hand on my boob. "Are you rolling your eyes again?"

I let out a laugh. "I can't help it!"

How does he know...?

Drew's fingers tangle in my hair, pulling me closer so our bodies press close, arms wrapped around each other.

Our breaths mingle, ragged and desperate, his mouth leaving mine so he can kiss my neck. Collarbone. Shoulder.

"You're going to be okay, Tess." He says against my hair, his deep voice low.

"I know."

And I do know.

My body has had a week to heal and I feel like I've done the right thing by telling my mom and family and letting Drew know right away instead of keeping it inside and dealing with the situation myself.

I can't imagine doing it alone and I can't imagine not being here, with him in this bed.

We don't say much of anything.

Just hold each other, the same way we were holding each

other in the shower, my head resting against his chest and his lips pressed against my hair.

Big teddy bear.

This time, I can feel the rhythm of his heart.

Move a hand between our bodies and press it against his flesh, over his chest, so I can feel it.

DEAR DIARY...

    It's been ages since I've written in here—I'm home for the weekend and thought it would be a lark to crack this open and read everything back what I've written over the past years. Wow, I was a dedicated little thing when I was young, there are barely any pages left for me to write in. Diary if there's one piece of advice I'd give my younger self, it's: if you have a mad crush on a guy who doesn't notice you're alive, you should say yes to a date with the guy that does. WHAT WAS I DOING ALL THESE YEARS CRUSHING ON DREW COLTER?? Wasting time, that's what.

    Seriously Tess. The guy doesn't know you're alive. Doesn't look at you, doesn't speak to you, never comes home because he can't—and even if he did, he would never ask you on a date. I could be standing naked in his room and he would brush past me out of respect for my brother.

    And here I am again, talking about him STILL. Like a total fool, always wishing and hoping I was going to see him when he came home, which he never does, LOL. Do you have any idea how many times my friends told me to get over it? Even Miranda, the girl I met in the dorms my freshmen year—without knowing anything about him—told me I needed to move on. She said "To get over a guy, you have to get under a new one."

She was mostly right, not that casual sex has ever been my thing. I was buzzed at a party a few weekends ago and decided this guy I met was cute enough to bring home for the night; turns out he couldn't last longer than a few minutes and I had to finish ON MY OWN with a vibrator while he past out next to me. Ugh. I laid in bed next to him counting down the hours until daylight and I could kick him out. Instead he tried to hang out, wanted to get breakfast, like DUDE, NO. GO HOME. You came in two minutes why do I want you around?! You are not boyfriend material.

Anyway. The point is, I'm trying. I get literal second-hand embarrassment for myself reading some of these entries back to myself but guess we can't go back in time and change things—not that I would do anything differently other than...maybe say something to him? Tell him. Confess. What's the worst thing that would have happened, he would let me down gently.

Alright. Spending the weekend with family and going to dinner with my grandparents tonight, Nana is finally retiring from the job she's had for a billion years.

This is Tess, signing off....

CHAPTER 58
TESS

LIFE IS SHORT. YOUR ORGASM SHOULDN'T BE

THIS IS our last night together before I leave for Texas tomorrow.

Drew and I have had our ups and downs over the past few weeks, and I'm still not clear on where we stand, but at least things are more normal than they are when I arrived.

Ish.

Normalish.

I don't want to jinx it but the guy I thought I was in love with when I was a kid? Is a far better man than I could have ever predicted he'd be.

More sensitive. Stronger.

More caring.

Gentle.

Patient.

He's taking me on another date tonight—kind of a do-over from the last first date—but told me not to dress up and to keep it casual. I have no idea what we could be doing or where we're going.

Drew is dressed in a flannel plaid shirt and jeans, work boots, and a baseball hat and looks pretty darn edible.

"So where are you taking me?" I ask, giving him a playful sideways glance as we pull out of his driveway.

"Little Miss Nosy, it's a secret. You'll find out soon enough."

"It's a secret, but I still want to know. I hate surprises." I cross my arms, hating this surprise. "Come on, give me a hint at least. One little one."

He pretends to ponder for a moment, his lips pursed. "Well, let's just say it's a place where no one will bother us except nature, and you may be part of the buffet."

"Does this mean you're takin' me out to a field to murder me?" Because that sounds terrible. "That's the worst hint I've ever heard."

He concentrates on the road, his hand casually resting on the gearshift. "Just relax."

I cannot.

I have no chill, not anymore, not with him.

I've literally spent countless hours writing about this man in my diary as a child—and as a teenager, there is no chill with him!

The truck hums along, the quiet moments between our banter filled with a comfortable silence. But soon enough, his fingers start tapping on the steering wheel to a rhythm only he can hear.

"What's going on in that head of yours?" I ask, a playful grin tugging at my lips.

He glances at me and grins. "Just thinking about how lucky I am to spend this evening with such amazing company."

My insides melt a little. "Flattery will get you everywhere."

He chuckles, his gaze returning to the road. "Good to know."

As we approach a stoplight, he reaches over and tucks a loose strand of hair behind my ear, his touch sending a shiver down my spine. Ugh, I wish it wasn't so easy for him to give me goose bumps. Shouldn't I be playing hard to get or at least make myself less available?

Too late for that, Tess. You've been to hell and back with this guy. There's no backpedaling and giving him more of a challenge.

You will lose.

Every time, your diary says so.

Dear Diary, I think I love Drew Colter and he doesn't know I exist...

Me, aged 11.

Age 13, age 17.

Well, he knows now. I just don't know how he feels about me.

Drew meets my gaze, a playful grin tugging at his lips. "We're doing something romantic." He pauses. "At least, I think it's romantic. Daisy helped me out a bit. I got some things from the diner where she works."

Daisy.

I wonder what she thinks of me and Drew and our situation.

It doesn't matter what anyone else thinks. All that matters is us and what we think. It's hard to think that way when I want to be included in their family dynamic and have them like me. Accept me. I want them to know I only want what's best for Drew because I care so much about him.

I've spent my life worshipping this guy, and I think...

He's at the point where he worships me, too.

"Are we driving to the middle of nowhere?" 'Cause that's what it looks like. The city lights disappear behind us, buildings getting farther and farther apart until the streets fade away in the rearview mirror.

"Seems like it, yeah?"

Hmm. We can't be going on a picnic. It's in the middle of the evening!

Could we?

"Are we going on a picnic?" He mentioned food from Daisy's diner, and we are in a truck.

My wheels turn at the same speed as the wheels of this truck are turning, barreling down this long country road.

"Yes, ma'am."

A picnic? In the middle of the night?

I wonder how he's going to pull this off when the blinker

goes on, and he slows us down, turning off the road onto what looks like the entrance to a field.

An open gate greets us.

This feels kind of like home, and the ranches where we live, dirt roads and split rail fences and cattle roaming in the tall grass.

We drive and drive, hitting potholes, and then the ride gets bumpy when he veers off the road, driving into the field toward the top of a rise.

Up and up.

Then he slows to a stop. Having located just the perfect spot, he cuts the engine and the lights and turns toward me.

"Stay put, kay?"

I nod, mouth gaping a bit.

"And no peekin'."

Another nod. *What on earth is he up to…?*

Drew climbs out of the truck, hopping down onto the ground and disappearing into the dark.

I hear the tailgate open, then the scraping of metal against metal.

Thumping.

He climbs up, then hops down.

It's quiet for a few moments, then he's back up in the tailgate again, shifting things around.

I face forward, though I'm tempted to look back.

So tempted 'cause like he said, I'm nosy.

But in a good way.

Suddenly, after a bit of banging around and some more noise, the passenger side door opens, and Drew holds out his hand to me. "My lady, dinner awaits."

I have no idea what to expect when I step out of the truck, and nothing could have prepared me for the sight that greets me: blankets spread out in the field, layered on the ground, and a garden table arranged in the center with two chairs.

A tablecloth.

Candles in the center.

Lanterns on the ground with candles throwing light, casting a glow.

A few tiki torches burn, four total, one in each corner of the makeshift dining room.

"I…" I suck in a shocked breath. "Drew, what is all this?"

He takes my hand, leading me toward the setup. "This is a romantic dinner for two."

Romantic is an understatement. As my eyes scan the area, nothing surrounds us but a farm field and the open sky. It's pitch black darkness except for the coach lanterns and the stars flickering in the sky above.

Honestly, the scene before me takes my breath away. I can hardly believe someone could put so much thought and effort into creating a moment like this.

For me.

Like—*what is this life?*

As I step into the softly lit area, our eyes meet, and there's a mixture of anticipation and vulnerability in his gaze. How can he doubt this for one second? How could he think I wouldn't love this?

He holds out a chair for me, fingers brushing against mine.

From behind, he leans down and kisses the side of my neck.

"Welcome," he says a bit formally—as if he were a server in a fancy restaurant. "I hope you like it."

Like it?

Is he for real?

I love it.

I'm quite literally at a loss for words as I take in the scene. The stars above us shimmer their approval as if they're witnessing a moment that's just as magical as they are.

"I feel so special."

Drew takes his seat across from me, spreading a napkin across his lap.

"I *wanted* to do something special for you, something that would let you know how much you mean to me."

A lump forms in my throat, overwhelmed by the depth of his sentiment.

"Drew, this... this is the most romantic thing anyone has ever done for me."

A soft smile curves his lips, his hand reaching across the table to find mine. "You deserve it."

"Where did this all come from?" And how did I not notice any of it in the back of the truck?

The spread is ridiculous and more than enough for two people. He's set up an elevated charcuterie—or grazing board—with almonds, crackers and cheese, and a variety of meat. Grapes. Apricots. Mini pickles, olives, some other veggies.

Sliced apples.

I can't believe my eyes.

"Obviously, I had help." He clears his throat. "I thought for sure half the shit would break on the road here. Every time I hit a pothole, I almost shit myself."

"I'm sure."

Drew hands me a plate from a small stack and a few utensils. Even though it's all finger food and forks aren't necessary, the ambience is out of this world.

Amazing.

"Are you sad I'm leaving tomorrow after I threw that little fit?"

"I don't think it was a fit. You had every right to be upset about me callin' you a friend."

"I did overreact."

He doesn't agree or disagree with me. "You look cute tonight."

I spread my arms wide, the sleeves of this oversized crewneck billowing. "You told me to dress comfortable and casual, so here I am."

"I want to squish and cuddle you."

"Are you gonna?"

"Yup, totally. After we finish eating."

After we finish eating? "You planning on laying me down in the hay field?"

"Nope." He pops an olive into his mouth and chews thoughtfully. "Bed of the truck."

I shift my gaze, looking at the back of the truck. It's filled with blankets and square pillows.

"I was thinking we could do some stargazin'."

Stargazing?

I feel a rush of anticipation. "That's so romantic." I swear I can feel my heart fluttering inside my chest. Stomach, too.

He shrugs nonchalantly. "Hey, it's a classic move in the movies for a reason."

"Was it your idea?"

Another shrug. "Mostly." He pauses. "Drake and Daisy were excited to help. He wanted me to string up lights and have music, but I didn't have time to figure all that shit out."

Wireless speaker?

Speaker from the truck?

Stop it, Tess.

"Well, this is perfect. I wouldn't change a thing."

He considers my words. "If you could change one thing about the past three months, what would it be?"

Oh, we're going to dive right into the serious topics, are we?

I have to think about his question because if anything had been doing differently or changed, we may not be right here, in this moment. And right here is where I want to be.

"I don't know, actually. Probably..." I think. "I'd probably have said something to you sooner about my feelings for you. And I would have let you put the moves on me first, instead of going at you like a horny teenager." I laugh, despite being serious.

"I don't think there's a man on earth who would object to a smart, funny, and pretty girl puttin the moves on him."

"I know, but you know what I mean."

He nods. "I know what you mean."

"What about you—what would you have done different if you could go back in time and change things?"

He pulls a thoughtful face. "I have no idea. Maybe how things went with Grady. We've been friends for a long time and it makes no sense why he's pissed about us being together. He knows me. He knows what kind of guy I am, there's no logical explanation for his anger."

My eyes move to the spot on his face that had been bruised and I cringe. "I know. You're the best guy I know."

I say it because it's true.

Drew Colter is the best guy I know and the past two weeks have proved it.

"Stop you're makin me blush," he demurs, ducking his head.

"It's true." I eat an olive.

"Things would have been simpler if he would have stayed out of it."

Also true.

As the night unfolds, we talk and laugh, our words carrying the weight of shared feelings. With every passing moment, I can feel the connection between us growing stronger, the bond deepening in the midst of this enchanting setting.

How could it not?

And then Drew produces a small box from his pocket. My heart races as he opens it, revealing a delicate gold necklace. From it hangs a tiny star pendant with a small diamond in the center.

"I know it might sound cheesy," he says with a self-deprecating smile, "but, um…" He clears his throat. "Every time you look at this, or put it on, I want you to remember this night, these stars, the…" His voice cracks. "Baby. And how much I care about you."

Tears gather in my eyes as I take the box from him with trembling fingers.

"Drew, I don't know what to say," I whisper.

He stands, coming around to my side of the table, standing behind me and reaching for the necklace with trembling hands. "You don't have to say anything. Just know that I mean every word."

At this moment, beneath the stars and surrounded by the soft glow of candlelight, Drew Colter—the boy of my dreams—fastens the gold chain as I lift my hair.

It hangs, resting at a spot on my neck where my pulse beats, and I touch it, knowing that I will probably never take it off.

"Tess Donahue?"

My pulse quickens. "Will you be my girlfriend?"

Oh my god, why am I so emotional! Seriously!

"Yes!"

Duh.

"I've literally been waiting for you to ask me that since I was eleven years old."

The End...
is just the beginning.

ABOUT SARA NEY

Sara Ney is the USA Today Bestselling Author of the How to Date a Douchebag series, best known for her sexy, laugh-out-loud sports and contemporary romances. Among her favorite vices, she includes: traveling, historical architecture and nerding out on all things Victorian. She's a "cool mom" living in the Midwest who loves antique malls, resale clothing shops, and once carried a vintage copper sink through the airport as her carry-on because it didn't fit in her suitcase.

ALSO BY SARA NEY

Campus Legends Series
How To Lose At Love
How To Win The Girl
How To Score Off The Field

Accidentally in Love Series
The Player Hater
The Mrs. Degree
The Make Out Artist
The Secret Roommate

Jock Hard Series
Switch Hitter
Jock Row
Jock Rule
Switch Bidder
Jock Road
Jock Royal
Jock Reign
Jock Romeo

Trophy Boyfriends Series
Hard Pass
Hard Fall
Hard Love
Hard Luck

The Bachelors Club Series
Bachelor Society
Bachelor Boss

How to Date a Douchebag Series
The Studying Hours
The Failing Hours
The Learning Hours
The Coaching Hours
The Lying Hours
The Teaching Hours

#ThreeLittleLies Series
Things Liars Say
Things Liars Hide
Things Liars Fake

All The Right Moves Series
All The Sweet Moves
All The Bold Moves
All The Right Moves

The Bachelor Society Duet: The Bachelors Club
Jock Hard Box Set: Books 1-3